A MIDNIGHT SWIM
BENEATH THE STARS...

"Come on," he encouraged her. "It's really not so bad." He strode back to where she stood, him with a god's body limned with moonlight, emerging from the lake like a child of Lir, a swan come to life, one with the water. He splashed water on his chest and arms and ran wet hands down his face. Droplets shone on his tanned skin, the muscles beneath outlined and defined in stark relief.

She stood transfixed as he approached her, not realizing what he was about until it was too late. She'd been focussing on his body, every inch of his maleness, when he suddenly scooped her up to carry her like a baby, then turned his back to the shore, walking determinedly into the water with her in his arms.

Lumau Publishing
Brandon: Bad Boy of Kinsale © 2017 by Sonia Gay
Cover image © Idutko/Shutterstock
Book and cover design © 2017 by Sonia Gay
and Lumau Publishing

ISBN: 978-0-9958376-7-6

Lumau Publishing
lumaupublishing@gmail.com

BRANDON:
BAD BOY OF KINSALE

Book Three of
the O'Farrell Legacy

S. M. Cross

BOOKS BY THE AUTHOR

The O'Farrell Legacy Series:
Mulligan's Dream
Double Take
Brandon: Bad Boy of Kinsale
A Winter Sky
C'Mere to Me

Celtic Dreams

By S.M. Gay

I'll tell a tale of Ireland's blood
Where love and turmoil grow.
Where Cupid's bow hath touch the hearts
And vanquished every foe.

***

A tale of Hank, so strong and true
And of his love, fair Laura.
Of broken hearts and broken dreams,
Of mending lives with honor.

***

Of Niall, whose love for Michael
Was censured and love forbidden.
But in the dark and in their hearts
That love was never hidden.

***

Where Liam found his lovely lass
Though Sine, fair uncertain
Against them though the world contrived
His love she learned was certain

***

'Twas Brandon, like a jester's son,
Who lived his shattered past
Whom Aine fed and nursed to health
To keep and hold him fast.

***

So hark ye now and learn the tale
Of Ireland's children, free.
Of lives and loves, of romance sure
And O'Farrell's Legacy.

***

BRANDON:
BAD BOY OF KINSALE

Chapter One

Brandon O'Farrell awoke to the sounds of the sea birds crying their high pitched 'eee-eee' outside the window and a brisk breeze blowing across his face, the scent of salt heavy in the air of Kinsale's harbor. Other sensations, a warm body hugging his back, while he in turn had his arm about another warm body spooned into him in front. It left him feeling hot but for the breeze through the gauzy curtains over windows cranked wide open. His eyes opened slowly to the bright, summer dawn.

Events of the night before came rushing back as he lay in limbo between sleeping and waking. It had been a marvelous ménage à trois. He viewed the blonde head tucked under his chin, saw the dark strands mingled with the blonde; a brief acknowledgement that she'd colored her hair. Nevertheless, she was lovely; she'd been perfect, her breasts so firm with hard nipples, and smooth skin, nearly as soft as a baby's over a bum ripe for caressing.

And in between her legs, her juices had coated him, smoothed his way. He was hard again, just remembering. Did he have another rubber? It was a brief thought, and then gone as the body behind him stirred and he felt a kiss pressed to his neck behind his ear. The stubble from the man's chin rasped against his skin. Is that what Niall liked?

Niall, his younger brother, one of a pair of mirror twins. Liam, the first twin, an actor, out-going and into the women; Niall, a techie as nerdy and reserved as they came, and gay. Niall had, Brandon knew, a very good-looking boyfriend. Michael had showed up at his half brother's wedding last year, and he wondered, briefly, what men saw in other men, until the hand behind him cupped his nads and rolled them through his fingers like dice in a game.

The massage of his nads had him mellow out. Still flaming from the drink last night, he was half in a dream as his mind wandered back to his family. They had all been living in Inishannon once upon a time, except for Henry, who lived in Killarney with Siobhan and young Emily. But now everyone except Ciara, the youngest, had left home.

Brandon, himself, had recently relocated to Kinsale in County Cork, south of Inishannon and on the coast. He'd rented a room at a local hotel for the summer because flats were few and far between and it was too hard to sneak a different woman every night into a B&B. They usually frowned on that sort of thing. So he'd settled on the hotel, loved it for its amenities and didn't mind paying the outrageous sum they were asking. He was getting a good wage, after all.

He loved Kinsale, a picturesque little town with a lovely marina, perfect for sailboats, fishing boats, and a few yachts. A port too small to accommodate the big cruise ships that docked farther up the coast in Cobh, and thankfully so.

Tourists flocked to Kinsale in the summer months and the likes of Brandon entertained them. He hadn't started out to do that, to play host to a bunch of gawkers, but he'd found out quickly that they paid well, especially if they liked you.

And Brandon was someone they liked. No, they loved him. Especially the two in bed with him. The two, the man and a woman, had been in a tour group he'd taken around yesterday, and they'd soon made their desires known. It had begun over a racy song Brandon had sung, his old guitar humming with renewed vigor as he accompanied himself to the obvious pleasure of all. The couple had come up while he was packing his instrument away and began asking questions. Questions that led to…

Well, he knew where they were headed before they got there. She was pretty, curvaceous; he was handsome, very masculine looking but with an affectation that spoke volumes. He was so very obviously an arse bandit.

"How did you two end up traveling together?" Brandon had asked, curious.

"We both wanted to travel through Ireland," explained the woman in her foreign accent, which Brandon thought was possibly Dutch, "and decided it was much cheaper for us to travel together. Neither one of us had a partner, so, it made sense, *ja*?"

Brandon wasn't convinced that was the whole story but it was okay by him if that's what they wanted. Each to their own, his mam would say.

He felt the masculine hand move from his nads, the

3

fingers splayed out in a caress that reached for that part of him that had hardened while the man had caressed his clackers. Brandon stretched, reluctant to let the woman he was spooned around go, but it felt so good to have a large hand on his flute. Especially one that was doing such grand things to him. He'd drawn a line last night, though. No fella was going to kick in his back door without a fight.

The woman before him stirred and turned to face him. Immediately she put her lips to his, invaded his mouth with her tongue, and began fondling his flat, male nipples with vigor. Between the man on his lad and the woman on his mouth and chest, Brandon was nearly beside himself. She grasped his hand and placed it on her crotch in silent instruction. Brandon was no fool and sliding a finger inside her, found her wet and willing. He was so hard. He wanted her but didn't have a rubber ready. No matter, between the erotic vision of the man on his lad and the scent of the woman's juices, it might not matter that he wasn't inside her.

His breath was coming in gasps. His climax was imminent. And then stars exploded inside his head.

* * *

Brandon woke to a headache that had him retching. Furthermore, he was a mess. And alone. The couple was nowhere to be seen.

The room was spinning wildly, made worse when he closed his eyes, and gripping the sheets in shaky fists, recognized in some corner of his brain that he was dealing with a concussion. The next thought that came to him was the two who'd been with him were not your usual tourists and as soon as he was able, he was going to check his pants to see if his wallet was still there. It wouldn't surprise him if he'd been robbed as well but until the room stood still, or at least slowed, he wasn't about to get out of bed.

Bed. It was not such a comfortable place at the moment. The room reeked like a toilet and one look through blurred vision told him a bigger story. Bodily fluids were smeared on the sheets, dark and red.

Blood?

His first instinct was to check his head. The goose egg sized bump had bled, but not profusely, and only on the pillow. That meant that perhaps it wasn't his blood.

That was just manky, thinking of whose it might have been and furthermore, why. Pushing himself to a sitting position, he squinted through the brightness of day coming through the two large windows with their multiple panes, and struggled to focus.

The room had been ransacked. Whatever they were looking for was now likely gone, although he didn't have anything here beyond some clothing, his wallet, and his guitar.

Tripping on the crumpled sheets as he attempted to climb out of bed, he landed hard on the floor, just missing the side table with his forehead. "Just grand," he muttered to himself, and laid there with his cheek on the floor until the room slowed. "Just feckin' grand."

Resisting the urge to sleep again, he pushed himself

upright, and with a hand on the bed for support, stood slowly until fully upright to survey the room. The once orderly space was anything but. The guitar he'd played on last night now hung by its strings on the back of a chair. In pieces. Two large pieces, in fact, and several smaller splinters, which were scattered in a wide area. The thirty-six-inch television on the built-in desk had been the instrument's undoing. Bearing unmistakable signs of damage, he doubted the TV would still work.

His guitar, though. He had loved that guitar. It hadn't been new when he got it but it had a tone that spoke to him. A sadness crept over him at the thought of never hearing it again.

His gaze searched the built-in where he'd laid his car keys the night before. Nothing. The wardrobe was also emptied of any contents that had been inside, namely articles of clothing, now lying on the floor. Scanning the area through eyes blurred in pain, he found nothing that resembled car keys. Or his wallet, he amended, as he picked up his jeans and checked the pockets in vain.

There was no hope for it. He couldn't let this one brush by as he had last year with the two girls. No, make that three. He'd forgotten about the one who'd come knocking on his door in the wee hours of the morning. That had been a bit messy, what with her caterwauling and carrying on and then trying to get her own piece of him by hauling the second girl from his embrace just when he had been about to get a mouthful of nipple.

That poor girl had lost a fistful of hair fighting off her attacker, but her friend wasn't about to be left out of the fray and came to her rescue. They ganged up on the interloper, and before Brandon could figure it all out, had her out the door. A quick call to hotel security had taken care of the mess in short order, with one of the girls hiding in the bathroom to defend the propriety of their position. Couples, after all, were a common occurrence in hotels. Not so much a ménage à trois.

This, however, could not be explained by simply playing the injured party. Hotel security wasn't going to like this one little bit and the garda would be called in, no questions about that. And once the shades were called, well, his mam would be there, followed quickly by his older brother, Henry.

Henry would know exactly what had happened, and for that, Brandon felt ill. His big brother, who had taken over after their da had been killed in a roll-over when Henry was fourteen and himself just ten, leaving the twins, Liam and Niall, then eight, and Ciara, their youngest sibling and the only girl, four, to be brought up by a mother who worked odd hours as a nurse at the big hospital in Cork, and a brother who was just into his teens.

No, Henry would not be pleased and if Brandon didn't get a beating from Henry, he'd be surprised. That's how it was. If you got in trouble for fighting at school, you wouldn't get sympathy at home, you'd get another beating. And you likely would have deserved it, too.

Reluctantly, Brandon admitted to himself that he deserved

7

this. He'd ventured into something that was too deep, even for him. Not only had he been taken advantage of, robbed, and beaten, but now, after thinking about it, he'd have to wonder if the two had some disease? He'd been careful. He'd used rubbers last night. But then he remembered something about this morning, just before blacking out. And if that memory was correct…no, he'd blacked out just when it was getting interesting.

He glanced down at himself, at his flute hanging limp between his legs. Christ, he needed to get cleaned up!

The evidence of last night's antics was all throughout the bed sheets. He made a mental note to clean up as much as he could before he called housekeeping.

He rubbed his head where it was throbbing and felt the great lump there, the matted blood in his hair. Had the woman bashed him on the head with something? He glanced at the telephone on the bedside table. It was crooked, as if someone had thrown it down, not caring how it landed.

"Aw, fooooook!" He wanted to hit something but his head hurt too much to move. Add to that the worry that he'd probably been the recipient of unprotected sex. That thought lay on him like a death sentence as he tried to dismiss it from his mind. No sense worrying over that until he knew if he had something.

In the meantime, there was the matter of his car, confirmed stolen if the empty spot in the parking lot out front said anything, and his missing wallet. He couldn't get away without calling the shades and reporting both the theft of the car and his wallet. He could try and claim the hotel room was broken into but he had a sinking feeling it wouldn't wash.

First things first. He needed to get clean, so going into the bathroom to step into the shower, he stopped dead in his tracks at the scene before him. Smeared along the mirror over the sink and the clear glass walls of the shower stall were obscenities, written in lipstick, the very shade the woman had worn last night. Christ, he didn't even know their names!

Standing naked in the bathroom, he began to shake, and recognized he was in shock. At least, he figured so, as much as his brain could think just then.

Grabbing the sink for support, he waited until the wave of nausea and dizziness left him. Somewhere in the deep recesses of his mind, he knew he needed help; this was much more than he could manage on his own. Worse yet, he had pain, low down in his gut, and he couldn't think straight.

In his entire life since the death of his father, Brandon had one person besides his mam he could count on, and that was Big Brother Henry. So before he showered, before he passed out again from shock, fear, and injury, he went to the hotel phone and placed the call. No sense looking for his mobile phone. He already knew it was gone.

* * *

Henry resisted the urge to throw his phone out the window. Of all the idiotic, lame-arsed things his brother could have done, Brandon had proved himself to be real bollocks. If Henry didn't care so much about their mam or grandparents, he would have called the garda himself. As it was, he said he'd get there as soon as possible but Kinsale wasn't quite next door. It was going to take him the better part of two hours to get there, although with his knowledge of the backroads, he might be able to shorten it a bit. In the meantime, Brandon had been instructed to put a 'do not disturb' sign on the door and clean himself up.

And then Brandon had told him about the stolen car. That did it. This wasn't something that could be hushed up and swept under the carpet. They'd need to involve the shades.

"Are ye sure the car's been jammered?" Henry had asked him.

"Of course I'm sure. I parked it where I could see it from my room and it's not there. Ye can't miss a yellow car in a sea of white," he'd exclaimed, wondering why he hadn't noticed until now that all the other vehicles in the lot seemed to be white.

"Yellow? Yer not talkin' of Grandda's car, are ye? The yellow Mini?"

There had been a very pregnant pause on the other end of the line and then the voice quietly saying, "The very same."

"Dickbrain!" exclaimed Henry, "That car has been in the family since God was a teenager. How could ye let this happen?"

"Well, it's not like I planned it, is it now! It was safe where I left it, only I hadn't thought it would be taken like it was."

Henry had to give him that. They all loved that little car; had all learned to drive behind its wheel, everyone from

Henry on down to Ciara. It was a forty-year-old car that his grandda had bought when new, when he had loved the color yellow and thought everything he owned should be yellow. *Well*, mused Henry, *it wouldn't be hard to identify it*. He'd never seen another car, anywhere, quite that shade. It was like a lemon on wheels without the connotation that lemons and cars usually had when put together. That little car could do anything.

And now it was gone. Hopefully, it could be recovered and still in one piece.

He finally got off the phone with his brother and resisted the urge to flatten something. He'd love to flatten his brother but figured he was likely already in a bad way. As he climbed into his car to make the trek to Kinsale, he dialed his wife, Siobhan, to tell her the news, thanking the fact that he'd had Niall install a hands-free calling system for him in the vehicle.

"He did what?" Her voice was not as shocked as it was tired. They were all tired of Brandon's antics. He'd been in trouble since the day he was born; but without Henry knowing anything else about the situation, only that whomever Brandon had slept with last night had clocked him a good one and stolen him blind, he couldn't yet fully express his opinion.

"I don't know everything yet although I expect we'll find out soon enough."

"So you're heading there now?"

"I am," he said as he pulled through the roundabout on the way to Cork. "It's sorry I am that I likely won't be at

Emily's birthday supper tonight. I doubt I'll be back in time. I'll make it up to her when I get back," he offered.

Emily, his half sister's daughter. Em's mother, Meara, had died of a drug overdose and Henry's mam had adopted her. There had been no other family. But as she'd been in Henry's care when Meara died, Henry said he'd raise her, and his busy mother, a nurse and midwife with on-call hours, day and night, agreed. Emily had become as dear to him as if she were his own and he truly hated not being there for her birthday. Feckit, but his brother was a gligeen!

"Let me know when ye get there," said Siobhan, and then, "Drive carefully. I know you're pissed. So am I. But I love ye, so take it easy-like, eh?"

"Right, then. Love ye, too," said Henry as he signed off. He suddenly felt every one of his thirty-eight years.

Chapter Two

The banging was incessant. Brandon was hoping it would go away, but the pounding in his head just got louder, and he felt that, at any moment, he was going to be sick.

"Brandon, open the door!"

He heard his brother's voice—angry, insistent—on the other side of the door and realized that the banging in his head was made worse by the banging on the door. "Coming," he croaked out, and then, "I said I'm coming," he yelled, as loud as he could without waking the furies of hell inside his skull.

Pushing himself off the bed, he soon realized his naked state. He'd been about to go in the shower, he recalled. And then the image of lipstick smeared words scrawled across the mirror and shower doors. They were in Dutch and Irish. A strange combination, but he could read between the lines. *Striapach* was Irish for whore, along with some other phrases he and his mates used to write on the walls in the toilet at school. And then there were some Dutch words, *poot*, and *hoer*. He didn't quite know what they meant but he could guess. The trick with some Dutch words was to just sound them out and sometimes you could guess at their meaning. Right now, he didn't care.

He stared at the phone on the bedside table, the ear piece barely back in the cradle, and remembered he'd called Henry but then nothing after that. He must have passed out again. Christ, but he felt wretched!

"Brandon!"

"Whisht would ye, I'll get there," he mumbled, too wrung out to say more as he wound the sheet around his naked body.

Opening the door to see his brother on the other side, one fist raised as if to bang again, Brandon knew both relief and a great sense of dread all at once.

"Jaysus Christ, look at ye," exclaimed Henry, pushing his brother back inside the room. "Ye look like a car wreck after a hurricane. Could ye be more battered?"

Battered? He looked battered? He hadn't thought so when he first looked in the mirror but he hadn't really noticed because of the writing.

He was dizzy, felt like passing out again but grabbed the back of the chair just in time. The chair that held the remnants of his guitar.

Henry reached out quickly and grabbed Brandon's arm before he went down and guided him to the seat of the chair, extricating the guitar before letting go of him. "Y'okay now?"

There was worry in Henry's voice. No anger, just concern. That scared Brandon more than he cared to admit. "I don't know. I think I'm goin' to be sick," he said, beginning to retch.

Henry grabbed the tail end of the sheet and held it up for Brandon to use but Brandon shook his head. "Let me get to the loo," he said, rising and stumbling his way to the bathroom, only steps away.

"Brandon," Henry began, but Brandon was insistent on getting to the bathroom, regardless of the writing.

"Brandon!" This time it was Henry who had taken on that insistent tone.

Brandon turned. His stomach heaved but nothing came out. Just dry retching as he held his gut, straining as the pain rifled through him.

And then his brother's words, the expression on his face, his color turned pale as he half whispered, "Oh, Jaysus feckin' Christ, Brandon, yer bleedin'."

Brandon slunk to the floor, his arms over his gut. "Oh Christ, it hurts," he moaned.

Henry rushed to his brother's side, lifted Brandon's chin, and did what their mam would have done, drawing down the lower lid of each eye to check for signs of blood loss. *Pale, not a good sign*, thought Henry as he dialed for an ambulance on his mobile.

"What are ye doin'?" asked Brandon weakly. Henry didn't like the sound or looks of his brother.

"Getting' help," he replied gruffly, and then doing a double-take at his brother, he pocketed the phone without calling, said, "C'mon. I'm goin' to get some clothing on you and then we're goin' up to Cork."

"Huh? Wha'?" asked Brandon.

Henry thought the guy was about to pass out again but held fast to his decision. He was not going to allow the locals to get hold of his brother and spread rumors. Brandon had already achieved the worst reputation a man could possibly have and remain respectable. If respectability had a fine line before falling into ill repute, then Brandon was straddling it. In older times, his brother could be referred to as a rake. There might have been a stronger word in use for those that straddled the line between rake and debaucher but Henry knew Brandon never did anything with anyone that they didn't want, although he couldn't say how he knew.

As he struggled to help Brandon into a t-shirt and jeans, he tried to ignore the carnage in the bed. The smell alone would have knocked a weaker man over; stale sex, something akin to feces, and God-knew-what-else. He didn't particularly care to know. First he'd get his brother to the University Hospital in Cork and then he'd call the garda.

"No, no hospital," protested Brandon as Henry manhandled him into the car. He'd managed to half carry, half drag his brother through the lobby to the car with a minimum of fuss, taking advantage of a group of tourists crowding their way into the lobby, effectively covering their escape.

"Why not? Ye need to see a doctor and I'm not lettin' the people here see the shape ye're in. The town's too small and our grandparents too well known and well liked to have your antics rubbed in their noses."

"But Mam works there," he pointed out.

His voice was still weak, but a little stronger in his

objections than Henry would have given his brother credit for. "Yeah, she does. And this'll likely break her heart, it will, but ye must be seen. I don't need ye to tell me what ye did last night. I already know."

Brandon had the decency to look flushed, but whether it was from exertion or embarrassment, Henry couldn't tell. "Just sit tight," he said, and started the car.

Throughout the drive into Cork, Henry kept glancing at his brother, watching as the guy's head lolled, sometimes appearing lucid, other times wincing in pain. It was the pain part that Henry didn't like, but in less than forty-five minutes, they were at the hospital, having avoided the tangle of traffic from the airport and gone the backroad up to N71. Henry knew the roads well and navigated them as if he'd invented them.

Moments later, Brandon was on a stretcher and under the care of the emergency department doctor, and Henry was being bombarded with questions. "I don't know," he tried to explain. "Ye'll have to ask him when he's more with it," he said of his brother, who had passed out again. He knew it was the chicken's way out. He could have told him his brother had been raped but it somehow stuck in his throat and wouldn't come out.

The doctor nodded grimly and indicated the waiting room while he pulled the curtain across the cubicle to examine Brandon.

Henry sat down to wait, knowing it wouldn't take long before his mam appeared, especially if she was working today. In the meantime, Henry made a phone call to the tourism outfit that had hired Brandon. He'd got that much out of his brother during the lucid periods. Someone would need to know he'd be unavailable for a while. He just didn't know how long a while it would be.

His next duty was to inform the hotel that there had been a break in. Henry had no idea if that was the case or if Brandon had invited them there, but he knew there were two people involved and he knew that Brandon wasn't innocent of the goings on. The fact also remained that Brandon had been victimized, no matter that he'd invited them in, and felt it wouldn't hurt to save some of his brother's pride. The hotel needed to be onside, after all.

He was just sliding his phone back into his pocket when he looked up to see his mam standing before him, looking as worried as he felt. *Mam never looked worried*, thought Henry. Pissed off, angry, frustrated, but never worried.

"They raped my boy," was all she said before the tears began. And then she was in Henry's arms and he was holding her as she got herself under control. Fear. He forgot to add that he'd never seen her afraid.

"Ye'd best sit down and I'll tell ye all I know," he said.

"Okay, but not here. I'll take ye to the staff lounge, it'll be more private there."

Nodding, he followed his mam, her tears wiped away and looking strong once again as she led him to the lounge on the next floor. Opening the door, she said, "This one isn't used much. We should be able to talk in here."

Not much more than a room in which to soak up some peace and quiet, the room contained a window that overlooked the main road and had a vending machine stationed just outside the door. "I've got some change, would you like a coffee?" asked Henry, about to get himself one.

"No, I've just come from lunch but thanks all the same."

They sat down on the vinyl seats and faced each other across the small accent table in between. Henry began with Brandon's call earlier that morning, and as he spoke, his mam held back tears but whether of frustration, pain, or anger, Henry wasn't sure.

"The eejit!" she exclaimed vehemently. "What on God's green earth did he think he was about?"

Henry had nothing to add to that. "What he told me on the phone was that they'd approached him after his performance and somehow talked him into a night of, well, sex, to put it bluntly. It isn't the first time he's had two at once but I think it was his first time when one was another fella."

His mam, Kathleen, shook her head. "I'd heard, but I didn't want to know. I kept thinkin', 'he's a big boy and can look after himself,' but, obviously, that's not true."

"Ye know," Henry observed, glancing out the window at the day that was becoming gradually darker with oncoming rain, "I think he would have been fine if he'd stuck to women he knew. Even the last time he was caught with two others, he managed to escape blame; but I wouldn't put it past him that he was at fault somewhere along the way."

"Ah, that would be the woman that was jealous because

he had someone else in bed with him at the time," she acknowledged.

Henry nodded. "Yeah, only there wasn't just one, there were two. The third got into a cat fight with the two already in the room."

"Oh. I hadn't known," she said quietly. "I thought it was just one."

"It's sorry I am that I can't tell ye more, or that I had to tell ye as much as I did. Especially about that previous episode. I would have liked ye to remain ignorant of that one and save ye some grief if I could."

"Ah, no bother," she said. "'Tisn't like I don't know me own son. I've known for a time that Brandon will do anything. I just didn't know what that 'anything' meant. And now I do."

Henry sipped his coffee quietly, thinking. He didn't have a fecking clue what his next move was.

"They should be prepping him for surgery now," said Kathleen, and Henry's head shot up.

"What?"

"Surgery. He was bleeding rectally. It looked pretty nasty so they'll operate to see what's what, do any repairs. I signed the consent form."

Henry nodded. Leave it to his mam to be there for that. "What did they do before ye got there? Anything?"

She nodded. "Oh, they'd done quite a bit, didn't waste any time. You're lucky ye came when ye did. They'd just got through an entire room of people and those left were in much better condition and could wait a bit longer, so as soon as they called me, I went down. They'd already ordered blood work to cross match. He was still losing a lot when I got there, I could tell. His consciousness level was poor, going in and out, and they'd begun the IV for fluids. They'll do a coagulation profile, you know the rest from what I've told ye over the years. He's been catheterized, he's that bad."

"They'll do a, what do ye call it, an endo-something?"

"Endoscopy, yes that's the plan, to see what they can and make any repairs. From the amount he's bleeding, there could be a very bad tear. I just hope to hell he doesn't get peritonitis."

"It's a possibility, then?"

His mam nodded, grim-faced.

"That's partly why they didn't waste any time getting him prepped. It's good ye brought him here. It's what this hospital specializes in, with the big trauma center."

"Too bad we won't know more about what happened until he wakes up," mumbled Henry, half to himself.

His mam ignored the comment. "I heard ye makin' phone calls when I saw ye downstairs. Who'd ye call?"

Henry told her, and she nodded.

"Do you think the hotel will call the garda?" she asked.

"They may, but I'll have to for sure. They stole Grandda's yellow car."

"The Mini?"

Nodding, Henry sighed. "The very one."

Kathleen's shoulders began to shake and Henry thought to himself that he'd finally seen his mam brought to her knees until he realized that she was laughing. Laughing!

"What's so funny?"

"That wee car," she said between bursts of laughter. "That wee car has handled all o' ye's and survived. I think we'll find it again but mayhap the culprits will be long gone. Still, they might have left somethin' behind to give themselves away."

Shrugging, Henry cracked a wry smile, glad to see his mam had put her professional mask back on. This was the mam he preferred, not the worried one. That one scared the hell out of him. "Like maybe their passports?" he joked.

Kathleen swatted at her son. "Don't be a gligeen. I mean like fingerprints or blood stains or somethin' like that. Maybe they have files already."

"Oh, well, and that could be true. The woman had a Dutch accent according to Brandon but I guess the guy didn't say much because Brandon didn't mention a whole lot about him."

"Well, he's the one did the damage," said his mam. "It's because of that plonker that Brandon is here. And thank God ye brought him here instead of Kinsale. They're good down there, they are, but it's too close to home and they haven't the facilities as they do here."

Henry couldn't disagree with that. "It's why I brought him here. Besides, I didn't think they'd do much down there except send him here anyway."

Standing, and having discussed the matter as much as they could, Henry said, "Let's go downstairs and see what's going on. We should be getting some news eventually."

Kathleen nodded and led the way. "Our one saving grace is that we know Brandon doesn't use drugs. Alcohol he's not a stranger to, but one thing I know about my son is that he's not a drugger."

"No, and thank God for that," agreed Henry.

Chapter Three

Aine Donahue flipped open the chart and marked her findings. His BP was low but that was to be expected, he hadn't fully woken from surgery yet. Everything else, though, seemed within limits.

As if her thoughts on his blood pressure had triggered something within him, her patient, Mr. Brandon O'Farrell, according to his chart, groaned as his eyes fluttered open.

Aine's breath hitched in her throat. His eyes, the most amazing shade of blue, froze her on the spot, all professionalism gone out the window.

Getting a grip on herself, she put her professional mask back in place. "How are ye feeling?" she asked in her fair, Dublin accent.

Brandon's eyes squinted and she recognized the signs of someone having difficulty focussing.

"It's alright, ye don't have to say anythin' if ye don't want to. I'll be back soon to check on ye."

She walked away, still taken in by Mr. O'Farrell's deep blue eyes. His hair was black, she knew. Even stuck to his head with the remnants of blood, and the shaved area where his wound was tended orange with antiseptic wash, she could see from his brows that the very dark brown was much closer to black.

His features were pale, not unexpected after surgery. From his chart, she knew he'd been attacked, that he'd acquired his head injury in the incident and that his surgery had been to repair the damage caused by a brutal rape.

She hadn't been nursing long, not quite six years, but she'd seen a lot in that time. At nearly thirty years old, she'd lost her innocence long before.

Innocence. It was a term she used sparingly. A rape victim herself at thirteen, she swore at the time she'd never let it stop her.

Only it had. For two years she'd never spoken unless she had to. Never went out, never socialized until she turned sixteen and met a woman who changed her life. Another survivor, someone Aine could identify with. Gradually, over time, her confidence grew and she became stronger, began working with other girls in a women's rape clinic that had suffered the same misfortune. Her volunteerism eventually led to an application to nursing school in Dublin, where she was from.

And here she was, a graduated nurse and midwife, and enjoying every minute of her job. Well, almost every minute. Like every job, there were the things she hated to do but it all came as a parcel. And although the hospital in Cork hadn't been her first job, she liked this one better than any she'd had before.

A noise in the room she'd just left made her turn. From the

crack of the opened door, she saw the man falling, reaching for something to grab onto and missing, sending the trolley cart with the water jug rolling across the floor and the jug itself landing with a wet splat on the floor.

Racing the few steps back to the room, she opened the door wide to see her patient half in and half out of the bed, IV lines pulled taut and a look of pain and confusion on his beard-roughened face. With another step she was at his side, easing him back into bed, pulling the steri-pad straight so he wasn't discharging fluids onto the bed linens. He was half out of it still and she had to fight with the leg farthest from her to get it back onto the bed. He'd somehow got it stuck under the one nearest her.

Eventually, she got him righted and eased the pad beneath him, noting that he'd made himself bleed. From the shelf next to the bed, she pulled a new pad, and with a strength her small stature belied, had the old one replaced in record time. She tried to ignore the bulge at the front of his hospital gown. It wasn't professional, but for some reason, she couldn't help herself. Was the hair down there as black as…

Brandon sighed his relief, apologizing profusely. "I'm sorry, I didn't know what I was doin'."

"No bother," she said, "just use the call bell if ye'd like to get up to use the toilet or need anythin'. I'm on shift until eight but I'll be back to see to ye before then. Right, then, there y'are," she said, straightening the covers and re-checking his IV line.

Brandon watched the nurse, a real beauty with classically

26

honed features, the high cheekbones pink with health, eyes a lively gray, and blonde hair with red highlights. Even in his state he could see that the red highlights weren't natural. No one had hair quite that shade of red. It was like the red on the toy truck he'd received for Christmas when he was five. No, it certainly wasn't natural but it was flashy, and she seemed to carry it off well.

She left him to himself then, and he lay back on the pillow, debating his next move. His attempt to get out of bed had proved stupid, and he didn't think he could eat anything yet, although the pain in his gut was gone. Come to think on it, so was the pain in his head. Immediately, his hand went up to feel the bump and came across the spikey feeling of hair clipped short and the knotted threads of nylon stitching. At least, it felt like nylon.

He was just ruminating on what the material actually was when his mam and Henry peeked around the door. "Ah, you're awake," said Mam, looking a little stressed, especially since she was in work clothing. When Mam wore her uniform, it seemed nothing could shake the positive attitude she displayed on a nonstop basis. It wasn't until she left the hospital that the mask disappeared and she relaxed and let go the stress of the day.

"Ye're lookin' cleaner than when I last saw ye," observed Henry, taking a stance against the wall, leaving the only available chair for their mam.

Brandon scowled at his brother. "Don't start," was all he said.

"I don't mean to. It's serious I am. Ye do look cleaner. There's no blood drippin' down yer face, although the bruisin' is creepin' in."

"There's more to come of that," said his mam, indicating with a nod of her head. "Ye'll be lucky if yer forehead and left eye aren't black-and-blue by tomorrow. I don't even want to imagine the other end," she finished, a stern look to her features.

It was that look that Brandon understood where words would have failed. She wasn't just angry, she was pissed. And Mam pissed was not a good thing. Before long he'd be on the receiving end of her wrath, and God help him but it was unavoidable.

"You and I need to talk," was all she said.

Brandon nodded, felt tears sting the back of his eyes. He felt like a ten-year-old again, that same ten-year-old that took the news of his da's death harder than the others. Henry had been his da's pride and joy, the one who'd taken to working the stone just as his da did. Henry, like a golden child, got to go everywhere with Da, while Brandon was always too young.

The twins were special in his da's eyes, too. "Look," he'd crow to his cronies, "I made not one, but two perfect boys." Brandon sometimes wondered what his da would think of the twins now. Not Liam. Liam was a man's man, outgoing, popular, a real lady's man. But Niall was different. Had been all along whether his da wanted to acknowledge it or not. Niall was as gay as they came.

That left Ciara, the only girl, which was why she was special. "Such a pretty cailín as ye'd ever see," his dad would boast. And she was.

That left Brandon. Nothing-special-lots-of-trouble Brandon. It was what he excelled at. If he couldn't get attention by being good—he'd tried that and failed many times—then being mischievous or outright naughty ought to do the trick.

He got noticed alright, and a beating usually followed. Da was good with the beatings, he was. But eventually Henry had taken Brandon aside and taught him how to use his fists. Brandon never asked where Henry had learned and Henry never divulged the secret, if secret it was. But Brandon learned, and after a time, his da never beat him again.

As weary as Brandon was now, he needed to stay awake, take whatever his two mentors would throw at him. He wasn't going to let a little discomfort slow him down, never mind that he'd fallen just trying to get out of bed.

"The garda will be comin' soon," Henry advised. "They'll have lots of questions and I advise ye to just tell the truth, never mind how embarrassin' it may be to you. I know what went on there, Brandon. I saw the rubbers, the mess on the sheets, everything. I saw the writin' on the bathroom mirror. Everything, Brandon. I. Saw. Everything!"

Obviously Henry hadn't realized he'd gained volume as he spoke because on his last words their mam shushed him with a look.

"We know ye did things ye're not proud of," she began.

"Don't start, I said. I know it was bad. All of it. And I don't feckin' care right now. I want ye's all to just leave."

"Brandon…"

"I said leave, and I mean it. Now go." He turned his face away, the tears were so close and he refused to let them see him cry.

"Right. But I'm comin' back later before I go home and I'll have some answers, my son," said Mam, turning on her heel and walking out the door.

"I'm stayin'," said Henry. "I don't want you alone when the shades come. I'll go once they leave."

Brandon stayed the way he was, his face turned to the wall, and refused to acknowledge Henry's words, relaxing only when he heard the door close in a soft shushing noise. When the silence of the room began ringing in his ears, he let the tears come.

And come they did until he was sobbing as if he were still that ten-year-old child, and no one to comfort him. But this time, a warm hand touched his arm, startling him out of his misery.

"Can I get ye anything, some water or juice?" she asked, as if she calmed a thirty-four-year-old baby every day of her life.

All Brandon could do was shake his head.

"It's tough, I know. The physical healing is the easy part. It's the mental healing that takes the time."

"Ye'd know that, would ye," he said, tight-lipped and between sniffs. How much snot could someone produce?

She seemed to ignore his sarcasm, for sarcasm it truly was, and handed him a tissue. "The garda are here to see ye. I thought I'd check on ye first, to see if everything was alright before I let them in. I can tell them you're not yet fit and to come back tomorrow if ye'd like."

She spoke kindly, and if grades were given for someone's efforts, she should make the top of the class. "No, it's alright. I should see them now and get it over with."

"Here's another tissue, then. I'll wet a cloth for your face." She handed him the tissue box and he heard the water running as she did just that. He turned to face her as she held out the cloth, warm and comforting. "Do you want me to do it or are you alright to do it yourself."

God forgive him but he wanted her to baby him. Just this once. "Please. Can you?"

"Of course. You're sure you don't want me to hold them off for another day?"

"Yeah." He waited until she'd gently rubbed his face with the warm cloth, spreading a healing touch across his features that went straight through to his soul. When she was done, he said, "Would you mind seeing that my brother comes in as well? He said as how he'd like to be here when they came."

She nodded, smiling sweetly. "Sure. I think he's with them now."

In a blink she was gone. *Did angels live on earth?* wondered Brandon. If so, he'd just been touched by one.

Unfortunately, the feeling of goodwill from his face wash didn't last long. Two burly officers came in, looking more like thugs than police, and Henry slipped in afterward just before the door closed. Brandon was as trapped as if he'd been hog-tied.

And then the interrogation began. How many, who were they, what did they look like, were the basic questions. Then the words between the officers…"we'll get the security footage from the hotel cameras…" and other talk Brandon couldn't take in. His head was beginning to ache again and the nausea was coming back.

He hit the call bell with everything he had. He knew it wouldn't make it ring any louder but he'd had enough for one day.

The angel came back, suggested the "gentlemen" come back another day, and shooed them out of the room.

All except Henry. "I won't stay long," he promised, so she left again.

"I'm going back to Killarney. I might just get there in time for Emily's birthday supper. We were takin' her to Murphy's. She likes the music there," he said.

"Ah, it's wee Emily's birthday. I'd forgotten," he sighed.

'Not so wee now, she's turning into a young lady, sweet sixteen and all that," Henry said. Was that pride he heard in his big brother's voice?

Brandon yawned. He was so bone tired.

"I think they've got what they need but I'll be back if they decide to come back tomorrow. In the meantime, I'm for Killarney, right?"

Nodding, Brandon said, "Thanks."

"For what?"

"For telling them I was a victim, not a player."

"Don't thank me, thank Mam. That's what she told the surgeons. If it'd been up to me, I would ha' told them the truth." He turned and walked out the door, and any feeling of brotherly love that Brandon thought he'd detected in Henry went with him.

So that's why the nurse had been so sympathetic, he mused. She thought he'd been raped, not that he'd been a willing participant in that part of it. Whatever he'd done while lucid the night before, he hadn't let the man do *that*.

Perhaps it was rape, if it was done after he'd been knocked out. Well, he wasn't about to correct her. He'd keep the sympathy going as long as he could, at least until he got out of here, he figured. After that, it wouldn't matter. He'd never see any of them again because as soon as this had blown over, he was going to take Hank up on his offer and try his luck in Canada. Hank had invited him over, said he needed someone to help rebuild the cabin.

Brandon had no idea how long that would take but he was always up for a challenge and he really needed a new start. Ireland was getting old.

Chapter Four

The shades had come and gone once again, as had Mam, finally seeming satisfied with the answers he'd provided. Brandon hadn't bothered calling Henry back. He'd feel more inclined to open up to the officers if his big brother wasn't breathing down his neck, listening to every sordid word.

The officers, at least, understood. They dealt with this stuff and worse, every day, he theorized. One simple mugging and theft, albeit after a night of salacious sex, was not over-the-top. And he wasn't the first male victim to be raped and left bleeding. No, things went better without Henry there.

The nurse came in. The one he liked, whose name he hadn't yet learned. He tried to read her name tag but his eyes still hadn't focussed yet. Come to think of it, he was still trying to get one eye to cooperate but maybe it had to do with his head injury?

This time, though, he could make it out as she stepped closer. Aine, it said. He liked that she used the Gaelic spelling. "Anya" was often used simply because it was easier for English-speaking people to pronounce but it seemed more Russian. And that was close to Dutch. He was still angry with them for producing such a good-looking woman, built for amazing sex but with such a sadistic attitude. He loved sex. He hated people who used sex to hurt others. It defiled the act, in his mind.

"I've come to check your dressing," she said matter-of-factly. "Can ye roll over for me?"

He paled. She was going to check *that*? "Can I not just tell ye it feels okay?"

"No, sorry. I just want to make sure you aren't bleeding. There's not too much prodding involved. Just peeking."

"Oh, right, just peeking. I'm sure that makes it alright then," he half joked.

She giggled. It was a lovely sound, like tiny bells ringing far away on a breeze. Light. Airy. Like her touch.

He rolled obligingly, felt her hand on his hip while the other peeled the dressing back. It pulled a bit where he imagined some bleeding had occurred, and then she put it back and he rolled back over. He waited for the comments about his arse end. Women always loved his arse end. But he waited for nothing.

"It looks okay," she said, removing the rubber gloves she'd donned. "I'll be back later to do rounds," she said, a smile on her pretty face and a sparkle in her eye.

"Wait," he called before she could leave.

"Oh, is there something ye need?" she asked.

Need? Oh yeah, he thought. A sponge bath. By you. "Em, ah, when will the doctor be in?" It was all he could think of at short notice. He just wanted to keep her there a little longer.

35

"I think about noon. Is that alright?"

He nodded. "And me mam. D'ye know when her next shift is?"

"Yer mam?"

"Yeah, Kathleen O'Farrell."

She stopped and came back into the room, and if her smile could have broadened, it did. It lit the room as she came closer to the bed. "I'd no idea she's yer mam. Such a lovely lady to work with, although I don't know where she gets her energy from. She fair wears me out and I'm maybe half her age."

"That's Mam," he smiled back, "She's got that much energy."

Again the laughter. He'd keep her here all day just to hear it.

"Sorry, I don't. Haven't seen her yet today."

"Right," he answered, trying vainly to come up with something else to stall her departure.

"I've got to go but I'll come back when I've some free time, if ye'd like?" she offered.

"Grand. Thanks. I would."

"Right, then, I'm off."

He watched her leave, and as the day was becoming warm, the door was left open. The breeze from the window was light and fresh and the curtains around his bed fluttered. A garda uniform caught his eye and he silently wished the curtain would flutter away so he could see what they were about. It appeared they'd buttonholed the doctor and he wondered if perhaps they were talking about him?

He wasn't wrong. The officer and the doctor made their way toward his room and he held his breath unconsciously while he waited for their arrival.

After minimal introductions, the officer said, "I'm happy to report we've found the car that was stolen. It was located just south of Dublin and a quick scan of it seems to check out. It's still in running condition. We've impounded it to dust for prints and will retain it for further investigation. As for the two involved, nothing yet; but with the prints we pull and the footage from the hotel security cameras, I'm sure we'll have them caught in no time. They fit the profile of two that have done this type of thing before." He gave Brandon a knowing look. One that said he knew what had gone on, in no uncertain terms.

Brandon had the grace to blush. He felt the heat up the side of his face like a hot iron and imagined he was just as red as if he'd touched one. "So I'm not the first," he stated.

The officer shook his head. "'Fraid not. But this time we know what they look like. We weren't so lucky last time."

"And just where were they, last time?"

"There was an incident down Bantry way. Maybe they like the coastal towns," he suggested.

"And maybe they like gullible musicians," offered Brandon.

"Is that what ye are then? A musician?"

Brandon shrugged. It was as good a job as any. "They wrecked my guitar. Guess I'm not a musician any more. At least not until I can replace it."

The officer nodded in sympathy. "Well, we got your car back. Found what was left of your wallet there but nothin' in it. If ye've credit cards or anything of the like, I'd suggest ye contact the company."

Brandon nodded his agreement, and thanking the officer, watched him leave. The doctor remained.

Brandon watched as the doctor flipped through the file he was carrying, checked the IV briefly, and then closed the file, laying it on the meal trolley. He was a tall, spindly man, with graying hair that stuck out in odd places as if it was in need of a wash or a cut. It wasn't that he didn't seem well groomed, just that he appeared to be a rather eccentric type. Brandon hoped he was at least competent, but knowing his mam, she wouldn't allow an eejit near her son.

The doctor pushed his glasses up his nose, nodded as if to himself, and then looked at Brandon, his shrewd gaze assessing in its scan. "I'll have the IV removed but I'm going to keep you for another day. I'd like to make sure there's no bleeding and that all your levels are correct." He took his glasses from his nose and wiped the bridge where a red line was left. It was easy to see that his glasses did not fit well and were causing him discomfort.

All this Brandon took in within the space of a heartbeat.

"You will forgive me," the doctor began again, "for approaching this next bit plainly. I won't pull any punches for your sake.

"The fact remains you had anal penetration in an

38

unprotected manner; whether by consent or not, that fact is clear. So," he took a deep breath and continued on without waiting for any kind of reaction from Brandon. Brandon didn't care. He just wanted the man to spit it out and was grateful there was to be no preamble. "So," he continued, "you must realize that this has put you at risk for a variety of STDs, not limited to and including HIV. There is no sense in testing you yet. I would recommend, though, that you get in for a test in three weeks' time. It will take that long for any antibodies to be detected. Until that time, I would highly caution you to not have any intercourse of any kind even with a condom. And that includes oral sex as well."

He must have seen the look on Brandon's face, because although Brandon had tried to school his features to remain blank, it was clear he had been shocked. Fuck! HIV? Wasn't that like AIDS?

"I can tell you have questions." The doctor's plain manner of speaking showed in his neutral expression.

Brandon took a deep breath to stem the shakiness he was feeling. It had felt like doom was at his door as soon as the term HIV left the doctor's mouth. It wasn't that he hadn't thought of it before. It was that the bubble of speculation had become the hammer of reality. He wasn't in a cocoon of safety anymore.

"Why not oral sex? Why total abstinence? I thought rubbers were safe."

"Safe to a point," the man agreed. "But the only purely safe thing is abstinence. It isn't forever, only until you know for sure whether you have HIV or not. You should plan on having a test again at three months and then six months. If you are still clear after that, you would be considered healthy, provided you maintain a clean lifestyle."

"What, you think I wanted this?" The little voice in Brandon's head shouted out his lie but Brandon would have none of it. He was going with the victim role, despite what was in the police report. He hadn't seen the report, but from the doctor's manner, he suspected everyone was on to him.

"It isn't my place to know what you think or to pass judgement upon you. You are not the first person I have seen in that bed whose anal canal had to be stitched back up because of rough play. Whether warranted or not, you were in a worse position than you perhaps thought and now you are healing. I am only warning you of the pitfalls and advising you how to go forward. And if you're half the man your mother thinks you are, you'll heed my words. Good day, Mr. O'Farrell."

The doctor turned and left, leaving Brandon feeling as if the dirty words scrawled on the bathroom surfaces were a label he wore for everyone to see.

Minutes later, the nurse Brandon liked so well came to remove the IV line. "So, you're getting better, that's good news," she said, smiling as she got tape and cotton ready to staunch the wound the needle would leave.

"So it seems," answered Brandon. He really liked this woman but the doctor's words were like bitter lemon in his mouth. There was no way he could approach her and hope for a relationship. Not when he could be carrying HIV, or worse. Whatever else Brandon was, he wasn't the kind of man to take someone else's life lightly. He loved sex, loved to have sex and give sex, but he wasn't cruel. If there was one thing he was truly good at, it was loving his partners.

He watched her fingers manipulate the tape with gloved hands. How she managed to do that without the tape sticking to the gloves he had no idea, but manage she did, and quickly and painlessly, too. She had the needle out in no time, the cotton pressed against the wound to stem the flow of blood trying to ooze out, and then the tape across to hold it in place.

"Just put some pressure here for a moment," she instructed, effectively handing his one arm over to his other for safe keeping.

Their hands brushed and Brandon looked up. Her eyes met his, warm and gray and bustling with life. They sparkled as the light from the window was reflected in their smoky depths. God, but she was lovely!

He pressed the spot over the cotton and tape and left it there while his eyes followed her around the room.

"I'm not in tomorrow, so I likely won't see you if, as I suspect, the doctor will discharge you then. But I'm happy to have met ye, and I'm happy ye seem to be on the mend." A pause, and then, "If ye need anything…" she began, but didn't finish.

Brandon was hoping for her phone number. "If I need anythin', then what?" he asked brazenly, a bit of a smile

41

turning up the corners of his mouth. It was the first time he'd smiled since it had happened.

"Oh, well, I was goin' to say something silly but thought better of it. After all, ye don't know me except as a nurse here."

She looked away from him as if she were afraid to meet his eyes.

"I wouldn't think it silly at all," he said honestly.

Her breasts rose with her deep intake of breath, as if she was thinking long and hard before saying her next words. "I don't know if ye'd be interested," she began.

"Try me," he answered, hoping for that phone number.

"It's just that, well, there's a clinic here at the hospital that ye might be interested in attending once in a while. I do a bit of work there with victims of rape. We don't get many men, but when we do, it sometimes helps the women along to know that it happens to men, too. You don't have to do anything, just show up. I can get ye some information if ye think that might be something you'd like to try?"

It was an olive branch, something he could use to see her again. And maybe, over time, she might want to see him, too? It was worth a shot.

"Sure. I guess. I mean, I don't know if I need it but if ye think it may help others, I'll give it a try."

She smiled, her gray eyes crinkled in laughter. No, she wasn't just out of her teens, she had a few years beyond that behind her. The little telltale lines were just beginning around her eyes, but Brandon thought, at least he hoped, they were because she laughed a lot.

"I hadn't meant that it would be just for the women there, but that it might do you some good, too. Ye never know."

"Then I'd like the information."

Nodding, she said, "I'll get the pamphlet for ye. And you can always call the hospital if ye need more information or ask for me and I can call ye back."

Aha! It was a moment he'd been waiting for, a name, maybe more than the single name Aine that was on her badge. "Oh, that would be grand, and who do I ask for?"

"Aine. Aine Donahue. I'm a nurse here, plus I help out at the clinic on Thursdays."

"What's today?" So much had happened in the last couple of days that he couldn't be sure how much time had passed. At least one, maybe two, of those days was a total write-off.

"It's Monday today."

"So Thursday, then."

"Yes." She tidied up the bits left from removing the intravenous line, and taking the IV pole in hand, said, "I hope to see ye Thursday, if not this week, maybe next. Bye."

She waved and was gone out the door before he could blink. And there he was, still holding his fingers on the pressure point where the intravenous line had gone in. He released the pressure, was glad to see that the bleeding had stopped, and lay his head back on his pillow.

They had a saying in France, one of his buddies who had traveled extensively through that country had once told him, and it went, *"Out of manure piles grow roses."* Well, he'd been in the manure pile, and a more accurate description did not exist as far as he was concerned. So maybe, just maybe, he'd get to find the roses, too.

Maybe.

Chapter Five

Aine left Brandon's hospital room with a lighter heart than when she'd gone in. She'd hesitated about informing him of the rape clinic, but only because she was the one who ran it. Every Thursday, from seven until nine in the evening, she counseled victims of rape, usually in a group, occasionally one-on-one.

They rarely had men. Men were too focussed on their bravado to think that a simple thing like talking about a problem could possibly help them. More often they turned to their cronies in the pubs after they'd had too many to count, or ignored the problem completely.

She was ecstatic that Brandon was going to come! A little voice in her head told her that she wanted him to come, not because he'd been raped, but so that she could see him again. She told herself that she wanted to hear his story in order to understand him better, but she knew there was another reason. She just wasn't ready to face that yet.

Aine had come a long way from the child who'd been raped by the neighbor who'd caught her alone one rainy afternoon. He'd come over on the pretext her da had asked him to look after something for him and she, being naïve and far too trustworthy, had allowed him entry.

It happened quickly after that.

Years later, she could still go back to that place of fear and ugliness. All it took was the smell of the same aftershave he'd worn and she'd be trembling in her shoes but for the tools years of counseling had given her.

She understood Brandon's hesitance. He would likely be the only man there. But again, she had to question her joy in his promising to attend.

No, not promising, but he did say he would go, and that was more than she'd hoped for. There was something about him that spoke to her. She saw a gentleness in him, a kindness that seemed to radiate from his eyes, and although she'd heard garda and the doctor speak about his attack, she knew that even consensual sex sometimes went bad.

Aine hadn't had a boyfriend in her entire life. The incident, as she referred to it, at thirteen had halted any thoughts of a loving relationship, no matter that her parents were proof it could happen. After years of her own therapy, she knew she was strong enough to move on. She could help others. She just couldn't help herself to an intimate relationship.

The job at the Cork University Hospital had come at precisely the right time. It was close to her flat, and at the same time she acquired the job at the rape clinic, which was held in a meeting room across from the main hospital at the Bishopstown Library. She would have been happy to do just that, if that was all there was. It was her calling now. She faced her attacker every Thursday along with the people she helped to counsel, and every Thursday she became stronger for it. But she was lucky enough to find a nursing position at the hospital as well, and so she'd done both for the past six years.

Her musing led her to the cafeteria and she bodily ran into Kathleen, who she now knew was Brandon's mam, and who was, luckily for them both, carrying an empty tray, not having chosen anything yet.

"How's my son today?" asked Kathleen, once Aine had properly introduced herself as Brandon's nurse.

"I think he's goin' home soon," she said, happy to be able to impart some good news. Thinking of the past as she had been always brought her to a dark place and she recognized the need to lighten up.

"Are ye in for lunch then?" asked Kathleen, looking at the food and nodding in acknowledgement of Aine's statement.

"I am. Shall we get a table together?"

"Let's. If ye don't mind, I'd like to talk to you," said Kathleen, tilting her head in query.

"Right, then, let's go."

They found a table over by the windows that had a view onto the busy roadway and sat facing each other. As they began to eat, Aine asked, "So, what's on yer mind? Is it your son's condition? If so, he's doing very well, has a positive attitude, and has agreed to come to the rape clinic this week."

"Has he now?" Kathleen remarked, a strange expression on her face.

"Oh, you don't think he'll come?" Aine was curious because she'd been so sure he would show.

47

"Oh, perhaps he'll attend, perhaps he won't. I suppose it depends on where he's staying."

Quickly finishing what she was chewing, Aine asked the obvious, "Doesn't he live in Kinsale? It's not very far."

"Ah well, and he does rent a room there, but it's in the hotel where he got the contract for the tours and entertainin'. He doesn't have a home other than that."

Aine thought about that. "So he really doesn't have a home to go to, then?"

"He could come home to Inishannon with me, but I doubt he'd want to do that. He'd have to put up with his younger sister there. It's just her and me now. His da's been gone these past twenty-four years."

"Oh, it's sorry I am to hear that. So, he never had a da to raise him. Ye did it yerself?"

"No," Kathleen answered honestly. "His older brother, Henry, was a big help to me. He took over when their da died, and him only fourteen at the time. They grew up fast, did those kids, all five of them."

Aine thought about that. Whatever growing up she'd had to do at thirteen, she'd at least had her parents to be there for her and support her. But Brandon'd had only his mam, and a busy one at that, working long hours to support five kids. She hadn't realized that the fellow she'd seen with Kathleen yesterday had been Brandon's older brother. She'd marked the resemblance, but hadn't put two and two together.

"That must have been very difficult for ye. For all of ye," she amended.

Kathleen nodded and finished her soup.

"But ye don't think Brandon would go home to stay with ye, not even for a little while?"

"I'll put it to him. I can't say for sure what his answer might be." Kathleen fidgeted with her napkin. "I've somethin' else to discuss, I hope ye don't mind."

"Of course not," answered Aine, enjoying hearing about Brandon from a different perspective other than what was in his chart.

"As his nurse, I know ye've read his chart, I know ye saw what's in it, how he got to be here. I just...I guess..."

"It's alright. Ye can speak plainly with me. I work at the rape clinic on Thursdays. I'm used to hearing things."

"It's just that, well, Brandon has always got himself into trouble when others wouldn't. It's like it's his trademark or somethin'. But I tell ye truthfully that he would never harm the hair on anyone's head. Whatever happened to him in that room, whatever started out, whether he wanted it or not, he didn't deserve what happened to him."

Aine's heart went out to Kathleen. She'd seen her son at his worst and still had the belief that he was a good man underneath it all, even if he'd brought misfortune upon himself. She placed her hand over Kathleen's where it rested on the table beside her coffee cup.

"I would never judge anyone by what I read in their charts. That's just medical facts. It has no bearing on how they got there, and there were no notes to indicate that this was anything but rape. If it had begun consensually, it didn't

49

end that way. And I fully understand and agree with you that he doesn't seem the kind of person that would want to harm anyone. I can't believe he'd invite this kind of treatment."

Tears started in Kathleen's eyes but she blinked them away and Aine could tell how difficult this was for her.

"I thank ye for yer understandin', and I'm grateful he's got you as his caregiver. He needs some help, does my son."

Aine couldn't disagree. "We'll just have to hope he comes to the clinic."

"I'll see he does," said Kathleen, standing and picking up her tray. "Thank you for takin' the time to sit with me and join me in some lunch. You're a lovely young woman with a good heart. I hope you can work some magic with him. He could sure use it."

Kathleen left Aine to finish her lunch and hustled off to Brandon's room to visit with him before she had to go back to work. She walked into his room just as he was attempting to get out of bed on his own. She stopped for only a moment before the realization dawned that he was quite shaky on his feet and liable to collapse at any time. In two steps she was at his side, her arms around him, supporting him.

He quickly turned away and leaned on the bed, shunning her help. "I can do it myself," he said gruffly.

Years of single parenting and dealing with difficult patients had given Kathleen a backbone she might not otherwise be credited with. "I'm not askin' after yer permission," she stated, "I'm stopping ye from hurtin' yerself more. Ye've enough on yer plate for both of us."

"It's okay. You can leave me. I'll be fine. I just need to stand for a while."

"Ye should have just sat for a while instead o' trying to do it all at once. Why didn't ye ring the call bell?"

He had the impudence to say, "I know how hard everyone here works. I didn't need to bother them with this. I can handle it."

"Ye would have fallen flat on yer arse if I hadn't walked in just now. And then there'd be hell to pay. Ye might even have hurt yerself more, eejit."

He was beginning to tire, his face had gone a pasty white, no sign of the summer tan he usually wore. Unwilling to be bullied into leaving, Kathleen put her arm under his in a move that brooked no argument.

"C'mon, back into bed with ye."

Brandon had no choice but to do as he was told, especially when she took that tone with him. By the time she got him settled again, he was breathing hard.

"Ye may have brought this on yerself," she began, "but I'm not so coldhearted that I won't help ye out. You're my son. My child. And I don't care how old ye are, ye always will be. I won't see a child of mine hurtin' if I can help it. So when they release ye, ye'll be comin' home with me. Ye'll need lookin' after for a few days until ye can get back on yer feet."

Brandon lay on the bed, stone-faced. It was clear he was mulling it over, looking for a way out of it.

"I was talking with Aine just now in the cafeteria. We

had lunch together and she told me ye said ye would go to the rape clinic this Thursday. I want ye to know I think it's a good thing for ye to do. Ye won't yet have the strength to drive so I'll take ye." She stopped her list of demands and thought a moment before continuing, thinking about what it was she was going to say and how to say it.

"I also want ye to know I know it wasn't rape. I know ye went into this with yer eyes wide open." She held up a hand to stay the words he was about to say. They would be words of denial, she was certain, but she wasn't finished yet. His words could wait.

"Ye didn't deserve what happened to ye, but if ye play with fire long enough, ye'll get burned. Ye didn't plan for this to happen, but it did, and so now ye've got to deal with it. And part of that is gettin' better, so I'll be takin' ye home with me. I've some holiday time comin' that I was goin' to use to go with yer gran and grandda to visit some folks up north. But I'm goin' to stay with ye 'til you're back on yer feet and join them later."

He'd closed his mouth, lips forming a thin line of refusal. Still, she wasn't quite done.

"Brandon, if ye've any decency left in ye, I beg ye, you've got to turn yer life around. You're thirty-four and still a waif, not knowin' where you're goin' or what you're about. It's time to get on with it. And this'll be a start. I know it in my bones. Now ye can speak," she finished, crossing her arms in defiance of whatever it was he was going to say.

"This is nothin'," he began, but didn't get any farther.

"T'isn't *nothin'*, ye gligeen. Ye could have died!"

"Ah, I would have been fine. Just Henry panickin' at the sight of a wee bit of blood. Besides, it was deadly craic! At least it was until they smacked me on the head."

"Craic? Ye thought it was fun? I'm gobsmacked, I am," she breathed out, angry beyond caring. "If ye've got such little regard for yerself, however do ye intend to go on? Ye may as well go drown in the ocean for all the use to humanity ye are. I love ye so much, ye've no idea; and ye've never let me in. I tried, even before yer da was killed, I tried, but ye never let me in."

He turned flashing eyes at her, "No one cared about me, never has. Only cared about Henry. Henry could do no wrong. And the twins, they were the perfect wee boys according to Da; and once Ciara came along, I didn't exist. No one fucking cared!"

She rounded on him, all fury and not caring who heard. "Ye're bollocks, y'are if ye think yer da thought so highly of Henry. Gave him a beating at least once a week if the lad so much as turned sideways. But I'll give ye the twins and Ciara. Ye're right about that, though I don't know how he'd feel now with Niall bein' gay."

"He'd think Niall was doin' it just to get back at him."

"Ah, ye maybe right there, too. But Brandon, I tried so hard to be there for ye. Every chance I had, I tried." She'd calmed a bit, her anger making her feel older than her years.

There was no reply from Brandon for a time, then a slight nod of his head and the words, quietly spoken, "I know."

"Then how can ye say no one cared?"

"I always wondered where Henry learned to fight. I guess Da showed him by example."

'Yes, that's the way of it, but don't change the subject. I asked ye how you could think no one cared?"

"I forgot, that's all. I was so busy tryin' to keep ye out of trouble with Da that I couldn't accept what you were tryin' to do."

Her eyes widened in surprise and she felt almost speechless. Almost. "Ye mean ye were tryin' to protect me?"

He nodded, turned blazing blue eyes to meet her green ones. Those blue eyes, the very same as the ones that had made her fall in love with Henry Ryan O'Farrell Sr. in the first place.

"Silly child. Yer da would never have harmed me. And he never went after you boys until after he'd acquired his other family. I can't blame Hank or Meara, or wee Emily, or even their mam. It was yer da's fault. He didn't have to go to bed with her. He had a perfectly good family here. But I think as the pressure mounted, the expenses of two families, the lies he had to keep until he was forced to admit all, well, it was just his frustrations and he saw you boys as a way to work those out, sad as it was."

"Why do ye think he'd never go after you?"

Her shoulders began to shake as she tried to hide the smile that insisted on creeping across her face. "He was afraid of me," she said simply.

"Afraid? Da? Of you?" His mouth hung open in shock.

"Um-hm. I was the respectable one. The one with a university education. He always saw me as a step up the social ladder, although it was never that. He was a stonemason, and a talented one at that. Was why he ended up all over the south of Ireland for work. People wanted what he could do.

"But I was the one people looked to for other things. I had some experience givin' parties and behavin' like yer da used to term a 'social butterfly.' I loved havin' people over since we had such a grand house, but after the first few years, yer da, who was very shy, refused to be there if there was company. So I'm partly to blame for him bein' away so much. But even so, I was known for havin' the talented husband so much in demand, and he was known as the man who had the educated wife who threw some of the best parties in town. Now, talk about deadly craic, and ye'd be describing those parties," she said, a smile on her face with remembering.

"Well now, I'm the one who's gobsmacked," he remarked, not bothering to hide his grin. And then, "Alright, ye win, Mam. I'll go home with ye and I'll go to that clinic, at least this time, but after that, no promises. As soon as I'm able, I'm off again."

"We'll see," she said with a look that was meant to be the final word.

And it was. She left Brandon's room with him still in bed and under control. At least, for now.

Chapter Six

It was a quarter past seven. Kathleen had let Brandon off at the door, promising she wouldn't go in with him, wouldn't be a part of whatever took place inside the meeting room. Instead, she said she'd go have tea with a good friend she hadn't seen for a while. It would be a good two hours spent for them both.

The solid wood of the meeting room door remained closed before him and Brandon couldn't bring himself to open it. He wanted to walk away, to pretend he needed to be back in hospital when they'd actually let him go earlier that day. In the end, he hadn't been released until he'd had a bowel movement and that was the worst thing he'd ever experienced in his life! Besides the associated discomfort with the action, he knew that everyone, absolutely everyone, would know that he had taken a crap. Feckit, but that was embarrassing! Everyone he saw afterward had smiled, nodded at him, done something that made him realize that they *knew*.

By the time his mam had come to collect him, all he could think of was how happy he'd be to go somewhere where no one knew if he could shite or not!

And here he was, his heart thumping in his chest so hard

that he felt as if he could pass out. His mouth was dry. He was going to walk away.

Just then the door opened and someone came out, and with heads turned toward the person exiting the room, he was clearly seen by everyone inside. Before the door could close, his eyes met a pair of gray ones, staring back, above lips pressed into a hopeful smile.

He couldn't walk away now. He had to go in.

"Brandon, I'm so glad ye've come," she said, and if the smile on her face was any indication, she was truly glad to see him.

"Sorry, I didn't mean to be late."

"Oh, it's no bother," she said, brushing his need for an apology aside. "Come and have a seat here," she indicated a vacant chair in the semi-circle around her.

When he was seated and the person who had left had returned, she introduced Brandon to the group of women, five of them. As she had said, there were rarely any men.

"Brandon is also a victim of rape," she said after introducing him to the others. "I know we don't get many men through here and I'm so pleased that I could convince him to come. It takes a great deal of courage to come here, and especially for someone who is, if you'll pardon the expression, the odd man out." This last comment drew chuckles, and women gazed at him either covertly through their lashes or outright. Only one kept her eyes deliberately away from him, and for that he was grateful because he must have looked a fright with his bruising faded to an eerie green and the stitches in his scalp still there in the shaved patch on his head.

"Tonight, I thought we'd try something different. I've brought some paper and some colored pens and other drawing materials. I'd like you all to take a seat at a table, anywhere in the room, wherever you feel comfortable. I don't expect you to be artists. I just want you to draw, paint, or color what you feel."

"I've never drawn anything in my life," said one woman, who genuinely looked horrified at the thought of having to produce a piece of art work.

"Oh, no, this is not a piece of art that you need to display to anyone. It is simply a different way to express what you may be feeling. I've had others go through this exercise and color the entire page black. There is no artistry in that but there is great expression. So, off you go. Get a paper and whatever medium you'd like, find a spot, and get started. I'll give you until eight o'clock, and then we'll stop for a fifteen-minute break and have a discussion afterward."

Brandon took a piece of paper, decided on some paint, and taking a small container of water, went to a table at the back of the room. Opening the first container, a light blue, he painted a swath of what he thought might be sky. A bit of white became some fluffy clouds. His mind was detached, not really paying attention to what he was doing, and before he knew it, his bright-summer-day painting was filled with black streaks, red splotches, the colors smeared and ugly. He stood back as if horrified at what he'd done and then took the small container of water and poured it over the paper.

It soaked into the watercolor paper, ran onto the table, and dripped on the floor. He threw the brush down and with his bare hands began to smear the colors together until there was nothing but a murky mess.

It's me, he thought. *I'm nothin' but a feckin' mess!*

Unwilling to let anyone see what he'd done, he quickly folded the stiff paper and began ripping it in strips and then in pieces. He didn't want anyone to see it.

Tears pricked at the back of his eyes. *This is crazy*, he thought, *I wasn't raped, it was just craic!*

He wanted to run, to leave the room at least. But he was the only guy there; someone would be bound to notice. And that someone, if no one else, would be Aine.

Instead, he stood, looking at the mess in front of him, breathing hard as if he'd just run a mile.

"Brandon? Are ye alright?"

Her voice, so soft and serene, materialized beside him and he hadn't even realized she was there.

"Fine. All good. Nothin' to be concerned about." He schooled his features as best he could, tried to calm his breathing. From his six-foot frame, he looked down into her eyes. She was so petite, a good six inches shorter or more. He noted the crazy red streak in her hair, the gorgeous gray eyes, assessing, worried.

"Good, then." She looked down at the mess on the table, the scraps of paper with the water-smeared paint, and said, "There is no right answer in this exercise, merely letting go of the feelings trapped inside. It doesn't matter, except to you," she explained, her soft gray eyes trying to penetrate the storm raging inside him.

"So, ye've no concern for the people who attend?" He was baiting her, and he knew it. For some reason, it was important that he put some distance between them, however that was achieved.

"This venue is for personal expression and letting go of feelings that stand in your way of progressing. If I feel concern, as you put it, over and above what can be accomplished here, I make a recommendation that the person I feel concerned about seeks other, more individual, attention." She was boring into his eyes with hers, never flinching, never giving any quarter, despite what he might have said.

It was an epiphany for him. She was going to do her job regardless of what he might feel for her. Or vice versa.

Checking her watch and turning away from him, she announced that the coffee was ready, as were the baked goods someone had volunteered to bring. "Let's all thank Sarah for the treats tonight," she said, clapping her hands.

Everyone joined in, and Brandon followed suit, walking with Aine as she went to where the coffee urn was bubbling away.

As everyone sat enjoying the coffee and butter cookies that the woman named Sarah had brought, Brandon took a look around him. He saw that most had left their artwork on the tables when coffee was called. A feeling of shame came over him as he realized that his piece was the only one that had been destroyed. Furthermore, the only thing Aine had said was to enquire after him, to see if he was alright. There had been no criticism, no berating him for bad behavior. Only concern for his well-being. It was a sobering thought.

After everyone had partaken of the coffee and snacks, Aine called them all back to their chairs. Brandon was already seated, paper cup in hand, sipping the last of the brew. He hadn't hung around the table to talk with the women there although he saw some eyes look hopefully his way. He was used to that, to the fact that he had pleasant enough features that women were attracted to him. It was what made finding a sexual partner so easy.

He was also outgoing. But not tonight. Tonight he felt shut down as tight as he could possibly be. He didn't want to share any part of himself, and that scared him. He was Brandon, the here-I-am-come-and-get-me fella. The fella who could make a good time out of a shipwreck. But the humor wouldn't come, and that scared him, too.

"Would anyone like to start, to express their feelings about the exercise?"

The woman who had refused to look at Brandon spoke, her voice quiet and shaky. "I didn't know what to color, so I closed my eyes and my hand picked up the red pen. And then I just scribbled. It reminded me of…" her voice faltered. No one spoke. The silence in the room was palpable.

Brandon thought Aine was going to say something, she looked about to speak until the woman began talking again. She said, still keeping her eyes downcast, "Blood. It reminded me of blood. It was everywhere. I just wanted to wash it off but I couldn't. Every time I looked, there was more."

Very gently, Aine encouraged her, "Go on."

"And then I took the yellow and covered up the red. It turned it to orange, but it was changing it, making it better. And I think that's how I feel. I'm changing. Getting better."

For the first time, Brandon saw her lift her eyes, noted the black lashes around deep set brown eyes. He thought her pretty, despite the lines of age she sported. Not young, but not his mam's age, either. Somewhere in between.

When it was clear the woman had stopped talking, Aine thanked her and moved on to the next person. Brandon wasn't the last one but he had to come up with something to say and felt his heart start to beat madly in his chest. What would he say? What *could* he say?

And then it was his turn.

"Brandon? What did you get out of the exercise?"

He thought a moment. Thought of the blue sky and the white clouds and the black and red splotches that marred the brightness of what he'd started and realized he was describing himself.

"I didn't realize until I painted it that it was a self-portrait."

When he didn't expound on it, Aine moved to the next person.

And so it went until it was nine o'clock and time to go.

When people began to leave, Brandon hung back, hoping to be the last. He wanted more from her, he knew, but others had the same idea and she ushered them all out with the professionalism that she wielded so well.

Still, he was hoping.

"Brandon? Did ye forget somethin'?" Her clear Dublin accent was like a breath of fresh air.

"Forget? Ah, no. I, uh, I was just wonderin'…I mean, ye never called me on rippin' up my art work."

She laughed, and once again, the thought that there were bells in a far off breeze, or a wind chime tinkling in his ear, filled his senses. He was heady with her nearness.

"Everyone has a different reaction to what they paint or draw. Sometimes it's nothing. Sometimes they view it as a piece they'd like to display, like actual art. And sometimes it is.

"But there are some pieces that are true feelings, like yours. None of them are wrong; this isn't about that. This is about getting those feelings out, expressing your hidden thoughts. No one really knows what the pictures you draw or paint mean. Only you. But they're expressions from your soul. And hopefully, they'll help you work through those things that block you from moving forward."

He observed her through her little speech and wondered if she gave everyone the same spiel. She seemed honest, as if she was speaking truthfully, and not caring if he agreed or not.

"I see…em...perhaps this is a bit premature, but I'd really like it if…?"

"Brandon," called Kathleen from the end of the hall,

"how did it go?"

Brandon cursed his mother's timing. Just when he'd got up the nerve to ask her out, even if just for a coffee, his mam had shown up and broken the mood.

"You were going to say something?" Aine asked Brandon.

"Oh, em…just…well, it's been enlightening, to be sure. I'll see you next week?"

"Of course," she said, smiling that broad, beautiful smile of hers. "I'll see you then."

Aine walked down the hall, past his mother, exchanging glances with her that had his mam smiling. He couldn't imagine what it was. Or maybe he could. He didn't doubt his mam would question Aine once she was back at work, even though he knew such things were confidential; but he really thought his mam might find a way around it. However, since Mam was on holiday, he didn't have that worry. And by the time she went back to work, this whole affair would be behind him.

But not Aine. He wanted her in the way he'd become used to viewing women. He'd see beautiful women walk by and think to himself how wonderful it would be to be in bed with them, make love to them, stroke them, bring them to peaks of pleasure so high they'd ask him to do it again. It was what he did, who he was. He showed them a good time and they all came back for more, so for him to feel that way about Aine was nothing new. It was just going to take him longer to get her beneath him in that way.

And then he remembered the doctor's warning about

HIV. He hadn't been tested yet. He wouldn't know for six months if he was infected or not. Not even a rubber would be safe enough. Despite his reputation as a bad boy with the women, he was always a gentleman. And gentlemen didn't go around spreading filthy, deadly diseases.

The sensations in his crotch that seemed to ignite whenever he saw Aine fizzled away at the possibility of infecting her. It was like getting doused with a bucket of cold water.

"Let's go," said Mam, and he allowed her to lead the way down the hall to the main doors. Whatever strength he'd gained over the last two days in hospital after being allowed out of bed had just left him.

Chapter Seven

Effects of trauma on rape victims, on any victim of aggression, really, can be mitigated. But it needs to be understood. Where the pain is coming from needs to be understood." Aine looked at the panel of rape survivors before her and knew she had to make them understand.

"You have all been traumatized by what has happened to you. But it doesn't mean that you have to be stuck there. There is nothing wrong with you, no sign on your forehead that screams 'victim.' You aren't bad people, nothing of the sort. But if you believe that, then you're stuck.

"However, if you understand where the pain is coming from, then it's possible to let it go."

"I know where the pain is coming from. I was raped," said one woman, her voice filled with anguish and unshed tears.

"Yes, and that's a start. But you have already admitted to the group that you pass the evening with a bottle of wine because it's the only thing that dulls that pain. So what I am saying is to let us take that and analyze it." She waited for the woman to acknowledge her words and then continued on.

"If there is a desire to hide in a bottle of wine, or drugs,

66

or any other substance, then you have to ask yourself, 'What am I escaping from?' because it is a form of escapism. And the answer is that I'm escaping from pain." She could see the women, and Brandon, watching her intently, wondering where she was going with this.

"The next question, is 'How did I get that pain?' and of course, in this case, the answer is, 'I was raped.' So again, the next question is, 'Why?', and that's the tough one. We don't always know why. Often, it's because the person who raped you was a rape victim, too, or a victim of other types of abuse. It's sometimes true that violence begets violence, but it doesn't have to continue. The point is," she took a sip of water to moisten her suddenly dry throat. It was getting to her tonight. She was headed back to "that place," and she was fighting to keep abreast of the feelings that were threatening to overwhelm her.

"The point is," she started again, "we don't have to see ourselves as victims. We can acknowledge that this thing has been done to us. We know where our pain comes from and we aren't stupid. We're all quite normal, there is no sign on our forehead that invites unwanted attention or screams 'victim.' Sometimes, things just happen. What we do with that knowledge, how we handle ourselves and move forward, becomes easier once we identify our pain, acknowledge it. That's the important part. Acknowledgement."

She felt Brandon's eyes bore into her, studying her, and she'd give anything to know what he was thinking. At first, she'd been delighted to have him come to the sessions, but now, three weeks into it, he hadn't participated in anything other than to sit there and listen. And tonight, it felt as if he were trying to read her mind, to see what was hidden there, the dark secret she harbored.

Someone had told her she should let the classes know that she, too, had been a victim of rape but Aine refused. She'd been through these sessions as a victim and others didn't usually care to know if their counselor had been an abuse victim. She had preferred not to know, and on that basis had decided that it was something in her past that no one else needed to be aware of.

After her little speech, a lively discussion ensued, through which Brandon, although attentive, was quiet. Should she poke the beast, she wondered, or would she get bitten? She wanted his participation in more than just attendance, and so she looked him squarely in the eye, trying not to listen to the voice in her head that kept remarking on how fine he was to look at. Not just the blue of his eyes nor his thick, dark hair, but his broad shoulders, muscular physique, visible as it was in a tight-fitting t-shirt and jeans. It was now July and the evenings were still warm from the heat of the day.

"Brandon? Ye haven't said much. Do ye have any thoughts on it?"

He was quiet for a long time, thinking, and then said, clear-eyed and looking directly at her, "What if we asked for it?"

It had been totally unexpected and stopped her romantic notions like a blaring horn in her ear, shocking her back into the moment. "Asked for it? Ye mean, asked to be raped?"

"Well, if ye ask for it, then it isn't rape, is it." His voice came out flat, matter-of-fact, not a query at all.

She felt like a fish suddenly out of the water, mouth open, gasping for air where there was none. "If ye mean, when it seems fine, and then, suddenly, it isn't, and the person won't stop when ye tell them, even though it's hurting and ye've begged them, and…" She stopped suddenly, realizing she'd been instantly back in that place. Pleading with the neighbor to stop. He was hurting her. The memory left her shaking but she took a deep breath and swallowed another gulp of water, which seemed to help. Getting herself under control again, she went on, "If ye have a considerate partner, they'll stop if ye tell them."

"But I went in with eyes wide open. It was just to be a bit of craic. But I ended up with a bash on the head and needing emergency surgery to repair the other damage. But. I. Asked. For. It!" He was forward in his seat, hands white-knuckled on the chrome arms of the thinly padded chair.

"No, Brandon," she said softly, feeling tears prick the back of her eyes but refusing to let them fall. She swallowed roughly and the tears disappeared before she spoke again, her voice stronger. "No one asks to be abused, no matter how it begins. There are those that thrive on that sort of thing, I know, but that isn't you, nor any of us here."

"How do you know? I might be that depraved," he exclaimed, and she could see by his expression that he was ready to blame himself for what had happened to him; that he was thinking he was a very bad person regardless of what she knew of him.

"Brandon, do you remember what I said earlier? That we don't have signs on our foreheads and that we're not bad people? No matter how it began, you did not ask to be bashed on the head or have your insides torn up."

Brandon held his head in his hands, having difficulty stemming the tears that threatened to overflow. He wouldn't cry. He took beatings from Da without crying, he wouldn't cry over this.

The woman who had always kept her eyes downcast and away from him said quietly, "That happened to me, too. But I didn't think it could ever happen to a man. I'm so sorry for you."

She still wasn't looking at him but Brandon acknowledged her words with a nod and a quick, "Thank you," before accepting the tissue Aine held out for him. He hadn't realized his tears had fallen or that he was sniffing them back.

"That's enough for now, I think," said Aine, and Brandon was grateful there would be no more to come. Not tonight.

It was a somber group that filed out of the room, unlike the other evenings when they'd left on a positive note. For once, Brandon didn't want to stop and chat up Aine and it seemed no one else was really wanting that either. He made to leave when Aine's voice stopped him.

"Brandon, would you mind staying, just for a minute?"

Had she asked him that last week, he would have been ecstatic. But tonight, he just wanted to leave.

She waited until they were alone in the room and then said, "I want to thank you for speaking out tonight. I know it was hard, and that was a tough question. I think it's helping Helen. That's the first time she's expressed what happened to her. It's taken her months of coming here to be able to voice it. So, thank you."

Brandon didn't know what to make of the situation. He'd helped a woman, the woman who had refused to acknowledge him even when he'd offered her the cream for her coffee. He'd thought she was rude. Stand-offish. He hadn't realized she'd been so badly abused. Images of her with a bashed head and torn up insides didn't sit well with him, but now that he thought about it, he saw her with a new insight: the eye that drooped slightly, the side of her mouth that didn't seem to work quite right.

"That woman," he began, "I mean, I know ye can't tell me anything about her, what happened to her and stuff, but did she have a severe head injury?"

"What makes you ask?"

Clearly, she was not going to make it easy for him. "Oh, I just noticed that the one side of her face seems a bit different, ye know, her eye, her mouth."

Aine surprised him with her answer, "She may give you details if ye really want to know, but yes, she was battered so hard it left part of her face paralyzed. She's come a long way. She's had lots of different types of therapy, not just this kind."

He was about to say something when she continued. "Ye've done her a great service tonight. It's been a big step

71

for ye both."

Whatever he'd been about to say went out the window. "Both?"

"Yes, both of you. Brandon, don't minimalize what happened to ye. Ye have to know it wasn't your fault, despite what ye said about asking for it. You are just as much a victim and deserve to be here as much as anyone. I'm very proud of you for sticking this out."

He hadn't expected that. Hadn't expected any of it.

Seeing her gathering her things, and having noted upon his arrival that she'd come on foot tonight instead of her usual car, he asked, "Can I give ye a lift? I saw that ye had no car."

She smiled sprightly, and he had to wonder how much of that smile was bravado. "That's alright, I don't live far."

"But it's dark, and ye've all that to carry. I'd rather ye let me see ye home."

Whatever he'd said must have made sense to her because she finally nodded her acquiescence. "Thank you, then. I'd be happy to have a lift. This is rather heavy," she said of the leather briefcase she sported.

He took the case from her, saw her blush and look away as he strung the leather strap over his shoulder. The weight took him by surprise; it wasn't light. "What have ye got in here? Bricks?" he joked.

Her laughter made him feel good. "No, just papers, things I thought we might need tonight."

They walked out of the library and into the parking lot where his mam's car winked into life at the press of the button on the key. The little Mini was still being held by the garda and no further information had come about the couple that had assaulted him.

Aine gave him her address and he cursed the fact that it was very near to the hospital. It wouldn't take them any time to drive there, so he thought he'd see if a stop for coffee might be alright.

"I don't know, I have to work tomorrow and it's already almost half nine. And you're a patient. Ye come to these sessions."

"Then I'll stop coming."

The look of horror on her face was almost laughable. "Brandon, you can't!"

"Well, if I can't invite ye for a coffee just because of going into that room, then I'll not go."

"Let's be serious about this. Ye must continue your work. Because it is work. And ye've made strides but ye aren't through it all yet, ye've just touched the surface."

"What if I say I'll continue with someone else? I'll be moving down to my grandparents' place in Garrettstown in the next day or so anyway and I can't see me drivin' up here on a Thursday evenin'. Not unless..." his voice drifted off.

There was only silence from the other seat and just when Brandon had thought she'd remain steadfast, she said, "I can give you the name of someone in Kinsale. It's a private counselor, not free like here. And it would be one-on-one. If you agree to go see this person, I'll have coffee with you."

If heaven existed, then Brandon was sure he was in it.

The joy he felt at her words was almost overwhelming. "*I'll have coffee with you.*" To himself, he thought that it would be a small price to pay for being able to see her again. The other thought that came to him was that he likely needed go more than once for it to be convincing. He hoped he could get well quickly because he wasn't sure that sessions with someone else would provide half the draw of sessions with Aine. But a deal was a deal.

Aine wasn't through making deals. "If I go with you tonight, I want to be home by half ten."

"Ye drive a hard bargain, ye do," he exclaimed, and couldn't help the grin that spread across his face.

Brandon thought he'd never been so happy in all his life.

Chapter Eight

The coffee shop was one of those all-nighters that had ghastly lighting, casting a garish glow to everything around. It made Brandon want to squint although it seemed dim at the same time.

They found a small table at the back where no one was near and took their coffee and a small pastry he'd tempted her with to share. Once seated and the pastry properly divided, he said, "I got the feeling tonight that there's more to you in those sessions than just an empathetic listener. Am I right?"

She seemed to hesitate before taking a deep breath and speaking. Some sort of mask was put into place when she did that, he noted, as had happened during the session.

"No, not at all," she answered, and stuffed the piece of pastry into her mouth, likely, thought Brandon, so she didn't have to speak more.

But he wasn't going to give up. She was hiding something, of that he was sure, and as delightful as it was to watch her lips work to stay together while she chewed, and while it was ever so difficult for him to not reach across and lick the delicate crumbs from that soft, pink flesh, he sensed the time was not yet right.

"It's just that ye stopped what ye were sayin', and ye looked, well, ye looked like ye were right there with the rest of us, ready to give in to what ye were really feelin' inside."

She finished chewing and licked her lips and Brandon felt his crotch tighten in response. Maybe stopping for coffee hadn't been such a good idea, after all. This celibacy thing was going to kill him!

"Perhaps I'm too empathetic, as you said," she acknowledged. "I've lots of training in the field, seen lots of survivors go through those doors, and I think I just get caught up in their emotions sometimes."

"Because ye're an emotional person," he offered.

"Yes, because I'm likely too emotional," she admitted. "It was probably the hardest part of my nurse's training that I had to deal with. I couldn't cry every time a patient died. I had to learn to guard my emotions so that I didn't get involved in their pain or their lives. It's like a mask I have to wear…"

"…that comes off at the end of the day," Brandon finished for her.

"Yes, exactly. How did you…oh, of course. Yer mam."

Nodding, Brandon elaborated, "Exactly. I remember picking her up after work once I learned how to drive. I had a job not far from here for a time during the summer when I was a teenager. And she was dead tired from work, trying to keep her emotions in check when, really, she's very involved in the lives of us kids. She rules us with an iron fist but she's just a marshmallow underneath. But she hid it all. And she was tough because she had to be. So I'd drive the way home to Inishannon so she wouldn't have to. Ye know, she was tired and it's a bit of a drive."

"That was kind of ye. Lots of young men wouldn't do that for their mams."

"Well, I'm not the same as most, I guess. I've always tried to protect her, even when it meant deflecting the anger my da might have had toward her to me. I knew I could take the beatings, wasn't so sure she could."

"Oh, I didn't know yer da was like that." She sipped the coffee carefully. It was hot, but not especially good, Brandon knew.

He chuckled but it wasn't a humorous laugh. "It's a long story, but to be fair, he wasn't always like that. It wasn't until things got rough with business that he began to take it out on us. I thought it was just me, but it was Henry, my older brother, too. And Hank. My half brother."

"You have a half brother? Goodness, what a load for yer mam to bear. Five children and a stepson." She shook her head in wonderment. Kathleen must have just attained sainthood in her eyes.

"Ah, no. No, ye see, Hank is why my da started takin' his frustrations out on me and Henry. He had this whole other family we knew nothin' about for years. Not until shortly before his death. Mam had kicked Da out of the house for the millionth time and we think he was headed back to see his other family in Killarney. But we didn't know about them at the time. Wasn't until Meara, Hank's sister, showed up on Henry's doorstep with her daughter, looking for her da. Our da."

He'd obviously gobsmacked her. She was speechless.

Aiming a cocky grin at Aine, a trademark of his that he knew the ladies liked, he said, "Told ye it's a long story, and that's only half of it."

"There's more?"

At Hank's nod as he sipped his weak coffee, Aine looked at her watch. "Oh, it's just about half ten. I'd love to hear the rest of your story but it'll have to wait. We'd best be off if ye're goin' to keep your promise to me. Oh, and here, before I forget," she rummaged in her purse and pulled out a card. "The fellow in Kinsale."

"Ah, thanks," he glanced briefly at the card in his hand before stuffing it into the pocket of his jeans. "Let's get you home, then. I'm a man who always keeps his promises," he grinned, hoping that when he stood up his wayward thoughts wouldn't be so obvious. In some part of his brain, he was still focused on the pastry crumbs that had stubbornly clung to her lips until she'd licked them off with her tongue. That tongue…he wouldn't go there right now.

Brandon pulled the car to the side of the road in front of the building where Aine lived. Besides her briefcase, she'd had a box of materials to carry as well, things like the paints they'd used that first time Brandon went to her session.

"Let me help ye get this stuff to yer flat," he offered, but she brushed him off.

"No. It's alright, I can manage. Thanks for the lift, and the coffee and pastry. Let me know how you make out in Kinsale," she called over her shoulder before waving goodbye.

She was gone before he could blink twice.

The road back to Inishannon would take a good half hour if he went his usual speed. He was very good at avoiding speed traps, but tonight, he didn't care to speed. He drove leisurely, pulling over to let drivers in more of a hurry pass him by whenever the road allowed it. Despite the late hour— it was after eleven—he didn't care to get home soon. He knew his mam would likely still be up, waiting for him so she could find out how the evening went.

All Brandon wanted was to go to bed, preferably with a warm, willing female by his side; but he knew that wouldn't happen. And it had nothing to do with the doctor's admonishment and everything to do with the fact that Brandon realized he was somewhat fixated on Aine.

He wondered how long it would take to get her into his bed? He sensed within her a passion that she likely knew nothing about. It was as if she refused to acknowledge that somewhere inside of her was a woman who wanted what he could offer. And by the remarks from the women he'd dated, and taking in his bad boy reputation, he had full confidence in himself. It was only a matter of time, he knew.

* * *

Aine put her box of materials down on the floor near the door. She would normally have put it away in the cupboard where it belonged, but tonight she was too tired to bother.

Brandon had struck a nerve with her, and for the first time in years, she'd found herself back in *that place*. She put the briefcase down by the box and wandered into the bathroom, flicking the light on and facing the mirror. No, she wasn't wearing a sign on her forehead and no, she wasn't a bad person. Despite knowing these things, she felt ugly and suddenly wanted nothing more than to have a shower and wash it all away. Showering usually helped. It made her feel clean again and helped to calm her.

Slowly, she stripped her clothing from her body, putting it all into the laundry hamper by the bathroom door; and facing the mirror once more, she scanned her nakedness, looking for something. Anything. An acknowledgement from her inner self that her body was okay. It wasn't flawed, at least, not horribly.

She touched her breasts, kneaded them like dough, felt the moisture grow between her legs, and ran a tentative hand down her belly. Slipping a finger between her legs, she found the moisture there and began to rub herself. The feeling inside began to build and so she stopped and stepped into the shower. Putting the nozzle on vibration mode, she held it up to her crotch with one hand while the other rolled her firm breasts around and tweaked the ruched nipples to hard little peaks.

In no time, she was wanting more, wishing that she could get past the part where the thought of a man penetrating her sent her into a full-fledged panic attack. This thing with the shower head, this she could do to ease the desire that flared when a good-looking man paid attention to her and the thought that it might lead somewhere was evident. It never failed to take the edge off, to leave her more relaxed and thankful because she'd dodged that bullet once again.

Aine knew she was pleasant to look at, not that she'd spent any time comparing herself with others. But she was smart enough to accept compliments when friends gave them. So when those sexual urges overwhelmed her, she could look at her body in the mirror and pretend that those hands belonged to someone else and give herself pleasure. She'd known for many years that this was how it had to be. And in the shower, while the thud-thud-thud of the massage selection on the handheld wand pounded her vaginal area, she felt her backside tilt upward, waiting for the penetration that would never come as her fingers tweaked her nipples and her climax overtook her.

Afterward, it was all she could do to stand while she soaped off the remnants of her body's juices, her legs still shaky from the climax. It had been a good one. Brandon had been the focus of her thoughts.

If she was normal, she thought, but then stopped herself and reworded the sentence in her head. If she had never been raped, she amended, she might have been able to let him help her bring the box upstairs. She might have let him come inside, and she might have let him stay the night. And then it would be his hands and his body that would be doing wonderful things to her and she wouldn't be standing on shaky legs. She'd be in bed, cuddled up to him like almost every other woman she knew would do with their partners.

But that wasn't her. Would never be her. Instead, she settled for the afterglow from the shower massage, telling herself it had been a good one and would help her fall asleep. But once in bed with the light out and the covers pushed back against the warmth of the night, she lay there wide-eyed, thinking of a man with hair as black as the night outside and eyes as blue as the sea, and wondered if he thought about her at all.

Chapter Nine

The breeze off the water at the beach in Garrettstown was too much for Brandon to ignore. He'd moved into his grandparents' home, to the little suite they'd had installed at one side of the house, a sitting room/bedroom combination with its own bathroom and a small counter with a coffeemaker. A microwave had been a later edition as well as the hotplate since there was no cooker. That was fine with Brandon. He liked his gran's cooking just fine.

They were still gone on that trip with his mam, though, and Brandon had the huge home to himself. The house was built on a large property with a grassy sward that flowed down to the thirty-foot cliffs that lined the shore. Even though it was early July, the long green grass had been cut already and sent to a nearby farm for silage for the stock for over the winter. It had enabled his grandparents to stay in their home and have help looking after the extensive property.

A large anteroom had been built on the front that overlooked the sea, the sweeping half circle of windows a perfect venue for the painting his gran loved to do. She was passably good at it but it didn't matter because she painted for the love of it. Her work covered the walls in the large room, colorful against the pale yellow backdrop of the walls and antique-style furniture. It was a beautiful room, and a showplace inside a home that was itself as grand as any.

The property to the rear of the house held a bricked lane and parking area, separated from the narrow, country road by tall, square brick pillars attached to a stone fence, with a wrought iron gate across the access, wide enough for two cars to pass at once. Of course, the gate was almost never closed, even Grandda had said it was mostly for show, but it was impressive and finished off the look of the stately home.

There were more windows that looked out over the bit of lawn and the bricked-in parking area and lane. They ran from the floor to the ceiling and if a person stood in the middle of the doorway from his gran's painting room, where the grand piano took up the near corner, a person could look both out to the cliffs and back to the road without having to move.

There were a lot of windows in that home and Gran was always cleaning them. When the kids were young and visited during the summer holiday, it had been Brandon's job to do them. Even now, when he stopped by to see his grandparents or stayed to visit for a while, he'd check the windows over and if they needed cleaning…well it had been his job, for as long as he could remember.

It was amazing to think that they had such a large house, that his mam still had the large home in Inishannon that she and Da had built shortly after they were married, and yet his half brother and half sister had grown up in near poverty in Killarney. Such a contrast, and yet Hank was a well-adjusted man, newly wed with his own family, and living in the mountains in south-central British Columbia. Not so Meara, who had died of an overdose of drugs. But her child, Emily, just turned sixteen and being raised by his own brother, Henry, and Henry's wife, Siobhan, was a lovely young girl.

He'd thought of going to see Hank in Canada, of helping him rebuild the home in the mountains he was calling a cabin. It sounded too palatial to be a cabin. At least, the idea did. *Maybe next year*, he thought. There were other things to do this year.

He'd lost his job in Kinsale since the incident that had landed him in hospital, and he needed to find another one. Starting tomorrow, he'd be job hunting. It didn't matter much what he did. He just needed something to bring in some money. For now, though, the surf was high and he was going to enjoy it. Donning his wet suit and grabbing a change of clothing, he laid his board in his grandda's van, the one they'd had forever and used to haul the entire family down to the beach when they visited, and left.

As soon as Brandon laid his board on the less rocky part of the beach, he met a crowd of his mates, lads that had surfed with him, girls that he'd dated, or bedded, or just had fun with. One in particular eyed him up and he found he wasn't immune to her glances.

"Sheila," he laughed, as she put her arms about his neck and kissed him solidly on the lips. "It's been a long time." He unwound her arms and stepped back out of her grasp to look her over.

She was tall, solidly built, with slight rolls that her wet suit held in check, and had a reputation almost as bad as his own. It was what he'd liked about her when they'd first met a few summers ago; that she could spend a night or two with him and then leave with no fixation on getting wed and no jealousy. It had been a grand way to have a fling and if it was a month ago, he'd already be leading her somewhere, to a lovely field of tall grass away from prying eyes or to the back of his grandda's van. Anywhere that afforded the slightest bit of privacy would do just nicely, but today he saw her in a different light. He was beginning to see all his friends in a different light.

They were all laughing, making off-color jokes that would normally have had Brandon jumping right in. But something had changed. Was it him?

He didn't have much of a chance to think on that because a large roller had just crashed and all heads turned toward the waves.

"C'mon, let's go," someone shouted, and at that, it was every surfer to themselves as they grabbed their boards and hit the waves.

Sheila was right beside Brandon, and when she stumbled with her board, he was right there to help her along.

"New feet?" he joked, and was delighted to see her laugh.

"Just clumsy," she admitted.

They waded into the water, felt the cool Atlantic chill their feet despite the heat of the day, and floated their boards. Brandon straddled his board, felt the incoming waves lift and carry him as he fastened the Velcro tie around his ankle.

He waited until Sheila had done the same thing and then they faced the ocean and began to paddle out. When they were farther out where the waves were merely swells, they faced inland, ready to wait for the perfect wave.

Brandon wasn't ready to go yet. He liked the view from here, the curving swath of sandy beach at low tide before the rounded rocks near the stone wall came into play. The sweeping view of the land was incredible to see; the cliffs to the west near his grandparents' home majestic and forbidding all at once, and to the east, the Old Head of Kinsale, where the golf course lay and the old lighthouse and tower now stood, a testament to the grit of the people who lived in the area. The tower had recently been restored and was a museum of the history of the area and a tribute to those who lost their lives on the Lusitania so many years ago. They'd erected a small monument out beside the road near the tower as well. Brandon had been one of the volunteers, working with the others when he had time, to help rebuild the Old Head of Kinsale Signal Tower. The tower, with its dark slate walls that had come from the Cwt-y-Bugail quarry in Wales, specifically chosen because they matched the original so closely, was one of eighty-one towers constructed, starting from Pigeon House Fort in Dublin, all the way around the south coast and then west up to Malin Head in Donegal. They were all built between 1804 and 1806, true relics of a bygone age. Everyone who'd worked on the restoration of Old Head Signal Tower, number 25, had called it a labour of love. To Brandon, it had made him feel as if he belonged. He hadn't been present at the unveiling of it just recently, but he could imagine the crowds that would have marveled at the masterpiece of restorative work.

Sheila was beside him. "What are ye thinkin'?" she asked. "Ye seem so far away."

"Oh, just looking at the view. I never get tired of it." He didn't, it was true. If he didn't enjoy surfing so much, he'd just sit out here all day. But the truth was he loved surfing, and so checking behind him and noticing a promising looking swell, he winked at Sheila and said, "Are ye ready?"

She looked back, her eyes widening in surprised delight. "Let's go!"

They began paddling for all they were worth, felt the wave come up beneath them, pushing them to the top of the swell, and then Brandon stood, guiding his board through the transition and into the curve, balancing and shifting his weight, working the board. The shore was fast approaching, and as the board began to lose momentum he jumped into the water, just before it hit the sand. It was still low tide but those rocks between the sea and the stone wall weren't that far away.

"Brilliant! That was grand," shouted one of the others as they came up beside him.

"No doubt," agreed Brandon, watching as Sheila ploughed her board into the sand and rolled off. She'd come dangerously near the rocks but expertly evaded them. "Alright?" he called to her, and at her nod, they put their boards back into the surf and headed out for another ride.

Several rides later, they wandered across the road, now half covered in sand from the ever-present breeze, where cars went back and forth to either the Old Head of Kinsale, or farther, into Kinsale itself. Brandon had debated on going to the pub where the road came to a T-junction that led out to the Old Head or over to Kinsale, but parking was at a premium and cars were chockablock along the roadway and along the sand-covered edge of the road opposite the parking lot.

Instead, he joined his friends and got burgers and chips, hot and greasy and exactly what they needed. Sheila was all for leading Brandon into the cow pasture opposite the food van and beyond the public rest rooms, but Brandon eyed it and decided the grass was too short. "Let's just go back and sit with the others," he suggested and though Sheila looked disappointed, she followed him.

They sat on the rock wall, having found a spot with smooth, rounded stones rather than the sharper, pointier ones farther down. Thankful for the extra padding of his wet suit, Brandon was further thankful he was wearing it because he could feel Sheila's hands checking out his backside as she sat watching the waves crash against the shore. The tide would soon be creeping back in, Brandon knew.

"I don't think ye're goin' to get very far," he joked when her hand tried to sneak across his hips to his cotch. Had he been that adventurous, that bold, too?

"Later, then," she said, and had assumed, as he had, that sex would happen eventually, like it usually did between them.

He gave a noncommittal shrug and finished his food.

"There's a rumor about that ye had a threesome that went bad," she said as blandly as if she'd made a comment about the weather. It could have been, "oh, look, there's storm blowing in" and it would have come out the same.

A storm. Yes. It was a storm and he was still in it, being flipped upside down so that he didn't know what end was up or how to go forward. Maybe Aine had been right. He needed to see the counselor she'd suggested, which meant he'd keep the appointment instead of a hundred other things he'd rather do.

"Well? Is it just a rumor? I'd heard they called the garda and y'ended up in hospital in Cork."

Rumors did get around and there was no denying what was true without looking like a real plonker, so Brandon nodded and sipped the cola to clear his throat. It gave his brain a moment to work.

"Yeah, it wasn't so great. The garda were called because they took me grandda's car. The rest was no big deal."

"I'd heard ye had surgery. That's pretty big," she pushed.

Again, Brandon shrugged. "Ye know how rumors go, 'twasn't as bad as all that."

"They catch the girls?"

Ah, he thought, the full truth had not yet surfaced, and with luck, wouldn't.

"No. I think they were Dutch," he lied. Only one was. The other, who hadn't really spoken, was either Irish, or knew an awful lot of Irish gutter-speak. "Likely gone from here now. They found the car just out of Dublin, so there's a good chance they hopped a plane or got a boat across."

"Well, as long as ye're okay," she said, and Brandon heard the hopeful tone in her voice, the unasked question, "can you still do the bold thing?."

"Oh, yeah. Everything's grand, why shouldn't it be?" He hoped he sounded convincing, because he sure didn't feel it. Everything was not grand, despite the surf and sun. He felt out of himself, as if he were role-playing at someone else's life.

"Let's get back into the water. The tide's coming in and I haven't had my fill yet," he said, climbing off the wall onto the nearby stairs leading from the parking area to the beach.

Hours later, when the tide had come in and the group had mostly left, Sheila and Brandon found themselves the only ones still sitting on their boards in the cold water. The sun was beginning to go down and the light had faded from the brilliance of the day to the subdued glow of late afternoon.

"Let's hit the hot tub," Sheila said. "I'm feeling a little chilled."

After a day of surfing, Brandon was feeling much the same thing, especially since they were no longer working their muscles but just sitting on the boards and chatting. He'd enjoyed those extra runs after lunch. Flying in on boards born on waves, stressing muscles unused and forgotten from a winter of little exercise and then paddling back out to sea. It had been exactly what he needed and if he'd been alone today, it would have been perfect. But Sheila was there, and she was expecting something.

Brandon wasn't sure if he wanted any part of it but everyone else had left and Sheila needed to get her board home, so Brandon offered.

As one, they carried their boards to the van, laid them side by side, taking up the space along the floor of the vehicle. Closing the back door, Brandon began stripping his wet suit off, displaying bare chest and torso, opening the suit down to his naval. The cool air felt good; his skin had felt clammy and there was gritty sand sticking to his skin in places. A quick swipe with a towel would fix that and then he could change.

"You could just take it off in the hot tub," Sheila said. "We could rent it for ourselves for the next half hour. No one would notice."

In another lifetime, Brandon would have been all up for that. Sex in a hot tub was fabulous, especially the thrill of knowing they were only a canvas drape away from prying eyes. Voices and noise, however, were only vaguely masked, and to make love silently, so no one knew what you were about, was something he'd learned to do at his first opportunity and added an element of excitement to the act itself.

But this time, it was different. He couldn't have sex, but he didn't want Sheila to know that, at least, not to know the reason behind it. So instead, he grinned his best grin, used his cheekiest tone, and said, "Ah, but I'm just out for the surf, nothin' else."

"Let's go anyway. I'm chilled," she said, and Brandon couldn't deny he was feeling a bit chilled himself.

They paid their euros for the pleasure of one half hour to themselves and slipped into the hot tub, screened by the heavy canvas walls surrounding it. There was almost no one left at the beach now and so it hadn't been a difficult arrangement for the owners, who rented the tub every day to hundreds of beach goers, to let Brandon and Sheila used it exclusively.

In no time, Sheila had removed her wet suit, peeling it down like a banana skin, sitting, leaning back against the walls of the tub, obviously relishing the warmth of the water against her cold skin.

"Strip down," she hissed at Brandon. "C'mon, we've only half an hour."

He grinned. Half an hour. Oh, what he could do in half an hour!

But that was then, and this was now, and he was never more aware of his enforced limitations than he was at that moment. His gaze took in her body, the full breasts bobbing against the bubbles of the jets, exposing dusky nipples that had him yearning for bygone days. She was fairly lean but with a good layer of insulation under her skin. It didn't detract from her beauty, but instead, enhanced it. Brandon was never a fan of skinny women, whose bones ground against his when trying to make love. No, he preferred someone with a little meat on them, helpful in cushioning hip-to-hip and bone-to-bone contact.

Although his wet suit was already down to his naval, he felt Sheila grasp at the zipper in an effort to pull it down farther.

"Wait," he said, staying her hand on his abdomen, "ye're goin' to get more than wet suit in there if ye try that and I've no desire to catch anything in it, hm?" he looked at her down the length of his short, straight nose and winked knowingly.

"Alright, but hurry. We don't have all night in here."

"Ah, but I already told ye, I'm not into that tonight," he said.

Sheila's face fell. "I didn't think ye were serious."

"Well, I am," he answered.

Leaving his wet suit zipped as it was, he ignored her pleas to pull it off.

She was pouty and he had a chubby. It was uncomfortable. But he had to endure it and ignore his body's natural urge to do exactly as she wished.

"Warm yet?" he asked.

"Of course. I can feel my bones thawing all the way through. If ye took off yer wet suit ye'd feel how lovely and warm it is."

"So ye want to stay in here for the full half hour?"

"I do," she answered stubbornly, and Brandon broke out into a sweat that had nothing to do with the temperature in the hot tub.

Chapter Ten

It had been the longest half hour of Brandon's life. He'd done as he'd said he would and ignored all of her pleas to have sex. She'd scoffed at his denial of being in the mood.

"Let me do you," she offered, and Brandon was tempted. It would release the tension he was feeling and make his chubby go away but he was steadfast in his decision. He knew, without a doubt, that she'd want to sit on him, and that he couldn't do.

Instead, he said, "I'm tryin' to turn over a new leaf. Get a new start. Challengin' myself, if ye will, to see how long I can go without sex. So far I'm a month in, and haven't died yet," he joked, gazing at her from the corner of his eye as he squirmed uncomfortably on the submerged bench.

Sheila burst out laughing. "Aye, right," she exclaimed sarcastically, face flushed with laughter and the heat of the hot tub.

"No. I'm deadly serious. Deadly."

Her laughter died as she scrutinized him. "Oh, my God. Ye really are. How sad."

Now that was something he could laugh at! "No, not

sad. Just growin' up, maybe. I've come to the realization that there's more out there than this. I want more out of life than just this." He indicated "this" with a wave of his hand that encompassed the hot tub, the beach, everything.

"Ah, but ye certainly don't mean me," she crooned, leaning over him and stroking his naked chest.

"Not you, no. It isn't about you, or me, or what we've done in the past. It's just that now...well, I'm suddenly looking at everythin' differently."

She gave him a stern, assessing look, and wondered out loud, "Did this have anything to do with what happened in Kinsale?"

If Brandon had been eating or drinking, he surely would have choked on it. "Kinsale? What makes you think it was Kinsale?"

"The stories I heard. You know, like I mentioned before; a threesome, the shades getting called in."

Inhaling deeply, Brandon thought that maybe he might be able to diffuse some of those rumors. He was almost always truthful to a fault but this time, he couldn't divulge all without embarrassing his grandparents, who lived in the area, or the rest of his family. For himself, he didn't care. But they deserved some consideration. He decided to settle for a little improvised storytelling.

"Some of that's true, and ye know I've had threesomes before, nothin' new there." There had only been two times but his reputation had made the number grow substantially.

Sheila nodded and he briefly wondered if she was jealous

that she hadn't been included in one of them.

"As for the shades, as I told ye before, me grandda's Mini was stolen and so they had to be called in. End of story."

"And the head injury, or the reason for surgery, or, you know, what was all that about?"

"Nothin' much. Again, I met with the wrong side of a desk phone, thanks to that skank, and needed stitches. Ye can still feel the scar here. See? That was the surgery part." He held his hand up to his head where the last remnants of his wound could be felt, some strands of hair still quite spikey, not having grown completely in yet, and the ridge of the scarring as it lay rope-like against his scalp.

"Oh, I see," she said, after giving the scar a good once-over, as if to ensure it really was real. "Does it hurt?"

Sympathy? She was giving him sympathy?

"Not so much now. Anyway, that's it," he finished. "Nothing more, nothing less. No big to-do. I finally got the Mini back, so all's well."

She was silent for a moment and then said, "So why won't ye let me do you? Yer lad's fair to burstin' it is," she remarked, staring overtly at his bulging crotch.

Brandon sighed audibly. How was he to explain this one? "Listen," he began, doubtful though he was that she really was listening, "I've truly decided to remain celibate for a time. It's in my own best interest and I'm discovering lots about myself through the process. Call it an experiment, if ye will."

Cozying up to him, lifting her breasts and offering the

ripe nipples for him to suckle, she almost pleaded with him. "Oh, come now, all this and more. Ye know ye love it. I know ye do. Can't ye make an exception, just this once?"

He had to admit she was hard to refuse, but he couldn't disallow the possibility that he could have HIV, or some other terrible disease, and so he stuck fast to his story.

"Sorry, no. Ye'll just have to take it at that."

"Ye don't want me." Another tactic, this one trying to lay the guilt on him.

"It's not that. Ye know it's never been that. It's just, this is somethin' I must do. For me. Just for me."

"So this half hour is wasted." She threw herself back against the side of the tub and pouted, her luscious lower lip stuck out like a ripe cherry.

His mouth watered. "No, ye know it isn't. Just allow me this time to say I'm okay not getting any, 'cause I'm really not in the mood."

A look of horror crossed her features, the pout suddenly gone. "What? Not in the mood? You?" She couldn't have said it louder if she had a bullhorn up to her mouth.

Rolling his eyes, Brandon said, "I think our time is up in here. Let's get out. I'll help ye get yer wet suit back on." He reached over to help her into the suit, zipping her up without comment. Noting her gaze, filled with a mix of anger and disappointment, he softened his look with a wink and a grin.

She turned away and scrambled out of the tub.

Nothing more was said until they reached the van and Brandon unlocked the doors. It was nearly dark. His wet suit was still half zipped and it was uncomfortable, not to mention the air had grown chilly, especially after the warmth of the hot tub. He desperately wanted to change into the clothing he'd brought, so he saw her into the passenger seat and hopped into the back where his clothing lay in a bag by his board.

"What are ye doin?" she asked, craning her neck around to see.

"Takin' off this wet suit," he explained, peeling the heavy material down his backside, feeling like he was a banana having the skin peeled off. He had turned so that his hip was to her, no real view of either front or back. Once he had the legs of the suit off, he grabbed his shorts from the bag and slipped them on. It felt good to have something loose on that let his skin breathe. The wet suit really was beginning to make him itch.

Her lack of comment while he was dressing surprised him. Sheila wasn't usually so quiet. But then, he'd already rebuffed her every attempt to get into his pants but as soon as he sat down in the driver's seat, her right hand landed on his thigh and began a rapid pace toward his crotch.

"Not while I'm drivin'," he scolded, pushing her hand away as he got the van moving. She withdrew her hand and turned her face toward the side window, but not before Brandon saw the look of disgust registered across her face.

The van was long but it moved well as he maneuvered it along the windy, narrow road, up the hill toward the house. They passed the B&B at the top of the hill where people were gathered to watch the sun go down. It was a good view and today, there would be a sunset. Maybe he could convince her to sit outside at his grandparents' place, where the lawn went down to the sea, and watch the sun go down.

And maybe he could spin gold out of his arse.

She wouldn't sit and watch the view, she'd be into his pants in no time. Brandon had to examine his own feelings on that. He really wasn't keen on getting his oats with her when he would have done so before without a doubt. Even if it turned out to be a hand job. So what was going on?

"Ye should just take me home. I need a fine fella tonight," came the voice from the other side of the van.

Brandon veered the van quickly to the left to make room for a large tour bus coming his way. In another life, he'd be the one driving that bus. "I don't think I like the connotation," he said, hands gripping the steering wheel, although whether from sudden anger or the need to stay away from both the oncoming bus and the stone wall that hugged the road, he couldn't have said.

"Well, ye obviously don't want me so I'm goin' to find me one who does."

"I'm as much of a man as any. I just don't happen to be…"

"I know. Ye've said it. Ye're not in the mood."

"So why is it alright for a woman to say it and man has to agree, but not the other way around?" He had never thought of that before but now that the tables were turned…

"Never mind. Just take me home, if ye would. Thanks," she added with a tiresome sounding sigh.

"Right, then." He wasn't going to argue. He was going to take her home, drop her off, and return to his grandparents' home to have a cold shower. And maybe never see her again.

The van wound its way through roads darkened by nightfall and the clouds that scuttled across the sky, shielding the moon from view.

So much for the sunset, he thought as they came to her place, just past Ballinspittle. It was out of his way but he hadn't minded. At least, not at first. But her attitude grated as he finally came to the realization that he was nothing special in her eyes. The fact that she was nothing to him hadn't occurred to him until then and the words he'd spoken in the hot tub came back loud and clear. He wanted more than this, "this" being the way his life had stalled and the mire he was up to his neck in. Up until the incident that left him jobless and with a bad reputation made worse by his own actions, he hadn't really cared.

He pulled the van up to the house, helped her get her board from the back, and waved goodbye as she strode into the place. The door closed behind her with barely an acknowledgement of thanks but Brandon didn't care. Having her close the door on him was like closing the door on a part of his life he'd just as soon put behind him and forget. It made him feel a little lighter, as if there was some hope at the end of it all.

By the time he returned to his grandparents' home, there were lights on inside. They had returned, and Brandon's wish to have the place to himself for a while evaporated. But with all that had happened today, he was glad of it. He needed company tonight; the kind of company that came with no strings attached.

Parking the van, he went inside and was welcomed home by his grandparents as if he were the prodigal son. It was exactly what he needed.

***

The following morning, Brandon drove the short distance to Kinsale, but instead of following the road down to the harbor as so many cars ahead of him were doing, he drove along Lower O'Connell Street, took the left, up St. John's Hill, and then left again onto Drom Daireach Compass hill. Like a switchback, he was effectively driving back the way he'd come but on a different road. Up here, where homes dotted the roadway high above the town, and the view of the River Bandon stretched as far as Charles Fort on the opposite side on a clear day, it was a picturesque place to be, one he'd always loved. The recent turn of events had left their mark on him though, and he was wondering if he'd ever feel as happy in Kinsale as he'd been in the past. Would he ever feel at home here again, or would the reputation he'd had the misfortune to attain make him feel more like a blight on the landscape?

It had never occurred to him before. He'd never given it a moment's thought. His reputation had suddenly been elevated to include a side of him that he had only just become aware of. He was indecent. He was crass, not the kind of person anyone with scruples would ever want to be associated with, so why had it not bothered him before this?

He was suddenly afraid to walk into the hotel he'd worked at, afraid to be recognized as the entertainer that had enchanted his audience, small though it was. He hadn't ever performed on stage, only brought his guitar along on those special bus tours where people stopped for photographs, for meals, for picnics on the beach, weather permitting. He'd pull out his six-string, tune it up, and in no time, have people clapping their hands and singing along and asking predominately for the old rebel songs. He knew them all like the back of his hand.

Now all of that had changed. He had no guitar and didn't really know if he would ever get another. He'd loved that guitar, had worked hard to get it; was loyal to his employer and done everything and more that was ever asked of him. But he feared that all of that had changed.

It was as if he had the sign on his forehead that Aine spoke of. Only this one didn't say victim, it said, eejit, loud and clear.

He'd been an eejit. A real plonker. All he'd ever thought about was who he could next coerce into his bed. And suddenly he saw himself as the biggest bollocks in the world. Who would ever want someone who never thought of anyone else, only of who they could find that would fulfill their baser needs? Brandon knew that he'd been shown his face in a mirror and it was one he didn't like.

He drove past the end house at the top of the hill and then a little farther along. The place he sought was nestled behind a stone wall, set back from the road, a lovely setting, very peaceful, a good place to do some difficult soul searching, he thought. Trees surrounded the house in a garden atmosphere but the grassy field around it was left in its natural state and Brandon knew that by the end of the summer, the sun would have baked it to a field of straw. But on this day, it was still green and wet with morning dew that shone like a field of tiny stars.

Leaving the car parked in a small area at the front of the building, he walked toward the entrance. It looked like a regular home, but following the directions on the note stuck to the front door, which invited people to walk in and sit in the waiting room, he realized it had been done over as a kind of clinic. Moments later, a man's face peered out of a door, asking, "Brandon?" At Brandon's nod, the man gestured him in, introducing himself. "Just call me, Sean," he said, after providing his full name. "I prefer to use my given name, makes it easier for my clients to relate to me."

That made sense, thought Brandon, and said so. "But I don't think I'll be yer client for very long," he finished.

"Oh?" ask Sean, gesturing at the comfortable-looking chair opposite his own in the compact office space. "Care for some water?" he gestured to the small cooler and paper cups nearby.

"No, thanks."

"Tell me why you won't be here long."

"I think I've figured it out. What I've been doin' wrong, why I ended up like I did."

"Maybe start at the beginning. Aine said very little, only that you needed to see someone closer to your residence than having to go to Cork every week. And since this is a clinic predominately set aside for victims of abuse, I'm assuming you're one of those."

His cultured Dublin accent left no doubt in Brandon's mind that Sean Graham—doctor of everything imaginable, according to all the letters behind his name and the price tag on the sessions—was well educated. Taking a deep breath, Brandon began. He told him everything, right from the time he began working for the hotel tourism agency, about his so-called reputation, to waking up after surgery, realizing that but for his older brother, he would likely be dead. Spilling the beans to this man had spawned more sobering thoughts than he cared to admit. Christ, he'd been such a Holy Joe! He knew better than everyone, could never be told something different. Brandon was always right, and if he had to, would prove it with his fists.

And then there were the women. He'd acted like a true Romeo; women fell all over him and never once did he discourage them.

Until yesterday.

"So I'm goin' to stay celibate until this is over and then I'm goin' to find that woman that showed me the error of me ways," he said. "And that's why I won't need to be here for long."

Sean nodded. "This woman you speak of. Does she know ye care for her?"

"Care? Of course I care."

"No. Care *for* her, there's a difference."

Brandon thought a moment. He cared about everyone. Was Aine just another number in that or did his feelings go deeper? And then he had to examine the idea that just popped into his head. Was he actually in love with her when he'd never been in love before? Did he know what it felt like to be in love? After all, he loved all the women he went to bed with but was that the same thing? Did being in love mean you enjoyed them in bed and out of it, too?

He turned a conflict-riddled expression on Sean before replying. "I have no idea," he said honestly.

Chapter Eleven

Sean watched the man in front of him as he talked, observed the casual way he spoke of his indiscretions and noted the circles under his eyes, the tenseness around his mouth. Despite Brandon feeling that he didn't need to be a client for long, Sean recognized the signs of someone in trouble.

He'd been sincere when he told Brandon that Aine had said little to him. But what he did get out of her was that this man had been hurt deeply, and Sean was positive it had nothing to do with recent events. The events that Brandon was speaking of were really symptoms of a much deeper problem and Sean meant to open his new client's mind to that fact.

"So, you tell me that ye've a reputation now and it isn't good. But didn't you have one before that? Or is this something new?"

Brandon had slumped down in the chair, long legs sprawled out in front of him. "No, nothin' new," he admitted.

"Then doesn't it show that recent events, as catastrophic as they were to you, have a root much deeper than a month ago?"

"What do ye mean?" A frown creased his brow as he listened to Sean.

His expression wasn't anger, Sean knew, but true curiosity.

"What was your childhood like?"

That got Brandon's attention and he sat upright, pulling his legs beneath the chair. "Christ, like everyone else's, I imagine."

Sean laughed. "I don't go with the notion that everyone had the same kind of childhood. What makes your childhood different from, say, mine?"

"Well, what was yours like, then?"

Oh, he was cagey, but Sean was only beginning. "See? You don't know what mine was like, so how about speaking clear. If you want to be a client who is in and out of here and done, as you say, then the sooner we get to the bottom of things, the sooner that will happen."

"Oh, fine then. My da beat the hell outa me and then I found that he'd done that with my older brother as well. Add to that he was killed when his truck rolled, on his way to his other family that we didn't know about until then. Mam and Henry, my older brother, raised us. If not for Mam's job, we woulda been raised in poverty like his other family."

Sean was gobsmacked. Of everything he could imagine, he hadn't expected this. "Now we're getting somewhere." He hadn't missed the frown that had deepened or the way Brandon didn't want to look at him, hiding the misting in his eyes. Crying wasn't something new to Sean. Almost all of his clients, men and women, succumbed to tears at some time or another. Only the brave cried, and they were all brave.

"Fine. I know my da's ways left a scar. I know his beatings were unjust and hurtful, not just physically but emotionally. I know all that, so why does tellin' ye make a difference?"

"There's knowing in here," said Sean, tapping his head, "and there's knowing in here." He tapped his chest over his heart and saw the look of pain that crossed Brandon's features. "It takes a while for the message to get through. Most people in your position blame themselves and I'm here to help you realize the role you may or may not have played in all this."

"Oh, I'm guilty as a bag of shite on a donkey's arse," answered Brandon. "I know I brought it on myself. No one asked me to act the way I did, I just did."

"Why?"

An eyebrow went up. "Why? Because no one *feckin' cared*," he stressed.

"Other siblings?"

"Yeah."

"Did they act out like you?"

"Nah. Henry seemed to be Da's favorite. First son and all that, although I've recently found out that he got beat, too. Mam said it was to do with the other family. The stress of him trying to keep it all a secret from both sides."

"So there's just you and Henry in your family? What about the other family?"

"No, I have three more siblings, the twins, next in age to me, and then Ciara, who's the youngest. The other family had

109

a boy around my age…"

"So if this other brother is your age, how old are the twins?"

"Oh, they're a couple of years younger than me."

"Right, then, go on."

"And then there was Meara, from the other family, a couple of years younger again, but I never met her. I learned she died of a drug overdose, leaving a daughter behind that my Mam adopted."

Sean's head was spinning. Jaysus, you needed a program to follow all the characters. "Okay, let's slow down and backtrack a minute. In your family, not the other one, there are twins after you?"

"Correct."

"Male? Female?"

Brandon nodded. "Male."

"And then Ciara, you said, younger than them?"

"Right ye are. Ye've got a good head for rememberin' things," Brandon smirked.

"No, I just write fast. But looking at all this, I can see why you've turned out this way, and it's surprised I am that you aren't worse."

Brandon shrugged at the statement, as if it didn't matter. What Sean saw was a man who was conflicted about where he stood within his own family. It was classic middle-child syndrome but Sean knew there was so much more to it than that.

From the little Brandon had told him, he was a man who had struggled to be heard, to be loved. As a young man, that desire for love had driven him into the arms of countless women, hence the reputation he had earned over the years. Sean wasn't surprised at all. Not one little bit.

The session ended an hour after it began, with an appointment booked for the following week. At this rate, Brandon thought as he drove away, he'd be broke very soon.

He thought back on the session. There had been no doubt the man was correct in all he said and perhaps his hurt did go pretty deep, certainly deeper than he'd thought. He'd always buried that hurt, and now Sean was encouraging him to bring it out and take a look at it, look at how it had impacted his life, and forgive himself for it.

Brandon wasn't so sure he could do that. He was filled with a feeling of hope but was harboring a sense of pending doom should the genie be let out of the box.

Already, he'd learned that a person could survive without sex. He hadn't felt as bereft as he thought he might and instead found himself gravitating toward the warmth in his grandparents' home. They'd never chastised him, had only ever offered him a safe haven, even when no one else wanted him. Even Mam hadn't been crazy about him moving home again but she'd allowed it because it was her duty. At least, that was his opinion of the situation.

His grandparents had been delighted to have him visit. They hadn't even asked if he would do the windows for them. To Brandon, that spoke volumes. They were genuinely glad to see him, not for what he could do for them, but because they loved him.

He pulled over to the side of the road and stopped the car beside an abandoned field, the stone wall of which lay in ruination but for a line here and there. His breath was coming in great gasps and he let it come, knew he was too tired to fight it off. He sobbed until he had no more tears, laying his head across the steering wheel, using his arms as a cushion. He could cheerfully have fallen asleep right then. Sean had said this was hard work and would be tiring. Maybe this was what he meant.

He leaned back against the seat then, watched the gulls swoop and call over the water below, and decided that next Thursday he would go see Aine, see if she would go for coffee with him once again. He needed to tell her so many things, to see if she returned his feelings. But mostly, he just wanted to see her. Not for sex, and not only because of the lingering threat of disease, but just to see her. That was new for him.

His gran was in the kitchen when he arrived home. He could hear her clanging pots about and smell the rashers she was cooking. His mouth watered. He hadn't had anything to eat yet. Despite needing a job, he didn't have the energy to be bothered looking just now so had come straight home to let matters mull about in his head for a while. But the smell of food ignited a rumbling in his stomach so he made his way to the side of the house where the kitchen opened onto a small garden.

His grandda was already tucking into his meal and looked up and smiled as Brandon sat down at the little iron table beneath the yellow-and-white umbrella, shielding them from the brilliance of the sun, now high overhead.

Gran called from the kitchen, "I'll get some food for ye, I imagine ye're right famished like."

Brandon nodded and called out his thanks to her. Famished didn't cover it.

Moments later a plate was in front of him and he dove into it with all the gusto of a man who'd been starved for a week. As he ate, he felt his grandparents watching him and knew they had questions. Perhaps this was a good place to start.

When he finished his last mouthful and took a gulp of his gran's best coffee, he leaned back in the chair, excused himself after he belched, and told them to ask whatever they wanted. "Go ahead," he offered. "It's time I came clean to ye. Ye've only ever given me the best of yerselves and I've only ever been a bowsie."

"Don't belittle yerself," chided his gran. "Ye've been through hell and back and I won't have ye thinkin' less of yerself for what's not yer fault."

Brandon shook his head defiantly. "That's where ye're wrong, Gran. I love ye too much to lie to ye or have ye believin' that I wasn't at fault." He swallowed...hard. Felt the food like a rock in his gut. "I invited those two to my room. I let them do what they did to me."

"Bollocks!" His grandda swore and banged his fist against the small table, sending a spoon clattering to the ground. "Ye no more invited what they did to ye than I did and ye know that. Ye may have invited them to yer room, to do those things to yer body, but ye never asked them to ransack the room or rob ye blind. And ye certainly didn't ask to be needin' medical treatment."

How could he make them understand? He'd brought everything on himself. He was the one to blame, the only one.

"If I hadn't been such an eejit in the first place..." he began, "If I hadn't been out lookin' for anythin' I could get..." For some reason he was having trouble telling them, the two people in the world, of whose love he was certain, just how bad a person he was. If he told them, made them understand, would they still love him?

"Brandon, ye've always been out lookin' for the worst life could throw at ye. I blame yer da for that," said his gran kindly. She was cradling his hand in hers, trying to look into his eyes.

"I can't blame all this on Da. Especially when he's not here to defend his actions. And if ye must know, I enjoyed what I did. It's why I kept doin' it. I loved it. Loved the women, even tried men." He took his hand away from Gran's aged fingers, noted the sad look she bore him as if willing him to stop.

"I'm as depraved as they get. Anyone who was willin' would end up in my bed. Or me in theirs. Didn't matter. And sometimes it was up against the wall in an alley if nothing near could be found."

"Brandon, stop," his gran pleaded with him. "Ye don't have to do this."

"Yes, I do. I have to make ye see I'm not the man ye

think I am. I'm not good. There is nothing good in here!" He thumped his chest and stood, ready to walk away but his grandda's hands were on his arms and Brandon knew he wouldn't shake them off. He could hurt his grandda with strength powered by anger, and that he wouldn't do.

"You are my grandson, as precious to me as any of my grandchildren. Ye might think ye're a bad person but I see only good in you. Ye're the one always lookin' out for yer family, protectin' them when things go wrong. Who rescued Ciara that day when she fell off her bike and nearly got run over? Ye risked yer own life, gettin' her out of the way just in time. We'd not have our wee Ciara now if not for you," he pointed out.

"Anyone would have done that."

"Anyone with a good heart. If ye hadn't cared, ye wouldn't have done it. I thank God ye were there with her. Have every day since it happened."

Brandon shrugged it off. He remembered that day. Ciara had wanted to ride her new bike; no one else was around and so he'd said he'd go with her so she didn't get lost. Lost, ha! Like him, she knew the area and could navigate it blindfolded. So off they went, against Mam's warnings.

All had gone well for the first while, but a car had come around the curve too fast, making Ciara start in fright, the front wheel of her bike suddenly caught in the narrow, weedy gap between the road and the stone wall. Over she went and Brandon had jumped to her rescue, righting her bike and scooping her up before the next car came racing past. She'd been scraped from the wall and the road but was otherwise unhurt. He'd been labeled a hero before being reprimanded by his mam for allowing her to ride on such a busy road. He'd brushed it off, knowing she blamed him for nearly getting his sister killed.

"It was my fault she was out there in the first place."

"Never mind that," Grandda said, "it was a long time ago. The point is, ye cared. Ye brought her home and tended her scrapes. Not Henry. Not the twins. You. And there've been other instances throughout your life that prove to me ye've more carin' in that heart of yours than in most peoples' little fingers."

Brandon looked into his grandda's eyes and saw the mistiness in them. Gran had tears rolling down her cheeks. Jaysus! Was it something in the air today?

Gran sniffed her tears back. "We know ye've done things ye're not proud of and we hurt with ye every time we heard. We didn't go to the hospital this time because we knew ye had enough to handle without us bein' there, too. We told yer mam we'd bring ye here after but she said ye needed to be at home so ye could go to those counselin' sessions. So we agreed. But we wanted ye here, so ye could heal, just the same."

"Sit ye back down like, alright?" said Grandda, and Brandon did. He hadn't the strength to do otherwise.

Wiping away his own tears, he then rubbed his face, feeling worn out, spent. "I just came from Kinsale, seeing a fella there on recommendation from the other clinic. Said it was closer since I wanted to relocate here."

"And?" His grandda wasn't being nosey, he knew, just curious.

Brandon lifted a shoulder in answer. "I think it's going to be good," was all he could say.

"How long will ye go?" asked Gran.

Again, a noncommittal shrug. "Who knows. I told him I didn't think I'd need to go for very long. I already know what I've done, where I've gone wrong."

"But ye don't know that ye're a good person," protested his grandda. "Ye deny ever having done anythin' good for anyone. Ye can't seem to get it through yer thick skull that inside ye're a good person who has maybe done some not so nice things. But those things don't make you a bad person. Don't ye see?"

A corner of Brandon's mouth turned up in a tentative smile. "Here I am paying this guy I-don't-know-how-many euros to see him every week when I should really just sit here and let you have a go at me. At least it'd be cheaper," he exclaimed, the smile having turned into a grin.

Gran shook her head. "No, boyo. Ye'll see the man; and if ye need funds, we'll see ye get them. He's a professional and right now ye've need of that. But we want ye to stay here, with us, until such time as ye're back on ye're feet. And by that, I mean hale and hearty. I don't mean just physically well."

Nodding, Brandon thanked her, feeling the lump in his throat as he did.

"I'm off to help Jimmy Cavanaugh with his garage door," said his grandda, standing. "I'd appreciate the help as ye seem to understand those things better 'n me. But if ye don't want to come, I understand."

"If ye don't want to go with Grandda," his gran piped up, "those windows at the front could use a washin' after that rain streaked them all up and down the last week."

At that, Brandon laughed outright. "Right y'are then. I'll come with ye, Grandda, and help you and Jimmy out, and Gran, I'll get those windows done later. If not by tonight, then tomorrow."

At her wink and a smile, he followed his grandda out to the little yellow Mini, now clean and looking none the worse for wear in the driveway. A little ray of sunshine in his troubled day.

God, but he loved that little car.

Chapter Twelve

It was just after nine in the evening and Brandon had been waiting for the last half hour, wondering if he would leave without speaking to her or be brave enough to stay. The past thirty minutes had been a rehearsal of things he would say, going back and forth, discarding one set of sentences for another. It was driving him mad.

Just when he'd looked at his watch for the umpteenth time, he saw the main library door open and the security personnel on the inside exchange a few words with Aine before she waved goodnight and left. The door was locked behind her and the security guard walked back to his post.

As she neared her car, Brandon sucked up his courage. His heart was beating a rapid tattoo in his chest and he felt ready to pass out. Would anything he rehearsed in the last half hour come out right?

He opened his car door in time to see her drop some papers she'd been struggling with in her arms. As she bent down to pick them up, the rest of them followed and she cursed under her breath. It was a relatively quiet night, with a lull in the traffic off the busy street, and so Brandon heard the curse word and couldn't help the chuckle that erupted from his throat.

Aine's head immediately shot up, a look of alarm in her eyes like prey that knows it's being sighted down a hunter's gun. He quickly stepped from the shadows into the light under the streetlamp, greeting her so she wouldn't panic further.

"Aine, it's me, Brandon."

An obvious sigh of relief was heard in the crisp, night air and she resumed collecting her papers from the ground. "Hi, how are ye…oh, just a sec, let me get these first."

He was there a moment later, helping her to gather them up, straightening them into a neat pile before handing them back to her. "How about I hold that while ye get yer car door open," he offered, and was pleased when she thanked him and did just that.

"Timin' is everythin', thanks again," she said, taking the piles from him and putting them in the boot of her car. "There, now that's taken care of." And then as if she'd just run into him on the street, said, "Hello, and how are ye doin'?"

Brandon stuffed his hands in his pockets. It was that or he'd be pulling her into his arms and that he couldn't do. At least, not yet.

"I'm well. Doin' well. And you?"

She shrugged in a halfhearted way. "I'm alright. You know, busy, what with work and all."

Nodding his understanding, and realizing they were both just making small talk, he decided to be honest with her. Above all, he would be honest with the one woman he wanted to be with in more than just the physical sense. He wanted to get to know her before they ever went down that road. "I was wonderin'…I mean, I know it's late and ye've likely a work day tomorrow…"

"Ah no, tomorrow I get to sleep. It's a turnaround day for me. I start nights tomorrow evening, so staying up late tonight is a good idea," she laughed.

"Yeah? Oh. Alright, then. I was wondering, that is, if ye wouldn't mind, maybe goin' to that place for coffee again. Just for a chat?"

Aine screwed up her nose. "Thanks, but they had the worst coffee. Why don't we just walk for a bit. It's a lovely night and I'm not yet ready for sleep."

That suited Brandon even better. Outside. There was fresh air and darkness outside. Easier to hide his emotions that seemed to be so close to the surface since that day in Sean's office.

As if she sensed his thoughts, she said, "So how is it going with Sean? Did ye go see him?"

"Oh, yeah. He's a likeable sort. We got on fine. I'll see him again next week."

"That's grand," she exclaimed, sounding truly happy for him. "I know it's early yet but do ye feel like ye're getting somewhere?"

Brandon laughed. "I think, between Sean and my grandparents, I can't help but get somewhere. They may be in league together," he joked. It may have come out as a joke but Brandon truly felt that his grandparents and his counselor were on the same wavelength, as if Sean had phoned them at the completion of the session and told them what had gone on.

Aine sighed into the night. "I'm very glad, I am, that ye've got someone like Sean in your life to help ye through this. He was one of my mentors while I was studying. That's why I recommended him," she confessed.

"He's a good man," agreed Brandon. And then, because he couldn't think of anything else to say at the moment, "I'd like to ask ye somethin', if I may?" They had stopped at a bench along the walkway and Brandon gestured to it. He waited until she sat and then took his own seat, slightly apart from her but turned so that he could see her. The night was bright with a nearly full moon, and glittering stars winked in and out in the black sky. The overhead lights from streetlamps helped to dispel any further darkness around them.

"I was wonderin' if ye'd be willin' to go on a date with me? I haven't much experience actually datin', for real datin', I mean. Not just meeting someone and then draggin' her off to shag somewhere. I mean, datin' so as to get to know each other."

He waited, unaware he was scarcely breathing until she spoke.

"I'm flattered, of course," she began, and Brandon could hear the "but" all the way across the bench before she'd uttered it. "But I was your counselor, Brandon. It isn't ethical."

"Ye aren't my counselor now," he argued, "and I was only there a couple of times. Besides, I knew ye before I went to those sessions and I know that ye can date yer nurse afterward. My mam's had a couple that way."

Nervous laughter crossed the space between them, quietly, shyly. "I know. Last year, wasn't it? I think there was a fine fella who'd ended up with a broken leg or something. Anyway, yer mam was fillin' in for someone on that floor because usually she's on maternity. But we were short-staffed and she'd said she'd help out. They got along right from the start and it continued on for quite a while. What ended it, do ye know?"

Brandon shook his head. "No, I don't. But Mam's like that. She's never settled on one person since Da was killed." He suddenly realized she'd redirected him and he fought to get back to the subject of a relationship with her.

"What about it? Could we date? Just see each other for a time to see if maybe there's somethin' here between us?" Brandon suddenly wished the light was brighter because he could swear there were tears in her eyes. Her voice, husky as she spoke, backed up his thoughts.

"I'm sorry, Brandon. I'd love to spend time with ye but I really don't think I can. Even though ye were only at a couple of sessions, I think I'd be breaking the rules if I said I could. I could lose my job," she finished.

Brandon understood all too well the limitations put on medical staff regarding relationships, confidentiality, and a host of other "rules," as Aine intimated. His mam was often restricted by them, careful not to overstep her bounds. The last thing anyone needed was to lose a job or be called up in front of the board for breaking one of them.

Still, he had to try. "Is this breakin' the rules? Us, sitting here, talkin' like this?"

A slight lifting of her shoulders told Brandon she wasn't sure. "I think this is alright because we aren't datin'. Ye're asking questions regarding the rules and I'm tellin' ye about them. But if it progressed from this…well, then we'd be on a slippery slope, as they say."

"What would it take for me to be able to date you? I mean, so there wouldn't be any rules broken or anythin'?"

"Nothin'." She shook her head and stood. "I'm sorry, Brandon. Really sorry. I didn't realize that ye felt anythin' for me, but ye must know it isn't reciprocated. I mean, I like ye, and all that, but…I just never thought of you in that way, is what I'm tryin' to say."

Brandon stood, too, took a step toward her so he could see her face more clearly. The glow from the streetlight illuminated her features and showed him the pain written across her face. Her lugubrious eyes; her mouth tight and drawn.

And then he stepped back and allowed her to lead the way back to the cars, staying beside her, not touching, not saying anything until they were standing beside her vehicle.

"Before ye go, can ye at least tell me that maybe you might have thought of me once in a way not fittin' for yer career?"

She laughed at that, and her laughter brought a smile to his own lips. "That's the funniest question I think I've ever had. And if ye mean, do I think ye're fine? I have to be honest, I do. But there's nothin' I can do about it so there's no use debatin' it."

She unlocked the door, but before she could get in, Brandon put his arm around her waist and pulled her to him, gently but firmly. "Then think on this," and before she had a chance, he touched his lips to hers, tenderly, testing the warmth of them, the feel of them and then felt the answering pressure and was lost. All his self-control flitted out the window with his words of self-denial. Pressing his body to hers, he felt her tense next to him and sought to reassure her. Splaying his hand across her back, he followed her spine, rigid beneath his touch, until he caressed her lovely round bottom.

Her answer was to pull his head toward hers, cup his nape with her hands, dance with their tongues in mouths locked together, her breasts flattened against his chest, the evidence of his desire pressed between her pelvis and his.

And then she pushed at his chest and forced them apart, a look akin to panic in her eyes. "No," she exclaimed, "I can't. We shouldn't have done that. Oh, God, oh, Brandon. I'm sorry. I have to go."

He quickly stepped out of the way of her closing the car door and watched as she backed up and drove off into the night without even waving goodbye.

"*We shouldn't have done that. Oh, God. Oh, Brandon. I'm sorry.*" What the hell was that all about? She was sorry, yet she wanted it as much as he did and the subject of HIV never even came up.

Likely it would have, he mused as he went to his own

car. The yellow Mini stood like a faithful steed in the harsh light from the streetlamp. No one else was about, the lot was empty, the library lights out except for the security desk in the front area.

He wasn't mistaken in her desire to be with him. He knew that in his soul. There was more than just the rules keeping them apart and Brandon couldn't help but think that if he could only get her to talk, to trust him, then maybe they could see their way around those rules.

* * *

His grandparents had decided they should all go to church on Sunday so they'd gone up to Inishannon where they used to attend as a family, years ago. It had been an age since Brandon had gone and he almost wormed his way out of it but his mam was having none of it. "It'll do ye good," she scolded, and so he went.

In the end, it had been alright. No one there seemed to know what had gone on with him. His notoriety hadn't gone as far as he thought, it seemed. That was a surprise to him. He wasn't as famous as he thought. No one outside of his current circle of friends—which was dwindling rapidly now that he was sworn off sex—knew anything about him, other than that he was Kathleen O'Farrell's second son. A voice inside his head spoke loud and clear. "*Wake up*," it said, "*you aren't the center of the universe after all*."

It was a relief of sorts, and the short drive back to Mam's for the after-church luncheon was quiet. Ciara, who had taken off for a two-week holiday, was nowhere to be seen, so it was just the four of them: his mam, his grandparents, and himself. The Mini would have been a tight squeeze so they'd left it at his mam's home and taken her car instead.

And now they were back and Mam and Gran were pulling food out of the oven, the aromas wafting over to where he and Grandda were watching the local hurling match. "Come and eat," came the command, and although hurling was right up there with football, no one dared disrupt the after-church luncheon.

Grace was said and they dove into the rare delicacies not sampled since the last great after-church luncheon. Brandon couldn't remember when that was. There was black pudding and white pudding, which he liked better because it wasn't so dry. There were piles of rashers, too much for them to eat all of, but not for lack of trying, and fried potatoes. Funnily, no one had wanted any eggs so their plates were devoid of those but there was fruit and coffee, tea and light pastries. It was like a celebration.

In a way, thought Brandon, it was. They'd all confessed their sins the day before and had attended church today, so wasn't that like a new beginning for them all? He didn't know about anyone else but he was beginning to feel more like himself, even if Aine had run off like a scared rabbit, disappearing into the night. It was what she let him do before she ran off that had Brandon filled with hope.

Chapter Thirteen

Aine had just finished her last night shift and was determined to enjoy her next couple of days off. The morning sun was lovely, the day not yet hot, so she made herself some coffee and took it out to the small balcony off her sitting room. Sunlight slanted across the patio deck, the rays just creeping around the cement wall at the side, making its way known as it pierced the iron railing along the front.

She sat, sipping the warm brew and thinking back to Thursday night when Brandon had met her outside the library after she'd finished. Seeing him was such a surprise, a delightful surprise, if she was honest with herself. He struck something within her, filled her with a kind of hope she hadn't yet experienced. In some far off corner of her brain, she knew she wanted him.

In that way.

A sadness came over her that had everything to do with wanting Brandon and knowing it could never be.

First and foremost, she had been his counselor. Nothing could change that fact and the rules were clear. It was wholly unethical for them to date.

The second barrier was not unethical at all. But it felt just as insurmountable as the first. She knew, without a doubt, that had neither barrier existed, they'd likely have ended up in bed together.

And then she amended that thought. Brandon had yet to be tested for HIV and they wouldn't know for certain, until six months had passed, whether or not he had been infected. He hadn't said whether they'd caught the criminals yet, but he had the yellow Mini back. She noticed it in the parking lot when they returned to the cars. It hadn't struck her until then that it was the car that had been stolen and she'd meant to ask, but then he kissed her, and…ah *feckit*, she was going to cry!

Tears fell from her eyes and she let them come, sniffing when she realized she didn't have a tissue handy. Her fingertips touched her lips in remembrance of the softness of his mouth, the bit of stubble of a beard just beginning to grow after a long day. His scent had clung to her and she hadn't wanted to shower it off. It was a light scent. It was him. Not something false that was heavy or cloying. It struck her that she'd been torn between staying in his arms and fleeing as if the bean sidhe were after her.

His mouth on hers felt so right and when she'd opened to him and his tongue darted in, she'd been both startled and thrilled. When she swirled her tongue around his, tasting, testing, it made her want to dive in, taste more of him. She felt a jolt of awareness dive straight to her core, felt a sexual excitement that she recognized as having everything to do with Brandon. Only Brandon.

And then he'd gripped her bottom, held her close to him so she could feel him there, his lad chubbed up against her belly. It had become a rod of steel in her mind and she had no doubt he knew the effect he was having on her. For the first time in her life, she wanted what he had, what he was offering her.

And it had scared her silly.

She'd pushed him away before the panic that had begun to build in the pit of her stomach reached the surface. She recalled shaking with terror at the unknown beast that was ever-present when thoughts of a normal relationship started to intrude.

She wanted it. She wanted Brandon. But she couldn't go there, couldn't bear the memories of *THAT OTHER MAN*. Because suddenly, all she could remember was herself as a thirteen-year-old girl, pleading with him not to do that, crying as he pounded into her, hurting her, making her bleed.

She still recalled the smell of his aftershave, and it could make her gag, even now. Swallowing the bile that had begun to rise, she put her coffee cup down on the small table beside the chair and breathed in deeply of the crisp, morning air. Focussing on the sights from her balcony, she vaguely remembered throwing up all over him, disgusting him, making him leave her but not before he slapped her hard across the face for defiling his clothing, never mind the fact that he'd just done the same to her body.

Breathing in steady, deep breaths was helping. Her hands had stopped shaking, although her heart was still beating rapidly, but it, too, was beginning to slow, back to its normal rhythm.

Thinking of some of the exercises she coached her clients with, she forced herself to close her eyes and think of Brandon, of his face, his eyes, the way he smiled. Tried to supplant his features over the other. She forced herself to remember how he'd looked when she first met him, bruised and swollen over his eye, the gash on his head still crusted with blood. And then the first sight of him post-surgery. He'd been pale, with a full twenty-four hour's growth of stubble on his chin and above his lip. She'd been so taken with his beauty, for to her he had been beautiful in that moment, and then he'd opened his eyes and she'd felt as if she'd fallen into them. She'd never seen eyes that blue before!

Perhaps it was that instant. Perhaps that was the moment when she'd fallen in love.

"Oh, this is a fine mess ye've got yerself to deal with," she muttered to herself, wiping viciously at her tears and giving a final sniff. "In love for the first time and ye can't have him!"

It was true. She loved him. He was all she thought about, night and day. He came to her in dreams and she daydreamed at work. Co-workers were beginning to ask her who the fella was that she was mad for. But she couldn't tell them.

Lucky for her, she hadn't seen Brandon's mam anywhere, thinking it wasn't usual to see her anyway, as they weren't often on the same floor. A nurse with midwifery skills wasn't often needed there.

How would she ever put it all behind her? How could life

continue on, now that she knew there was someone she cared for, and who had made it clear that he was interested to get to know her better, to see if there was something between them, so he'd said. For the first time, she wanted that, too.

Oh, yes. Her life was suddenly a mess.

* * *

Henry had just got off the phone with his half brother, Hank. Hank and his wife, Laura, were new parents of a strapping baby boy. They'd purchased a new house in the town they called home, nestled in the south-central mountains of British Columbia, Canada, and both had individual properties on the mountain.

Henry recalled Hank telling him the story of how he and Laura met. There'd been a blizzard that had gone on for days. Laura had been up the mountain, stranded in her cabin, and Hank had been on his way home to his own cabin, a few miles farther up, when an avalanche had knocked his truck off the road. The truck had been nearly wrecked in the accident and Hank had received a good knock on his head when it flipped over. He'd had to crawl through the rear window of the cab, dig his way to the top of the snow, and make his way a mile back to Laura's cabin, all in the dark and still-falling snow. The avalanche had prevented him from getting to his own place, which was in any case, as far as Henry understood, much farther away.

The two had spent days together before they could get back down the mountain. Days in which the weather held them prisoner and Hank's cabin had burnt to the ground.

Nothing like enforced captivity to encourage people to get along, mused Henry with a grin. Had he known Hank beforehand, he would have said it was a done deal anyway. The relationship just needed a starting-off point to get it burning. A year and a half later, Hank was rebuilding the cabin, or, at least, what he called a cabin. To Henry, it seemed more substantial than that.

And that was the crux of the phone call. Hank hadn't been able to contact Brandon and was wondering if perhaps he wouldn't want to come over for a time to help him rebuild. Hank wanted to get the roof on before winter, and it was already July.

Henry had taken the opportunity to tell him about Brandon's incident. He didn't go into things, stayed clear of details as much as he could; but Hank had had his own share of misdeeds, and Henry knew he'd understand where others wouldn't.

He hadn't been mistaken. Cursing Brandon for an eejit before asking after his health, Hank had then thought that perhaps Brandon might like to make a new start somewhere. Somewhere where no one knew him, where he had no reputation to hide. Somewhere like the wilds of Canada, as Henry liked to put it. "I'll send ye photos of the project so far," offered Hank.

"I'll mention it to him and one of us'll get back to ye," he'd told Hank before hanging up.

As he dialed his brother, Henry wondered how Brandon was doing. He'd heard that Mam and Gran and Grandda had got him to church, and confession, too. Perhaps Brandon's assertion that he was turning over a new leaf was more than just talk.

He finally reached Brandon at their mam's home. "How's the lad?" asked Henry, cheekily.

"Ya bollocks," replied Brandon. "It's a fine thing to ask a fella when ye know it's out of service."

Henry laughed and nearly choked on the coffee he was swallowing. The fact that Brandon could now joke about his enforced celibacy told him more than anything that his brother was doing well. "I've heard from Hank. He's wonderin' if ye've nothin' better to do, would ye go help him throw a roof on that palace he's buildin' in Canada?"

"Who says I have nothin' to do?" asked Brandon, back to his usual surly tone. "I'll have you know I'm tryin' very hard to get out of a piece of duty I'm told I must attend to," he said crossly.

"And what duty would that be?"

"Mam's trying to make me buy a ticket to the fund-raisin' luncheon for one of the charities at the hospital. Cancer wing, or something like that. Says the food's good and I should go."

"Ah well, she'd know. From the looks of her, I don't doubt she knows all about the food," Henry exclaimed, an imagine of their mam, as wide as she was short but with energy to burn. None of them could ever figure her out.

"Yeah, I'm bein' pressured to go."

In the background, Henry could hear their mam chatting Brandon's ear off, telling him to get off the phone and help her get the garage sorted like he said he would. "Oh, so she's put ye to work as well?"

"Hmmf," answered Brandon. "Not only am I being forced to go to this luncheon, and havin' to pay for my own ticket, I might add, but I've to sort through those boxes in the garage that have been there since God was a teenager. Lord only knows what's in them."

"You're about to find out, is my guess," said Henry. "So listen, I need ye to phone Hank as soon as ye can. Remember the time difference, and don't leave it too late."

"Yes, sir," exclaimed Brandon, and Henry knew it was a throwback to when he'd become the man of the house at fourteen, after their da had been killed in a motor vehicle accident. His younger siblings viewed him as a hard taskmaster and likened him to a military officer. It hadn't been far from the truth but Mam had depended on him and he couldn't let her down. And never did.

Brandon hung up the phone and finally acquiesced to his mam's rantings. "Alright, I'll buy a ticket to yer *feckin'* lunch but do I really have to go, too? Can't I just support it by buying the ticket?" he argued.

"No, because they'll make food for as many people as buy tickets, ye eejit. And if ye're buyin' a ticket ye may as well enjoy the food. Besides, it'll be good craic," she finished.

Brandon shook his head. "Ye've a strange idea of fun," he replied, but there was a smile on his face. He knew he'd be going. He was hoping to see Aine there because he knew that when there was a fundraising event that benefitted the hospital in some way, any staff who weren't working would usually attend. It often turned into a giant party. Good craic, indeed.

"Boxes," came the directive when Brandon would have slunk away.

"Hmmf," he answered sullenly. "What's so special about these boxes that we've got to do them now?"

"I don't know. That's part of the problem. I can't get rid of them and use the garage for what it's intended without knowing what's in them. It might be serendipitous, ye never know," she winked at him and smiled.

Christ, he hated it when she did that. It meant she was going to oversee and he would do all the work.

"When's this bloody luncheon, anyway?"

"Next week. Now get a move on."

Drill sergeant. That's what she was.

Chapter Fourteen

As Brandon had suspected, the luncheon was peopled with staff who were either on holiday or off work, as well as a generous helping of the general public. He scanned the crowd, hoping to see a familiar face, and wasn't disappointed. He'd arrived early and snagged a table near the door so he could watch and see when she arrived. Mam had arrived earlier and was off chatting up friends so Brandon was alone at the table when Aine walked in. She couldn't help but see him there.

He noticed the moment she saw him. Her eyes lit up and then died, and he wondered if she was going to walk past or say hello. He held his breath and steeled himself for the letdown he would feel if she ignored him.

Instead, she walked over to where he was seated, and as he stood to greet her, she stretched out her hand to say hello. Stretched out her hand? She was only going to shake his hand when they'd shared a kiss that'd had him ready to shag her on the spot? And then he realized that they were in a public venue, that people would be watching, and that she had been his counselor.

Ignoring his body's impulse to wrap her in his arms and

137

kiss her senseless, he instead shook her hand as if they barely knew each other, asking politely if she would like to join his mother and himself at today's event.

Jaysus, but he couldn't have been more formal if he'd got down on one knee. Her eyes twinkled with laughter, he noted, and his hopes took a jump. When she said yes, he tried to hide his joy although he felt his hands tremble when he pulled out her chair for her.

Soon after, his mam joined them along with two others. The table was nearly full, only one seat left, and that was on Aine's other side. Brandon was hoping a lone woman would fill it but his heart sank when a doctor he'd never met before greeted the couple sharing their table in a familiar manner.

He hated these affairs. Hated having to be seated with people he didn't know. As soon as the doctor introduced himself, he noted Aine's eyes light up in recognition of his name. Sounded like he was some bigwig in the research field. Grand. Just feckin' grand. He'd never before felt jealous of any woman he'd been with. Had only felt secure in the knowledge that whoever she was, she was with him because she wanted the best. And he was the best. Or was he?

He mollified himself by knowing that he was good at sex. Women liked, no, he corrected himself, *loved*, what he did to them. It was why he'd been so popular. That, and the fact that he'd rescued any number of them from plonkers who'd tried to take advantage of them. It was part of his reputation, that a woman was always safe with Brandon O'Farrell.

But Aine wasn't in any danger. At least, if she was, no

one knew about it, least of all him. But it didn't stop the green monster of jealousy raging within his heart when he saw her turn her attentions to the doctor and laugh at something he'd said.

If he was truthful with himself, the man was very interesting to listen to and he could understand what had Aine so fascinated. But when it came time for their table to go help themselves from the buffet, Brandon made sure it was he that was helping Aine with her plate, and not the delectable doctor. Brandon liked the man, for feck's sake. It would be so much easier to hate him.

Back at the table, while Aine and he tucked into their food, the doctor regaled them with stories of cancer research and the ongoing struggle to keep funding coming in so research could continue. "Do you know," he said between forkfuls of food, "we are using cancer cells that we've regrown for over thirty years. It's one way we can continue to do experiments without having to worry about needing another donor."

"Fascinating," said Brandon, truthfully, and it must have struck something within Aine because she smiled at him. A suddenly insight came like a slap to his face when he realized that Aine liked it when he showed an interest in what the doctor was saying, and that maybe, just maybe, if he participated in the conversation rather than sulking like a teenager still in school, she'd like him even better. So he wracked his brain and came up with a few questions and comments that had Aine including him in her conversation with the fellow instead of excluding him, as he'd feared.

139

Eventually, the lunch was over, the doctor excused himself, saying he had to get back to work and exclaiming what a pleasure it was to have met them all. Brandon's mam excused herself as well, telling Brandon she wouldn't be needing a ride home after all. She was going into the city to do some shopping with one of her friends. The other couple had left with the good doctor.

That left Brandon and Aine together and a nervousness that had been missing during lunch seemed to descend on them like a misty rain, not enough to spoil the day but enough to make things feel suddenly awkward.

"How about a walk?" asked Brandon, when Aine looked like she was getting ready to leave.

He saw her hesitate before agreeing. "Alright," she said. "It's a lovely day and the park across the road has some beautiful floral displays just now."

Brandon didn't give a feck about floral displays but he knew he would do anything to stay in her company just a while longer. Besides, he had to tell her he was going away for a while.

"Where?" she asked, with an expression that seemed to be a mixture of excitement and relief.

He hoped she was happy for him, and not happy that she would be rid of him for a time. "I'm goin' to help my half brother, Hank, the one who lives in Canada, to build his place up some mountain. He calls it a cabin but my other brother, Henry, says it sounds more like a palace."

Her laughter was like a boon to his ego.

"How long will ye be gone?"

Was that hope he heard in her voice…hope that it wouldn't be too long? "Ah, well, I expect about three months. I think I'm allowed to stay for ninety days, like here. Not allowed to work, just on a visitor's visa. I'll stay with Hank and his family. Maybe help him with the cabin. Enjoy some Canadian hospitality, I'm sure."

Her eyes were full of laughter, as if she were going, too. "It sounds grand," she said, "I'm very happy for ye. Ye need to get away for a while, like." And then, "Are ye still seeing Sean?"

Brandon nodded. "Yeah. And we'll continue the sessions over the internet. We've got it all figured out."

She smiled at that. "I'm very glad for that. It's so important."

"Aine," he stopped and turned toward her. They were near a bower of flowers growing on a tall trellis, white and pink blooms covering the surface, looking like a wall of flowers that followed the pathway. On the other side, enclosing them and shading them from prying eyes, was a similar trellis, covered in red blooms. A few bees buzzed inside the blooms, loading up on pollen before flying back to their hive in some unknown location.

She looked up at him and he was lost. Purposely keeping his hands in his pockets, he needed to try one more time. "I know ye've said a relationship between us is impossible, but I want ye to know that if ye ever find a way out of it, if there could ever be a chance for us, please don't let it go by."

Immediately her eyes misted and he knew she was feeling what he was feeling.

"I'm goin' away for a while," he explained, "not forever. And if it's alright, I'd like to be in touch with ye when I get back, to see if anything's changed. By then, I might even know if I'm okay or not." He was referring to his HIV status, and assumed she'd know.

"Ye mean if you've got it or not," she clarified, and he nodded.

"I can't believe that God would be so cruel as to let me find the one person that seems to mean somethin' to me, only to make it impossible for us to be together; and I'm assumin' you're in agreement with me. It's like ye're a wee treat on a line bein' dangled in front of me, just out of reach, and try as I might, I just can't have ye."

"It's true, Brandon. Ye can't. And the sooner we both realize that, the better off we'll be. I'll tell ye straight, I don't care if ye have HIV or not. There's ways around that, it's not the barrier it used to be. But it isn't about what you or I want. It's about what's right and what's ethical and I just can't see a way past that. It's impossible."

A tear slipped from her eye before she dashed it away. "It's no use talkin' about it anymore, Brandon. It's impossible, and we both know it, so let's leave it be. Let's just leave it be."

He didn't care who was watching, didn't care that it wasn't right, and pulled her into his embrace and kissed her well and good, feeling her respond before she pushed him away.

142

"I can't," she said, and the tears were running hard and fast now, breaking his heart. "I just can't."

He stood watching as she walked down the path and out of his life. He'd given it his all. He'd tried to reason with her but she'd have none of it. Of the two, she was obviously the stronger one, the one who knew what was right and would not be swayed by anything, let alone her feelings. That she was denying herself as much as him was not lost on Brandon.

He felt the tears start in his eyes as well, and like her, hastily brushed them aside. He'd save them for another time when no one could see.

* * *

"Why don't ye go cut the grass to the front of the house," suggested Gran. "Ye're mopin' around here like a month of rainy weather."

Brandon couldn't deny that he was moping. He was frustrated beyond belief. He wanted to hit something. Maybe that was why Gran had suggested mowing the front and not the back. They never mowed the front, usually leaving that for the farmers that came to harvest it for silage.

"Ye can't be serious," he said, looking at the tall grass that would bind the mower before he got more than a foot into it.

"Well, then, go find somethin' to do, something to take the edge off. And if ye go out, just don't come back hammered or I'll make ye cut that shite with nail scissors."

Hammered? Brandon hadn't been hammered in a while and a drink at the pub at the junction of the Old Head sounded like a good idea. He'd walk there. That ought to burn some frustration out of him.

He left, knowing it would be his last opportunity for a while to visit the pub. His plane was leaving for Canada tomorrow.

The walk past the Garrettstown beach was reminiscent of his meeting with his surfing buddies, and of course, Sheila. And although it looked like good surfing weather, he didn't stop to see if there was anyone he knew. Today, at least, it held no draw for him. On he walked, over the bridge and past the next beach, so similar to the first, and around the curve that led straight up to the pub.

Half an hour later he arrived, thirsty from his walk and looking forward to a pint. Stepping through the gate into the patio to sit at one of the wooden picnic tables out there with a view of the sea beyond, he noticed a new foal in the paddock next door to the pub. The thoroughbred mare that had been ensconced there had finally foaled and a new little colt stood on spindly legs beside her, the umbilicus still a visible nub on his belly.

Brandon went to the fence but the mare was wary and the foal even more so. He was patient, if nothing else, and so he just stood watching, careful not to look the horse in the eye but instead focussed on her withers while dangling choice grass and flowers in his hand. Eventually, his patience paid off and she stretched her graceful neck out and took the meal he offered before trotting off with the grass dangling from her lips.

Brandon smiled to himself and then outright laughed when the foal realized that his mother had left his side and went gamboling like a little lamb after her. It seemed to have sparked something playful in the wee colt because he did a turn or two around the mare, nearly throwing himself off balance before coming to a stop to snuggle up to her.

One of the barmaids from inside the pub came up to him. He knew her slightly, and supposed she recognized him as being one of the locals who frequented the place from time to time.

"Get ye somethin'?" she inquired.

"Guinness, please," he answered. And laughed when she answered with, "Thought so," before going back inside.

It was a nice day, so he sat outside and watched the horses, glass in hand, feeling as well as could be expected since Aine had dashed his hopes.

And then the old crowd came by, the surfers who'd tired of playing in the water and were looking for a meal more substantial than offered by the food trucks. Or maybe they were tired of beach fare.

Brandon acknowledged their greeting and saw with dismay that they were going to join him at the table outside. Ordinarily, he would have been happy to have them join him, but for some reason, they struck him as being immature and boisterous. Or perhaps he was just in a mood to be quiet?

He suffered through their jocularity, finding little to laugh at. Their humor was overly rude and especially inappropriate; there were children eating at the establishment as well as other clientele who cast censuring looks their way.

Brandon had had enough. His pint was done and he just wanted to be away from this group that he once felt so much a part of.

"Ye're not leavin'?" asked one of them, his expression one of incredulity.

"I am," replied Brandon. "I'm off for Canada tomorrow and I've yet to pack."

"Canada?" said another, "What the *fook* ye goin' there for?"

"Visitin'. Goin' to enjoy some good Canadian hospitality. Not like here, where every time I go for a drink a crowd of plonkers invades my space."

"Who're ye to call someone a plonker, ye gligeen?" said the first, laughing at his own joke.

"Ye're bollocks, y'are," said the other and it looked for a moment that they were going to do him in for his comments.

Instead, he downed the last drop of his drink, laughed, and agreed with them. "Yeah, maybe," he said, still laughing, "but it's adventure I'm out for and I'm sure to find it there. I'll see ye's all in a few months."

"Oh, so ye'll be back, then?" said the first, and at Brandon's nod, waved him off.

As Brandon walked back to his grandparents' home, he wondered that he hadn't gotten into a fight when it seemed it was headed that way.

Something had changed within him. He just didn't know what.

Chapter Fifteen

Have ye never been out of Ireland, then?" asked Hank as they drove up the hard-packed, dirt and gravel road that led to his and Laura's two homes on the mountain.

"No, never. Never even been to Ulster, and that's a fact," he answered, taking in the craggy mountain peaks surrounding them, the snowcaps that stayed all year long and the barren rock beyond the tree line.

Hank was a little surprised that Brandon hadn't set foot outside Cork or Kerry, but then realized that until he'd left for Canada, he hadn't, either. "Well, don't misunderstand me," he began. "I love Ireland. The scenery there is as beautiful as anywhere. But there are things ye'll see here that ye won't see there and they'll blow ye right out o' the water, they will."

Ahead of the truck, a gray shadow trotted up the road like it owned the place.

"Is that a wolf?" asked Brandon, and Hank assumed he'd never seen one up close and personal before.

"Ah, no. That's a coyote. Scrawny little buggers for the most part and always lookin' out for a good meal. They'll eat anythin' from rodents to small animals, including cats or small dogs. I've even heard of them goin' after toddlers. Don't know how true that is but we don't take chances."

"Do ye see them often?" He was looking at it as they drove by. It didn't seem too worried by the truck, only darting off the roadbed and into the trees at the last moment.

"Depends on the year. I think we must be comin' up to the final year of the cycle where the population peaks, then starts to dwindle. We've seen a lot this year, and even now, in midsummer when they don't spend much time near people, we've seen quite a few."

Brandon seemed to think a minute and Hank wondered if he was nervous to be out in the bush by himself. "Bears?" Brandon asked, a concerned look on his face.

"Oh, bears for certain, but not usually near the cabin. Not unless ye have some garbage ye've strewn about. They get addicted to dumpster divin', as they say here, and ye can't stop them from doin' it. The poor beasts usually have to be put down."

"Why don't they just relocate them somewhere's else?"

Hank laughed. "They have a range of hundreds of miles and will often come back to the very place they were removed from. And if there's garbage in between, they'll stop along the way for a snack or two."

"You're coddin' me."

"No, I'm not. I'm serious, not joking at all. There are special containers to keep bears out of the garbage, fairly effective. We take ours to the dump regularly so that nothing is left to chance. Ah, here's Laura's cabin, coming up," he said, indicating the tall, log structure with its floor to ceiling windows and peaked, metal roof, bright red in the sunshine.

"Holy *fook*!" exclaimed Brandon, and Hank knew exactly what he was thinking. It was the same for him when he saw the structure first go up about three years back.

"Pretty impressive, eh?"

Brandon merely nodded and hopped out as soon as the truck stopped, gazing at it from the bottom of the driveway. From there, it was like looking at a three- or four-story building, it stood so tall upon the rise.

"A loft is it, did ye say?"

"Yeah," said Hank and then gestured toward the stairs. "It was only one bedroom until after Laura and I were married. We then made an addition to the rear where there was lots of room and put on a couple more bedrooms and another bathroom. So now it's a three bedroom, two bath home, instead of one bed, one bath. We actually have room for visitors and Ryan has his own room, next to ours."

"How is the weyan, anyway?" Brandon asked.

"He's grand, growing like a weed and getting more like a person every day, rather than just a baby that eats, sleeps, and takes a shite."

* * *

It had been an impressive day, that first day. First the arrival at Vancouver and then the drive through the city and into the wilds beyond. And then, what seemed like hours later, finally arriving at the cabin. And now, several days later, he was well and truly earning his keep.

Brandon swung the hammer, pounding the nail through the wood, securing it steadfastly to the crosspiece. He stopped and wiped the sweat from his brow. It was going to be another warm one today; he put down the tool and went in search of his water bottle. It was around somewhere.

He found it near the sawhorse outside where the sun had warmed it. Brandon had half a mind to leave it and grab a cold one from the cooler but hated the thought of seeing good water go to waste. Instead, he downed the last few swallows and decided it wasn't really that bad after all. It was wet, at least, and took the dryness from his parched throat quite nicely.

He sat down in the sunshine, his face aimed at the sky, looking to get a bit of a tan going. He hadn't had time to really get out in the sun and just relax so he figured a couple of minutes would be okay.

Thoughts raced through his head like a mini-documentary of his time since his arrival. Seeing Laura's cabin for the first time, now her and Hank's home-away-from-home, he'd been gobsmacked at the size of it. It'd made him wonder if he'd be up to the chore of helping Hank rebuild his old place because if it was anything like that cabin, Brandon felt he might have just got himself into a task he wasn't equal to.

But in no time at all, they were inside and he saw how comfortable it was, and not as grand or palatial as he had thought it might be. It was the kind of place that made you feel instantly at home, from the hardwood floors to the beamed ceiling high overhead. Open to the kitchen at the back, or, according to Hank, what used to be the back, the new addition went on from there, another twenty feet farther to a sunroom with a view of the hillside that stretched up the mountain behind them. It was breathtaking.

Laura had come down the stairs just then, little Ryan in her arms, cooing and blowing bubbles happily. Brandon had laughed at his half brother's comments, could hear the pride in Hank's voice when he spoke about the baby and to see him now, with his son in his arms as he scooped the fat little thing from Laura's arms, he couldn't help but feel sentimental. He hadn't been exposed to babies except for his younger siblings, and that had been a long time ago. Babies, to him, were something that had to be tolerated or endured. They hadn't been real until they began toddling around and trying to converse.

That was when things had changed, and Brandon knew he'd have moved heaven and earth to protect his younger siblings if he'd had to, even though he hadn't been that old himself.

From down the road a vehicle could be heard approaching. It was not yet afternoon and Brandon thought it was too early to be Hank, back from town with extra supplies.

It wasn't. It was Laura, with the baby strapped in the infant car seat behind her.

Brandon shook off his musings and approached the car as it came to a halt. Laura opened the door and said, "Your mom called from Ireland. She said it was important, so I thought I'd come and get you. I tried calling your cell but you didn't answer, so thought I'd just drive over. Do you want to use the land line at the house?" she offered.

"Mam? Called here?"

"Mm-hm," she replied. "Asked if I could get you to call her right away."

"I didn't hear my phone," he said, feeling in his back pocket and looking around the area as if he'd dropped it.

"Oh, don't worry. I found your phone on the kitchen table when I called you. That's quite the ring tone you have," she grinned.

"Yeah," he laughed, "I thought it would get my attention."

"Yes, well, it got mine. It's not every day you hear Grieg's piano concerto on a cell phone."

"It starts off loud, and that's what I needed," he said by way of explanation. And then, "Let me just check the site, I'll be right back." He quickly checked things over, made sure to shut the generator off, then got in the car beside Laura to go back to her cabin.

"Did my mam say what she wanted?" he asked, watching as Laura steered the SUV expertly over a particularly rough spot. The baby had fallen asleep.

"Nope. Just that it was important. She left a number for you to call."

Brandon began to get the feeling that all was not well in Ireland but damned if he knew what it was about. Instantly he thought of his grandparents and wondered if something had happened to them. According to Laura, Mam wasn't up to sharing any information except to Brandon himself. That didn't bode well.

"The phone is on the table by the sofa," Laura said as they got inside and she carried the baby up to bed. "Go ahead. I'll be out back with the baby monitor. I'll hear him from there if he cries, and you can have the privacy you need."

"But it'll cost dearly from here," he objected.

"No. Not really. Hank does it all the time. What's one more call?"

And then she was gone upstairs and Brandon was left to make his phone call.

Moments later, he heard his mam's voice answering.

"What's up?" he asked, once they'd established that all was well this side of the pond.

"The garda called."

Immediately, Brandon felt the chill that went down his spine. Why it was so, he wasn't certain because really, they could be calling to say they caught the two and had them in custody.

"Okay," he said, encouraging her to speak more.

"Well, there's good news and bad news."

"Please, just spit it out. I don't care what ye say first, just tell me."

"Right. Okay, good news is they caught the two who did ye."

"Well, that's grand. Anythin' else?"

"Because ye ended up in hospital, and all the rest that went on…well, they got a blood sample from them both." There was a large gap in her sentence and Brandon was just about to urge her to get on with it when her voice cracked with emotion. His mam was choking back tears, Brandon could tell. "Brandon, that fella has full-blown AIDS."

He nearly dropped the phone. His heart stopped. He could have sworn it stopped beating. He couldn't breathe. The room swam before him, and if he wasn't already sitting, he would have fallen to the floor.

"AIDS? That bollocks has AIDS? And he did *that* to me knowin' he has AIDS?"

Just then Laura's footsteps could be heard in the loft, the soft cry of a baby, the soft whispered shushing of a mother's voice.

Only then did Brandon realize that he had yelled.

"Jaysus. God. Mam, what'll I do? How can I go on?"

"Christ, Brandon. It's not the end of the world. Ye haven't even been tested yet. Just trust that ye'll be alright, that's all I can say. And keep it in yer pants so's ye don't infect anyone, just in case. At least keep it there 'til ye know for certain."

"Thanks. Yeah. Thanks, Mam. That's real encouragin'. I needed to hear that!"

"Yeah, Brandon, ye did! Ye get angry and ye do all kinds of stupid things. Just think for once before ye do anythin', alright?"

He couldn't speak. He was so angry. So scared.

"Brandon, right?" It was his mam's turn to yell.

"Right. Okay. I hear ye. I'll mind what ye say." He was beginning to breathe again, but still not thinking straight. "I need to go. I can't talk about this anymore."

"Right." His mam sounded a little better, more in control. "If they need ye here, ye know, for anything, I'll let ye know."

"Yeah. O' course ye will. I'll be here in any case. We've made good progress. The roof's nearly there."

"Fine. As long as I can get ye if I need to."

He signed off then, told her loved her, and hung up. Only then did he notice his hands shaking, and Laura on the stairs, a worried look in her eyes.

"Brandon? Is everything okay?"

Brandon was still sitting. Still in shock. "Uh, sorry. I didn't mean to wake the weyan," he apologized.

"No, it's okay. He'll go back to sleep just fine. You look like you've just seen a ghost, though. Are you alright?"

He saw her take a step toward him, baby Ryan sleeping in her arms now that things were quieter. "I'm fine. I'll be fine," he said, shakily. "I could sure use a dram, though. Got any?"

Laura nodded. "In the pantry. There's a shelf there with some good Irish whiskey on it. The real kind; we brought it back from Ireland," she said, smiling, and Brandon was thankful. He'd heard the imported stuff was not as good and right now, he needed the real thing.

"Thanks. I promise I won't drink the bottle."

Laura nodded and took the baby back upstairs while Brandon got the bottle from the pantry and poured himself a good double. No ice. Just straight up, how he liked it. Taking it out to the sunroom with him, he had just sat down when Hank walked in.

"Slacking off already?" called Hank in a lighthearted voice.

Brandon had hit the lowest point he'd felt since the incident occurred so although Hank sounded all cheery, he was ready for a fight. "Eff off," he said sullenly.

Hank must have known something was up because he immediately went to where Brandon was sitting and sat down opposite him on the overstuffed sofa. "What's up?"

Brandon looked at Hank under furrowed brows and was deciding what he should tell him and how much. He was a brother but only a half brother. Until Hank had shown up in Ireland last year, Brandon had known nothing of him. Then deciding that Hank might as well know everything and then decide for himself whether or not Brandon should even be in the same place with the baby, he began.

"Did Henry say anythin' about me when ye called?"

"I'm not sure I understand," Hank replied, his voice calm but wary.

"I'm not stupid, Hank. I know Henry must have said somethin'," he snarled.

"Look, Brandon. I'm not inside yer head, y'eejit. If you mean did Henry tell me somethin' about what happened to ye a couple of months back, then, yeah, he mentioned somethin'. Just didn't go into any details."

Brandon finished the glass and laid it on the table, felt the whiskey slide down his throat, smooth and calming. He took a deep breath and began.

He told Hank everything, leaving nothing out and didn't

stop until he told him about the news from his mother. Hank hadn't batted an eye, making Brandon wonder exactly what Henry had said but not caring.

"And that's it. So, if ye want me to leave, if ye're worried over spreadin' anything to the weyan, or to you or Laura, I'll move on."

Hank shook his head. "No. That's not a problem. We've come a long way since AIDS was first discovered and everyone became paranoid. Holdin' Ryan, stayin' here, sharin' our meals, that's not goin' to transfer any disease to us. And besides which, ye don't even know yerself whether or not ye've been infected. Ye could be clear."

"I could have horseshoes up me arse, too, but that's not likely."

Hank sighed and leaned back against the cushions. "I don't disagree; does seem like the deck is stacked against ye, but Brandon, ye can't live yer life wonderin' if ye're goin' to drop off the twig at any moment. It'll drive ye crazy."

All Brandon could do was nod in agreement. Hank was right. There was nothing to be done by brooding about it. And they had a roof to get on before winter.

"Right, then. Let's go back to the other place and start workin'."

Hank looked at the empty glass and said, "How 'bout some nosh first. Looks like ye could use somethin' to eat to soak up that whiskey."

Brandon laughed, "Yeah. Not a bad idea," and followed Hank into the kitchen to make some lunch.

Hank thought about what Brandon had told him. Jaysus, the guy had the worst luck. But he'd brought it on himself, he knew. Would Brandon ever get out of the habit of having trouble follow him around like a sniffer hound, hot on his trail, just waiting for him to mess up? Somehow, he doubted it. And if Brandon ended up still healthy once the six months was past, well then, he'd have dodged a bullet. Brandon may not have horseshoes up his arse but Hank would bet rainbows there were unicorns!

Chapter Sixteen

They'd finished working on the house for the day and Brandon was still in a mood. He hadn't been able to shake the feeling of doom that had washed over him since Mam had told him the news. He'd been such a bollocks. If he got out of this one, he'd swear he'd never go astray again, although he wasn't sure how to avoid that. After all, he'd been working at being bad since he was a wee lad in short pants.

Now, though, he just didn't give a damn whether he got into trouble or not. He'd help Hank get as much of the house done as they could before he had to leave for Ireland again and then he'd just see what happened after that. He was supposed to have a video conference with Sean next week. *It couldn't come soon enough*, he thought, although two months ago, he would have scoffed at the idea of seeing a counselor. But he hadn't been in such deep trouble before.

On the way back to Laura's from the site, Brandon asked, "Do ye mind if I take the truck into town tonight for a while?"

Hank glanced at him, and Brandon knew what was going through his mind.

"I promise, I won't drink and drive."

"Alright. I'll hold ye to yer word," he said, and when they got out of the truck, handed Brandon the keys.

Brandon heaved a sigh as he got into the driver's side and began to drive down the road into town. It wasn't his first foray into town and he was getting used to driving on the right instead of the left. It was still a novelty and it gave him a bit of a boost to be in a different country, seeing sights other than what he'd see back home. Everything was new and that in itself was a boon to his mood.

By the time he arrived in town, he was feeling much more at peace with himself and went to the first place he could think of. The pub, or bar as they called it here, was not yet full and wouldn't be for at least another hour. That was fine with Brandon. He wasn't out looking for crowds. He just wanted a drink and maybe to socialize a bit. It was Friday night. Chances were there would be a lot of people filing in for a drink after work and maybe he'd get lucky and meet some nice young thing to chat up.

Sure enough, a group of women walked in, and taking a look at Brandon, seated alone at the bar, picked a table just behind where he sat. He heard their orders and the giggles that followed. They must have thought he was deaf or didn't speak English because they were talking about him in no uncertain terms. He couldn't make out everything they said, they were trying to be quiet at least, but every now and then he caught words that he knew were directed at him, "nice ass," especially. It wasn't the first time he'd been told that.

Smiling with everything he had, not because he was

conceited but just because he thought the situation humorous, he turned and asked if he could join them at their table. The answer was a resounding yes, and they moved over to fit in another chair.

There were three of them and one of him. Brandon liked those odds and at another time, he'd already be working out a way in his head where they would all sleep together at the same time. And if not a foursome, something he hadn't tried yet, then a threesome or even a regular one-on-one would do. He wouldn't have cared.

But now he knew they were off limits, and that was something that just sat in his craw and choked him. A timid soldier never won any battles, and so he decided to dive right in and see where it went from there.

"Are ye ladies all from here?"

One squealed in delight. "Oh, it's true," she exclaimed, "You're Irish!"

"Right through to me bones," he answered, broadening his brogue and liking how the conversation was starting out. After a few more giggles and questions and a refill of his drink, they were all getting more comfortable by the minute. At first, the ladies had all thought he was Hank, and had been pleasantly surprised to know he wasn't. Hank, it seemed, had a reputation as well. Or did. Brandon didn't suppose Hank had kept that reputation, and wondered briefly how he'd changed it.

Brandon's reputation had not followed him from Ireland; there was no one here to tell tales about him. And although he wasn't sure how to go about it, he was going to try to instill a different kind of reputation here. He was going to try to become known for taking care of people. It wasn't really so far from the truth.

* * *

Hank looked at Laura as she nursed their son to sleep. It was nearly eight in the evening and he was concerned. He'd already talked himself out of throwing Brandon out of the house just in case he really was infected, but common sense prevailed. There had been nothing to worry about in everything Hank had seen that would preclude Brandon from being anywhere near his son or his wife. Everything had gone on as normal.

But this afternoon, everything had changed. Brandon worked hard, and in that, all was well. Still, there was something eating away at him and though he was sure Brandon had told him all there was to know about his little escapade back home, he felt that the man was still processing it and the worst was yet to come.

It was that which prompted him to say to Laura, "Would ye mind if I drove into town? I know it would leave ye without a vehicle, but I'm wonderin' about Brandon, how he's faring." He punctuated his comment with a worrying bite to his lip.

"He said he wouldn't drink and drive. Don't you believe him?"

Hank wondered about that. "Yes and no. Did ye hear any of what Brandon was tellin' me just before lunch?"

Laura shook her head. "Some of it, but not all. I was busy with Ryan so I only heard something about him being in hospital and the garda looking for a car. Is that why he's here? Did he get run over or something and he's here to hide from whoever did it?"

Hank laughed outright and the baby jerked awake at the sound. "Oh, sorry," he apologized. "I didn't mean to wake ye, my son," he said as Laura shushed the baby back to sleep.

"Why did you laugh? Did I say something funny?"

"No," Hank was still chuckling. "It's just that Brandon has a way of invitin' trouble and what ye said would have been completely in character. But," and he emphasized the word, "that's not what happened." He then regaled her with the story, saw her tighten her hold on the baby and found himself encouraging her to relax a little. At the end of it, he wasn't sure if he wasn't trying to convince himself to relax as well.

"So you want to go to town because you think he will drink and drive?"

"No. Well, maybe. I'm just concerned because I don't know what he'll do. He's not happy right now, he's worried. I think he's in a strange head space."

"Well, you better go, then. If I really need to, I can ask the neighbors for a ride to town because I saw them earlier today and I know they're there. But I can't see why I would. We'd normally be up here anyway since it's the weekend."

Hank nodded. "Right, then, I'll call ye when I know what's up, and save a little o' that for me later, right?" He nodded to her bared breast where Ryan's chubby baby lips had let go of the nipple.

Laura grinned and he loved the gleam in her eye. "You're on," she laughed.

It was ten-thirty by the time Hank arrived in town. He hadn't seen Brandon drive up the mountain road so he knew he was still in town and the first place he was going to check was the pub.

No sign of the truck at the bar, so Hank drove the streets, keeping an eye out for his vehicle with its distinctive licence plate that said "Eire." He'd chosen it after he got the truck back from the body shop, thinking that it deserved a special plate for not killing him in the rollover.

Eventually, he found it, and saw two figures staggering down the street toward it. He'd been looking for almost two hours; it was nearly one, and it was only dumb luck that had him go down this particular street. He thought he'd covered all the residential areas in town but realized he'd missed this one when he noted the boarded-up shed on the corner lot. He knew he hadn't driven past that before.

He was looking for a place to park when he saw Brandon with the woman. They'd stopped and he had her up against a tree, kissing her wildly in a way that, at any other time, would have sparked the voyeur in Hank and had him watching, getting excited himself.

But that was then and this was now and Brandon was about to dig himself into something he'd never get out of if Hank didn't intervene.

He gave up on trying to find a spot to park on the crowded street and double-parked. Getting out, he strolled slowly to where Brandon now had his hands inserted up the woman's shirt, obviously enjoying the way she felt. She was enjoying it, too, from what he could see.

Oh, Christ, thought Hank. Would this come down to fisticuffs from him trying to get Brandon off the girl? He continued to stroll up the sidewalk where the two were so intent on what they were doing they didn't notice him standing there.

"Brandon," he said firmly, and got no reaction at all with the exception of the girl's eyes that opened slightly to peer at Hank as if he were nothing more than a pesky fly.

"Brandon," he said, louder this time and finally penetrated the fog that had enveloped his half brother.

"Mm?" answered Brandon, reluctantly pulling back from the kiss he was so locked into.

"Time to go," was all Hank said, hoping it was enough.

"I'm just getting' started," slurred Brandon, and Hank took another step closer before recoiling from the stink of booze off him. "Fer fuck's sake, Brandon, how much have ye had?" he said with contempt. "Ye smell like a *feckin'* brewery."

"Mind yer own business, I'm busy here," he mumbled.

Hank'd had enough of Brandon's attitude by then. Between what he'd heard this afternoon and Henry's request to "look after" Brandon, he was just beginning to understand what it all meant. He'd need to babysit the fiend if this went on much more.

He put his hand on Brandon's collar and hauled him off the girl, whose protests were loud and clear.

"Hey!" she exclaimed into the dark night, "Whaddya think you're doing!"

"Saving ye," said Hank. "Now get off home before I call the cops and tell them ye're trying to solicit yer wares on this fella."

"What?" She raised her hand to try to hit Hank but she was so drunk she merely stumbled and would have fallen down had Hank not caught her.

"Okay, that's enough of that, that is. Where d'ye live?" She pointed to the building they'd just come from and his heart sank.

"Christ, Brandon, did ye fuck her?"

Brandon had the decency to stand up straighter and look Hank in the eye, wavering slightly while saying, quite clearly, "No. I did not."

Hank eyed the woman, dusting herself off with ill-aimed movements. She was beyond drunk, he thought. She was paralytic. "Is this true?" he asked of the girl.

She looked at him with unfocussed eyes and Hank thought if she could understand what he'd just asked her, that in itself would be a miracle.

"'S'true," she slurred. "But he's gotta great mouth," she giggled, and like Brandon, was having difficulty standing.

"Right, then. Toddle off home, you. I'll wait 'til ye get inside yer building to make sure ye're safe. And Brandon," he glared at his half brother, "I'm takin' you straight home; and if ye give me any trouble, I swear on my mother's grave I'll lay ye out here and now. Understand?"

Something seemed to sink into Brandon's liquor-filled brain because he nodded and didn't resist Hank's help.

As Hank man-handled his half brother into the car, he looked at the truck, the way it was so sloppily parked, and before climbing into the car, made certain there were no extra dings in his precious truck. He still remembered getting it out of the shop after the avalanche had nearly banjaxed it for good.

Climbing into the driver's seat of the car, he glared at Brandon. "Ye promised me ye wouldn't drink and drive," he accused.

Brandon, who looked as if he were either going to pass out or break into song, merely blinked stupidly and said, "I didn't."

That didn't make sense to Hank. It was too far to walk to the pub from here and Brandon wouldn't have known the girl beforehand, would he? "Then how did the truck get here?"

"She drove," Brandon answered, head lolling against the window and humming softly to himself, and miraculously in tune, thought Hank.

"Mmf," he answered, starting the car. "Ye'd better hope there's no mark on it when I come back to get it in the morning."

"Mmf," answered Brandon, sounding remarkably like Hank, and then carried on with his wordless song.

At three forty-five in the morning, Hank and Brandon

walked through the door of the cabin to find Laura waiting for them. "I couldn't sleep, not knowing where you were or how things were," she said.

"I'm sorry, luv, I forgot to let ye know I'd found him. Go back to bed. I'll just see him to his own bed and be there in a minute." Brandon was ahead of him, stumbling, but basically okay to walk on his own. "D'ye need help or can ye make it on yer own?" asked Hank.

"I'm okay now." And then, "Thanks," Brandon said, like an afterthought of something that had been drilled into him from day one.

Hank nodded and made his way up to the room he shared with Laura. He stepped into her waiting arms, felt them go around him and cup his flute that had suddenly grown. "I believe ye said ye'd save somethin' for me," he grinned as he kissed her.

"I did. And Ryan's just been fed and changed so he's good for the next three or four hours."

"Mm, playtime for me," he said, taking her over to the bed where the sheets were rumpled and so inviting.

She pulled at his shirt until he shrugged out of it and then she started on his jeans, pulling at the clasp, letting him take the zipper down so she could cup his nads, rolling them around in her hand familiarly.

He moaned his appreciation and stepped quickly out of his pants, the night air cool but pleasant on his fevered skin. She felt so good in his arms.

Moving to the bed, he lay her beneath him and crawled

on top, nibbling at her neck below her ear, kissing her cheek, her chin, before settling on her lips to ravish her mouth. He felt her hands slide down his hips, felt her spread her legs in invitation and grasp his flute to guide it in.

But he wasn't ready yet. He wanted to prolong the moment, so he said, "If ye aren't too sleepy, I'd love to relax in the hot tub with ye," he whispered in the night. "Ye did say how wee Ryan would be asleep for a while yet."

"Oh, we haven't made love under the stars since last winter," she exclaimed.

"That's what I'm thinkin'," he observed. "And yon half brother is sure to be passed out by now. I'll check before we go down. Meet ye there?"

At Laura's nod, he padded down the hall to peek in Brandon's door and found his half brother sprawled across the bed and snoring, still dressed in jeans and t-shirt. He closed the door again and met Laura at the back where the hot tub stood in its new location, in a sheltered bower closer to where the giant shed was, and noted she had the baby monitor in hand, just in case.

The great thing about having a cabin up here, Hank reflected, was the fact that you could wander nude out your back door and no one would be the wiser. He sauntered over to the tub where Laura had the jets turned off beneath the heated water. Hank remarked on them.

"No. I just thought we'd work up enough blood pressure without worrying about water jets, too," said Laura, watching as Hank lifted his leg over the side of tub and then stumbled,

169

splashing into the water awkwardly.

A trill of laughter sprang from Laura's throat, "Are you okay?"

Hank guffawed and shook the water from his head. "Oh yeah, I'm fine. It's no bother," he said, spitting out the water he'd nearly inhaled. Laura sat back then and Hank detected that look in her eye. "Ah, it's goin' to be like that, is it," he said, a grin running from ear to ear.

Laura raised her delicate brows, her smile widened and she thrust her hand out to grab Hank's flute. He let her, stood before her as she handled him, and then stepped closer so she could take him in her mouth.

Brandon woke from a dead sleep. He lay still, wondering what it was that had him wide awake. He thought he'd heard something, like the cry of a wild animal, coyote or wolf, when it suddenly occurred to him that he had to pee like he'd never had to pee before. Getting up, he meant to go straight to the toilet but something caught his eye out the window, which was wide open to catch the cool breeze off the mountain. The moon was up and the back yard was in shadow, but not so dark he couldn't make out the two people in the hot tub.

It was Hank and Laura, he knew. He could make them out quite clearly from the window in his room but he didn't know if they knew that, and they were…well, they were doing something out there. He couldn't take his eyes away, couldn't help playing the voyeur. He hadn't meant to, but it was impossible not to.

Laura was doing him. *Oh, God*, he thought, *she's taking*

him all in. He couldn't help but get chubbed up himself, and he loosened his jeans, cursing the fact that he had to pee so badly. His lad was stiff, he hadn't got it off with that girl in town, although he'd brought her off a few times. Christ it was frustrating!

He was just about to tear his eyes from the scene before him, thinking they were finished, when Laura stood, a naked beauty, all curves and flawless skin, her long, wavy hair plastered wet against her shoulders. She turned and the moonlight glinted off water droplets that limned her breasts and dripped from her nipples.

Brandon felt himself quicken. He watched as Hank knelt before her, to put his mouth to her, much as she'd done to him, and when Brandon saw her knees buckle, he knew Hank had been successful. A moment more and Hank was inside her, pumping, bringing her to a full climax that she cried out to the moon above.

No wonder he'd woken up. It wasn't an animal he'd heard, but the two of them, outside, making love in the hot tub.

He quickly turned then, made his way to the toilet to relieve himself of both tasks, and praying with all his might that one day he'd be free to do that again.

Chapter Seventeen

Aine had done it. She'd figured out a way for herself and Brandon to be together. It hadn't been easy and it was likely the biggest decision of her life. It was certainly going to affect her life in a big way. She would have to move.

Taking a look at her cozy flat, she knew that most of what she had could be sold and the rest would fit neatly into boxes that could be easily transported to Killarney. She had resigned her post at the hospital, given her last counseling session a few days ago, and had been accepted at the hospital in Killarney for a part-time position. She was hoping something full-time would come up soon, but it was better than nothing for now.

She filled another box with keepsakes, things she knew she couldn't part with, and taped it up. Then, glancing at the clock, she knew she had to get ready for her final shift or be late. It was the night shift and she'd spent most of the day packing, too filled with emotion to sleep, knowing it would be a long night if it wasn't busy.

It was busy. As soon as Aine got onto the floor, an ambulance arrived with a motor vehicle accident victim. It was a young man, and he was critical. They'd got him stabilized as best they could before rushing him off to surgery. Soon after, another ambulance arrived. This time it was a woman, and she was so obviously pregnant. In and out of consciousness, one look told Aine she was in a bad way. If they didn't take the baby right then and there, they'd lose both mother and child.

Emotions welled up in her. It wasn't unusual for her to feel strongly about her patients but this one struck a chord in her. The poor thing looked to be a teenager still!

Aine turned around to get the cart when she bumped into Kathleen, moving as fast as she dared toward the cubicle with the young woman.

Suddenly a scream came from the bed and the woman half sat up, clutching her abdomen. Her knees came up beneath the sheet and a gush of liquid filled the bed.

Kathleen lifted the sheet and immediately went into action. "Ye'll not have time for a section, the baby's presenting," she called out to the surgeon who had just arrived and then went into action, doing what she was trained to do, trying to get the baby born safely and save the mother's life.

It was over very quickly. The baby slipped into Kathleen's hands and was whisked away by the neonatal team. Aine knew it was alive but didn't know if it would live. She didn't even get to see if it was a girl or a boy.

Kathleen finished up with the woman, who was now slipping into unconsciousness again. "Okay, now ye can take her," she said, stepping back and letting the surgical team step in.

Nearly three hours had passed since Aine got on shift and she suddenly felt like she could use a coffee. One look at Kathleen told her that it was likely the same for her.

"Coffee?" asked Aine.

"I could use one," said Kathleen as she removed the soiled gloves and wiped her brow on a tissue. The hospital tissues were rough but serviceable, and there was nothing else around. She dropped it into the dustbin near the bed and looked at Aine as if there was something on her mind.

"Let's go to the nurse's lounge down the way. I need to tell ye somethin'," she said, and Aine nodded and followed.

Inside the lounge and thankfully by themselves, at least for the moment, Aine sat down with a cup of coffee, then sat back, stretching her legs and arching her back until the stiffness from working in one position for a long time went away.

"Oh, that feels much better," she said, feeling a slight movement in her spinal cord and the resulting relaxation of a particularly tight muscle.

"I hope that woman makes it, and her babe," Kathleen said, shaking her head. "Crazy fools, taking the turns too fast and she so far along."

"What happened?" Aine hadn't been told anything but, obviously, Kathleen knew more about it.

"Ah, they were racin' to the hospital because the baby was comin', and them so young themselves. No time to wait for anyone so they thought they could get here faster if they just left. As I understand it, he took the corner too fast, ye know that rural stretch through Raheen?"

"Oh, they must have decided it was faster than headin' down to N71," Aine said, thinking.

"Mm," agreed Kathleen. "From what I was told, they took the corner wide and then tried to swerve to miss the oncoming traffic. Must have over-corrected as he ended up flipping the car. 'Twas only luck that no other cars were involved."

"That's so sad," observed Aine. "Here's prayin' to God they all make it. I hate it when families are ripped apart needlessly."

They sipped their hot coffee, enjoying the rare quiet that surrounded them. Kathleen put her cup down and said to Aine, "I heard from the garda about those plonkers that assaulted Brandon, did I tell ye?"

Aine shook her head and was quite sure Kathleen would have known if she had, but it was a way into a conversation that she seemed to want to have. She looked at Kathleen expectantly, inviting her with a raised brow to continue.

"Ah well, it seems they caught the two. Interpol had prints on them. Seems they do this a lot."

"What, make like they're out for a good time and then beat people up and rob them?"

Kathleen nodded. "It was just bad luck it was our Brandon that they chose. And worse luck may follow."

Aine was curious. "What do ye mean by that?"

Kathleen took a deep breath. *She looks scared to death*, thought Aine.

"If ye don't mind, I need to talk to someone, just to let it out, like. Someone other than the family."

"I understand," Aine answered. And strangely enough, she did. Kathleen and Aine had become good friends since Brandon's incident, despite the gap in their ages.

Kathleen rubbed her hands together as if to warm them, but it wasn't cold in the room. "Turns out the fella has AIDS. It was in the file they got from Interpol and so they were able to get his cooperation and get a blood test, just to confirm."

Aine sat back, feeling suddenly as if someone had smacked her in the gut. "Oh," she breathed out softly, and couldn't say why but had to gulp air to keep the tears from starting in her eyes. "And Brandon? Does he know?"

Kathleen nodded. "He does. I called him a couple of weeks ago to tell him. Hank says the boy went to town, got drunk, and Hank had to go get him. He's stayed up the mountain ever since, refuses to go anywhere or see anyone. Just works away at the cabin."

"Good for Hank but not so for Brandon," observed Aine.

"Ye've got the right of it," replied Kathleen.

"I've somethin' to tell ye, too," said Aine, knowing Kathleen would hear about it soon. She'd rather tell her friend now than have her hear through the hospital gossips. "I've tendered my resignation."

Kathleen's eyes opened wide. "Why would ye do such a thing? Ye've got an amazing career ahead of ye. Ye're talented, ye are. Why quit?"

"I'm not quitting, at least, not nursing. I've taken a

176

position in Killarney, away from here, away from the rape clinic. I can't do that anymore." She let that sink in before she continued. It seemed to be a night for confessions, after all. "I love Brandon, and I can't be with him and be a counselor at the clinic. And I don't know if I can be with him, either, if ye understand my meaning."

"But Brandon loves ye, ye must know that," said Kathleen gently.

"It's not that," Aine began, and then the tears began to fall. She felt Kathleen's hands on hers, encouraging her to continue. "I was raped when I was thirteen. I've done a lot of work, had a lot of counseling myself, and the rape clinic was a way to pay all that back. But meeting Brandon and falling in love. Well," she faltered, sniffed back the next flow of tears, and gladly took the tissue Kathleen offered. "I don't know if I can *be* with him, have sex with him. I've never. Not since the day it happened. I can't. I freeze. Panic. And then it turns out awful, the fella thinks I'm a tease, or that I'm horribly messed up, which I am. They walk away blamin' me and callin' me names. I can't do that anymore," she finished.

"These other men," said Kathleen, "did ye love them or they you?"

"No," answered Aine truthfully. "I didn't, and I'm certain they didn't love me. But I do love Brandon. And now there's a chance he's infected, could have full-blown AIDS, and I don't know if I can handle it."

"Well, I think that if ye really love someone, the sex part becomes easy. They take their time, take care to make sure ye're feelin' it, too. Ye know Brandon has a reputation with the ladies," she said.

Aine had to smile at that. "I'd heard."

"Well, and he didn't come by it without reason. But he's always been careful, always used rubbers," she hastened to add. "He's a good boy, underneath it all, and smart. Even AIDS isn't quite as bad as it used to be and there are ways around it."

Aine nodded and wiped her tears. It was what she remembered telling Brandon, when the threat had been simply HIV.

"Ye needn't worry with Brandon," said Kathleen, patting Aine's hand in a motherly fashion. "If ye tell him what happened to ye, he'd understand. He'd never call ye names or make ye feel like it was yer own fault. He'd only ever protect ye. It's what he does for those he loves. He protects them."

Aine's tears had stopped flowing and she blew her nose, standing and feeling somehow better. Her horrible secret was out and Kathleen had said Brandon would understand. Now all that needed to happen was for Brandon to have the test that would define their future.

"I've got to get back to my station," said Kathleen, standing and stretching, straightening her uniform, and looking as if she were feeling better herself. "Take a moment, get yerself together before ye go back out there, and I'll see ye later. How about at dinner break?"

Aine nodded and watched Kathleen leave. What had begun as a busy night with mixed feelings over leaving was progressing into something that felt more like a comfortable transition. She felt hope that all was not lost, that Brandon might still want her even if he found out about the rape. And then there was the move. Would Brandon want to move to Killarney, too? Had she done something that would irrevocably keep them apart? He seemed to love Kinsale.

She didn't know the answers to those questions, but she didn't have time to figure it out. Her pager went off, and she was back in action, racing out of the lounge and down the hall to the next casualty in line.

Kathleen checked in on their newest arrival, the baby from the MVA. The infant, a little girl, seemed to be doing well; the neonatal team had her well in hand. That made Kathleen happy. It looked like the little girl would live. She wasn't so sure about her mam or her da. Both were still in surgery and only time would tell. She would check on them before she went off shift, and in the meantime, pray that they would be safe.

She thought about Aine's confession. What drove some men to do that, and to a thirteen-year-old girl no less! It angered her more than she cared to admit. It made sense now, the passion she'd seen in Aine's eyes when she dealt with rape victims that presented in the ED or talked about breakthroughs with difficult clients. Of course, no names were ever mentioned but Kathleen knew it often helped to hear a co-worker's ideas and thoughts and to share in the successes that were sometimes hard to come by.

Would she tell her son herself, Kathleen wondered? No.

Not likely. She'd let Aine do that when Brandon returned.

As for Brandon, it didn't sound like he had taken the news very well. She felt scared for him, worried that even now the disease was rushing through his body, replicating cells and making him sick. Secretly, she was glad he'd decided to forego the trips into town, staying to work at the cabin instead. From what Kathleen knew of the place, it was in the mountains—she'd seen photos. Wilderness as far as the eye could see, lakes and rivers that looked so pristine and no one around for miles. It was a place that a body could heal, she thought, and if there was hard work to be done, that would help.

Eventually, the dinner break rolled around and as she had promised Aine, they met at the almost deserted cafeteria, both having brought their own meals from home.

Not one to waste words, Kathleen began with the thought that was most on her mind. "Are ye takin' time off between here and whenever ye start in Killarney?"

If Aine was surprised by the question, she didn't show it. "The job starts next month. I've a couple of weeks to get resettled."

"I've an idea, and I hope ye won't think me too daft." The more she had thought on it, the better it sounded to her; and seeing the expression on Aine's face, she continued.

"I was thinkin' that if ye had some time, and it sounds like ye do, ye could go to see Brandon, to tell him what ye told me. He's havin' a tough time, and so are you. Ye both could use each other right now."

"I'm not so sure that's a good idea," said Aine. "I've got to get myself to Killarney, find a place to live, and get settled before startin' my new job. I'm not sure a trip to Canada fits in with that right now."

"If it's money ye need, I'll help with that," offered Kathleen, knowing that she had a good nest egg tucked away.

"Ah, that's grand of ye, but no, it isn't money I lack. I never go anywhere or spend it on much except what I need to live, so I've got a bit set aside. It's just that, well, what if Brandon doesn't want to see me? It's a long way to go to have someone tell ye to eff off," she explained.

Kathleen couldn't help but smile at that. "I don't think he'd tell ye that, but he might be somewhat surprised to see ye there." She thought a moment before continuing. "I understand they've got the roof on, and so Brandon's workin' a little on the interior. He's decided to stay there at the new place for the moment rather than with Hank, Laura, and the baby at the main cabin where they're livin'. Seems they have a place in town as well, but Hank says that since Laura is still on maternity leave, and it's summer, they decided to take the time and spend it on the mountain. They've a spare room there. I think Laura might like some female company."

Aine sucked in her bottom lip and was quiet. Kathleen knew she was thinking about it, wondering if it was possible.

"My eldest son, Henry, could help ye find a place in Killarney. He's in the know out there. He also has a lorry ye could commandeer for your furniture or what have you. Ye'd just need to help pay for petrol."

The look of relief on Aine's face was obvious. "I'm gobsmacked, I am," she admitted. "I thought I'd have to sell everything, decide what I really needed to keep and then get rid of all the rest because I couldn't afford to hire a mover."

"Ah, now, we'll get it done, see if we don't. Let me call Henry, and when ye decide the date, we'll have it there for ye. In the meantime, I'll get him to scout out a few properties for ye. I'm sure he'll surprise ye with what he finds."

"The timing would be very tight, to figure all that out and go to Canada, too. I don't know that I can do that," she said, worriedly.

Kathleen was not to be outdone by pessimism and hadn't raised five children for nothing. "Here's how we'll do it. I've lots of room in that big house of mine. I've three spare rooms for ye to choose from. One day I'll sell that monstrosity but I love it and can't quite bring myself to do it yet. In the meantime, there's all the space and Ciara isn't home often enough to dirty it up. She's always off explorin' old ruins, climbing up where a body should never go and tellin' everyone down below how far she can see."

"It sounds lovely, and ye're very gracious for offering…"

"Ah now, it's a bit of a drive, I know that. But it's the national road all the way in so goes quick. Besides, it isn't forever, only a couple of weeks until we can get ye settled in Killarney and off to Canada. I'll take ye to the airport myself."

Aine couldn't believe what she was hearing. It was as if her prayers had been answered. Tears misted in her eyes…she'd have to stop doing that. It seemed all she did lately was cry.

"It'll all work out, ye'll see," said Kathleen, patting Aine's hand. "Let's get back to work and pray there are no more crazy drivers out there. I swear, if I have to deliver one more casualty from a car wreck, I'm going to scream."

"There was another one?"

"Mm hm," Kathleen answered. "Seems this one stepped out in front, not lookin' where she was goin', playin' on her phone, like. Don't know what this world is comin' to, people pay more attention to their mobiles than what's in front o' their noses."

The two walked back to their separate floors, ready to power through the rest of the long night ahead.

Chapter Eighteen

In retrospect, the move to Killarney had been easily arranged and everything had gone off without a hitch. Aine was now comfortably ensconced in her own place near Killarney Community Hospital, thanks to Henry, and was ready to start work after her two-week break. A break that would see her fly to Canada to surprise Brandon with her presence. She became suddenly nervous, wondering what he would say, or do, when he saw her. Did he even want her anymore?

Arrangements had been made with Hank to meet her at the airport and drive her the distance to their home in the mountains, and if she thought she wouldn't recognize him, she was dead wrong.

"It was like seeing a younger version of Henry standin' there, wavin' at me as I came through the doors," she laughed as they greeted and walked the distance to the parkade. "Ye look so much alike."

She had only one suitcase and a small carry-on that Hank had no trouble hefting along at a good pace. "I just kept lookin' for the Irish cailín with big gray eyes and blonde hair, nervous as a cat in a room full of rockin' chairs. As soon as ye came through, I had a feelin' it was you."

"I am nervous," she admitted. "All kinds of thoughts, crazy thoughts, are runnin' through my head. I'm not so sure keepin' this as a surprise was such a good thing."

"It'll be fine, ye'll see," Hank assured her.

They started the drive, winding their way through traffic until they were out of the city and on the long drive to the mountain. Finally, after more than two hours, they turned off the main highway onto the road that would take them to the cabin.

"If it goes badly between us," Aine said to Hank on the lengthy drive up the mountain road, "ye might have to put up with a mopey house guest for the next ten days."

"Ah, I'm sure Brandon will be happy to see ye. He's been draggin' his arse around the cabin for weeks now and it's making us all a bit crazy. I'm sure your presence will shake things up a bit. Maybe do him some good."

Aine smiled to herself. She was looking forward to seeing Brandon again, but she feared his reaction to seeing her unexpectedly, especially in light of what he now faced. If her worst fears were realized, and he didn't want to see her, then she would, as she had told Hank, become a house guest they hadn't counted on.

In no time, it seemed, the drive was over, although between exiting the city and driving to the town where Hank and Laura lived was long enough. And yet, when the tall log home on the hillside came into view, its red metal roof shining brightly in the sun, it had felt like no time at all.

"Wow," said Aine, and heard Hank laugh at her response.

"Yeah, that's what everyone says," he joked, and she knew he wasn't lying.

She looked up to see a woman standing near the railing, a chubby infant in her arms, his little arms flapping up and down. "Is that yer son and yer wife?"

"That's them. And that's wee Ryan's way of waving. Hasn't yet figured out it only takes one arm to do the wavin'."

They made their way up the stairs and introductions were made. Aine and Laura seemed to hit it off right away, leaving Hank the chore of dragging her suitcase up the stairs from the driveway.

Aine looked back guiltily. "Hank, I'm sorry, I should have taken that up myself."

"No bother," he said, huffing his way up the steps. "It just reminds me how fortunate I am to have built my own place on a flat piece of land with only two steps to climb to my front door."

After they'd had some refreshments and Aine was settled in, Hank said, "Do ye want to see Brandon now, or wait until tomorrow? It's been a long day for ye, and he doesn't know ye're here, after all."

She nodded. "It has been a long day. But if it's all the same, I think I'd like to go now. Is there something I can bring him? Groceries, anything?"

"He's got everything he needs," said Hank, "but I bought some ale for him. Ye could take him that."

"Oh," said Aine standing suddenly, "I almost forgot.

I've some good Irish alcohol for everyone. Yer mam says ye can't get the same stuff here so I brought some ale and some whiskey. Which would ye prefer?"

"One of each," joked Hank, and then, "You take the ale with ye to see Brandon and leave the whiskey here. I may drink the same brand here as there but I assure ye, it isn't the same at all."

Minutes later, they were back in the truck heading down the road to where Hank's new Irish cabin was being built. On first appearance, all Aine could see were large river rocks in a pile off to the side, but as they drew closer, she saw the chimney, which, as she'd been informed, was the one remaining piece left over from the fire, and along one side, stone skirting had been started. "Oh, it's goin' to be lovely," she breathed on a whisper, her voice filled with awe.

"That it is," said Hank. "I'm hugely impressed with what Brandon has done. I knew he did a little work with the stone, knew Henry had shown him a few things, but this, well, it left me speechless when I first saw it myself. Gobsmacked, I was."

Hank got out of the truck first and though neither of them could see Brandon, they both knew he was nearby. The sound of the generator going could be heard, coming from the rear of the house, and as they made their way to the back, Hank called out, "Brandon. Someone here to see ye."

He looked to Aine and gestured for her to come up beside him as he pointed to a spot just beyond the corner of the house. "He's just there. I'm goin' to take the truck back to the other cabin. When ye're ready to come back, Brandon can take ye on the four-wheeler. And if ye don't come back tonight, well, I'm sure ye'll be quite comfortable here." He winked at her, and before she could protest, left.

In fact, she felt ready to bolt. Sucking in a breath and mustering her courage, Aine stepped carefully around some short ends of lumber, scrap pieces that were left over and not big enough to be of use. About to put her foot down, she heard a voice call, "Hey, watch yer step!"

Looking down, she saw she was about to place her foot on something not very stable and so shifted it over to land on firm ground. Looking up, she was about to say "thanks" when she heard Brandon's indrawn breath and then, "Aine?"

She felt tears prick the back of her eyes and all she could do was nod. He covered the ground between them in less than a second, and before she could think, had her in his arms, kissing her like he'd never let her go.

"Ye're here? Ye're truly here?" At her nod, he stopped, as if it just occurred to him that this was maybe not the gift he thought it was at first. "Why?"

She had no answer except to say, "Because of you. Us. I heard ye weren't well."

He put her down and backed away from her, a sardonic look in his eye. "Oh, so ye just thought ye'd drop by and cheer me up? And how will ye do that, I'm wonderin'?" He turned and looked busy, as if he'd lost something and was trying to find it.

However prepared Aine thought she was, this wasn't

what she had planned. "It came out badly. I only meant that I needed to see ye. To tell ye…"

He swung around to face her, his demeanor like a threatened tiger. "To tell me what? That it's no matter I've likely got AIDS, that ye'd take me anyway? That ye can make me happy even though what I've got could kill ye? No thanks, ye can take yer pity elsewhere."

This was not how it was supposed to be at all. She felt the anger build inside her. "Ye bollocks! Ye think I came all this way to shower ye with pity? Bollocks!"

"Ye already said that!"

"Well, and I'll say it as many times until it sinks in. I came to tell ye I love ye." Her voice broke but she continued on, knowing it was too late to stop now. "I came to tell ye I want ye so bad it hurts and I don't know if I can ever lie with ye but it's not for the reason ye think."

Whatever Brandon had been about to say stuck in his throat and froze him in place. A pause and then, in a quiet voice, "Ye love me?"

"Yeah, I do, but ye're too pig-headed to listen," she finished on a sob.

Brandon stood still, his mouth hanging open.

"I don't think I've ever seen ye at a loss for words," she said, giggling through her tears.

"Ye love me?" he repeated, much quieter.

"Ah, Brandon. Ye really are thick, ye know."

He took her back into his arms then and showered her with kisses. She wanted him so badly that she didn't protest when his hands cupped her bum and pulled her close, or that the erection she felt as he pinned her to him was a clear indication of what he wanted to do.

She ran her hands, splayed out with fingers seeking, pulling the edges of his t-shirt up to caress the skin she wanted to touch. His heat struck her like a hot iron and she kissed him back with everything she had.

Brandon pressed his hands flat against her back, pulling up her t-shirt until he, too, was touching her bare skin. Fingers searched, groped until they came across her bra and undid the clasp. Aine gasped, suddenly unsure of herself.

"It's alright," he soothed, "no one around for miles. Just you, me, and the great outdoors. Isn't it grand?"

How could she tell him? Despite Kathleen's assurances that Brandon would understand, she was scared. Scared he'd step away, scared he'd continue. She tried to try to relax, to keep his face in focus and ignore the specter of that other time that loomed ever so near.

His hands slipped around to cup her breasts, lifting the loosened bra up and over her mounds before lifting her t-shirt off over her head. She was exposed to the sunshine, bared to the wilderness, and the feeling of empowerment that came over her at that moment was nothing short of amazing. She could do this, she thought, feeling strength bubble to the surface, reaching, hoping.

Brandon, wasting no time, slipped off his own t-shirt and pulled her to him. "Lord, I have wanted to hold ye like this since the first day I met ye. But how can we be like this now?

I thought, I mean, you said…"

She laughed, all traces of tears gone. "I know. And it was true. I couldn't come to ye while I was a counselor. But things change, people change. I realized I wanted more out of life than what I had. It was time for me to move on and so I resigned my place at the hospital and rape clinic. I moved to Killarney, to take up a post there."

"Killarney? But, it's so small compared to Cork," he exclaimed.

"It'll be a change, but I think a good one, don't you?"

"I don't know. I don't know where I'll go when I get back. Doesn't seem much for me in Kinsale anymore and I don't like big cities."

"Ye could try Killarney," she offered, a gleam in her eye.

"Ah, but my older brother is there. It may be too small a town for us both."

They stood a moment, him just holding her, and she suddenly realized she'd stopped shaking. She felt calm. It felt right to be held in his arms.

His hands began to move again and slipped into her jeans. They were tight, and before she could say or do anything, he'd popped the button on the front and drawn the zipper down, his hand following inside, fingers seeking.

"Wait," she said, feeling the panic rise.

"Ye're right," he said, "let's go inside. I've a pallet on the floor, not too uncomfortable and certainly better than standin' here like this."

She let him take her inside, through half-finished walls

and gaps where doors would be, a maze through which he didn't bother describing what rooms were what until he came to the one where he was sleeping. In this space, with the exception of window openings just waiting for the casements to arrive, the walls were solid, and no prying eyes, not even from forest creatures, could see what they were doing.

He eased her down on the pallet, a soft bed of memory foam complete with sheets and a blanket that gave with each movement of their bodies. She felt her heart beat madly, her breathing quicken as she struggled to get herself under control.

"It's alright, I won't hurt ye, I promise. I can't even shag ye, most I can likely do is a snog-act," he grinned.

"I think ye've done more than just kiss me," she said as he fondled her breasts.

"Ah, well, a little extra on the side is grand. But I made a promise that I won't break. I won't take ye until I know for sure if I'm clean. And I don't intend to worry on it until then."

He took in a mouthful of breast, clearly enjoying himself but it made Aine nervous. She loved the sensation, could get lost in it but she needed to stall him. "I heard ye weren't goin' anywhere, just staying here, mopin'," she said, buying time to get her nerves under control.

"I might have been," he admitted, releasing her breast with a tender kiss to her nipple, "but not now that ye're here. Ye're the answer to my prayers, ye are."

His hands roved, pulled her jeans and panties from her body and tossed them aside, then looked her over, a smile of pure delight across his handsome face.

Nervous or not, the look Brandon gave Aine made her smile at him as she sucked in her bottom lip in doubt. Her heart beat madly in her chest. She felt like a deer about to flee a hunter's arrow.

Brandon leaned over her, settled his weight between her legs, his jeans feeling rough on the tender parts of her inner thighs. He shifted, kissed her lips lightly, then traced a path down her neck to kiss her with gentle touches in the hollow of her throat.

She sighed her delight. This was nice, not scary, and though her heart kept up its rapid pace, she felt herself begin to want Brandon in *that* way.

His fingers traced a path down her hips, stroking the contours of her body while his mouth found her nipple and was busy laving it with his tongue. Delicious sensations engulfed her and she unconsciously tilted her hips toward him, seeking fulfillment.

He obliged, running his hands over the tops of her curls before cupping her heat in his palm. Aine's breath hitched as Brandon's mouth continued the ministrations to her breast.

Her hands slid down the length of his torso, feeling the muscles move beneath her touch, hard, steel-like ripples over a solid cage that moved like a feral cat. Lean, every movement a ballet of control and desire.

His fingers brushed the inside of her thigh and she felt herself open for him. Then suddenly he was rubbing his thumb against the tip of her own female erection and she felt herself begin to want more.

"Let it go," he breathed between mouthfuls of nipple, urging her to relax as he pressed a finger inside her.

Her hands grasped his arms, tightened their grip as she began to push at them. The darkness came over her and she felt herself falling and suddenly, she was screaming, "No, no, please don't hurt me," over and over.

Brandon stopped and sat back on his heels, watching as she drew away from him to curl up into a tight ball of quivering fear. "What the hell? I told ye I wouldn't hurt ye," he exclaimed. "What's this all about?"

Aine grabbed at the blanket and covered herself to her chin. She'd made a mess of it. She'd screamed, when she needn't have. He hadn't hurt her, he wasn't going to hurt her, and then the tears began to flow and she couldn't stop them. "I'm sorry, I should have told ye. It's what I meant when I said I couldn't lie with ye."

Brandon was clearly flummoxed. "What's happening, Aine? Why are ye like this? I kiss ye and ye're all fire and then I put my finger in ye and ye're suddenly off as if I was goin' to take ye against yer will."

Aine nodded. "I know. I'm sorry."

His face suddenly cleared and she could tell he knew. He just *knew*.

"Ye were raped, weren't ye? That's why ye had such insight to those people at the rape clinic, to me. Oh, my God, Aine. And I was about to do it to ye all over again." The grimace he wore radiated guilt, and something else that looked like pain.

"No, ye weren't," she said through her tears. "I knew ye wouldn't hurt me, it's just, I can't help it. I get so far and then all I see is blackness and *HIM*, and he's hurting me and it won't stop and then I just cry. It's horrid!"

"Ah, love," he pulled her into his arms and just held her tightly. "How old were ye?"

Her answer, muffled as it was by his holding her, was still audible as if she'd screamed it out. "I was thirteen."

"Fucking bastard," Brandon swore. "Fucking, fucking bastard!"

He was angry, Aine knew, but not at her. Kathleen had been right when she told Aine that he would protect her and she took heart in the feeling of his arms around her, that should she want to try again, Brandon might just be the one to get her through it. She had a feeling that if she could experience love in his arms, she'd be able to banish the ghost of that other time once and for all.

But Brandon could be infected with a deadly disease and so what did that mean for their future? A future that might not hold anything if she couldn't get past her own fears. She wanted to agree with him, that they wouldn't worry about the possibility of him being sick until they had to, but it was hard to get her mind to listen to her.

Chapter Nineteen

Would ye like to go back?" asked Brandon as Aine got herself under control. "It's alright. I understand. And ye've had a long flight and the drive here would…"

She cut him off with a curt gesture. "Brandon, would ye just whisht." And then, " Please."

He caught her eye just then, a glance from under half closed lids, the soft gray irises glistening with tears still but crinkling at the corners when she smiled. And she was smiling, or trying to.

"Sorry," he began again, "I'd offer ye somethin' to drink, but I've nothing. Just water. Would ye like some?"

"Actually, I brought ye somethin'," she said, pointing to what she thought was the front of the house. "Unless Hank left it in the truck and drove off with it, there's a bag out there with some ale in it for ye. I brought it from home. Yer mam said as much that it's not the same here."

Brandon couldn't have been happier if she'd given him a hundred kisses. "Wait here, I'll see if there's anything there."

He came back moments later, a bag in his hand and hauling out the ale. "Ah, this'll go down very well," he admitted, grinning. He pulled out two, opened them, and handed one to Aine. She kept one hand on the sheet that covered her breasts and reached out for the ale with her other.

"Do ye want me to fetch yer shirt?"

She thought a moment. Seemed to consider her options. "No. I'm…it's alright. It'll be alright."

"Ye don't have to do this, ye know." Cracking his own ale and taking a good swig, he swallowed, sighing appreciatively. "Ah, that's so good. I really had forgotten what good ale was like. The local stuff here is good, but the imported stuff isn't quite the same as at home. Ye'll soon see what I mean." The change of subject might be good. Might get her mind off the other.

"I don't know. I haven't had the stuff from here yet. Maybe I'll get a chance to try some tomorrow?"

"Maybe." He wanted to bring it up, the elephant in the room that stood between them, but was worried that it would set her off. Instead, he asked, "How long can ye stay?"

She'd just taken a healthy swig of her own and took a moment to answer. "Ten days. I leave in ten days, well, I guess nine now."

"Did Hank tell ye…I stay here, rather than at the house with them? I feel like three's a bit crowded and they've wee Ryan to worry about."

"Worry about…oh, ye mean that ye might be sick."

"Yeah. I'd never forgive myself if I passed something like that on to anyone, let alone a wee babe."

"It sickens me to think that they may have passed

197

something like that on to you. And they knew they were doin' it. What kind of people do that?"

"Ah, ye've spoken to me mam."

"Sorry, but yes. She needed someone to talk to, someone she knew wouldn't blab it to anyone else. Someone who cared enough to listen."

"Ye're good at that, ye are," he remarked.

"What?"

"Listenin'. I don't know where I'd be without ye."

"I know where I'd be without havin' someone like you," she said, a defiant look in her eye.

"And where's that?" He'd expected anything but what came out of her mouth.

"I'd be stuck livin' a life that was goin' nowhere. I'd end up alone, unhappy, and always wonderin' what every other woman in the world found so wonderful in men that had me cringin' in a corner, cryin' like a baby."

"Ye're welcome, I guess," he said rather sheepishly.

She looked away. She was having a hard time meeting his eyes. "Can I ask ye somethin'?"

"Yeah, anything," he answered truthfully.

"Will ye…I mean, can we…oh, for fuck's sake, Brandon," she exclaimed, "I need to know what it's like to have a man hold me, make love to me. I need to pass that threshold to see if I can bury the past. I'm nigh on thirty years old and never had a lover. Will ye help me?"

Brandon took another deep draught of ale, held it, felt it slip down his throat. His lad throbbed with wanting her. He'd been chubbed up since he saw her standing there and even through her fear, through her tears, it hadn't dwindled much. And now, here it was, as full as ever, straining at his jeans.

"I told ye. I can't do that. I can bring ye off. I can make ye feel good, do everything else, just not that."

"I brought rubbers," she offered, "good ones."

"But the doctor..." he began, but she stopped him with her own argument.

"I know what the doctors told ye. I know what they tell all of them. But rubbers were made for protection and they work when used properly. How do ye think married couples with AIDS get on? Some have even been able to have children."

"They're not a hundred percent. What if..."

She cut him off. "Nothin' in life is a hundred percent. I want this Brandon. I want you. Not anyone else, just you. And if I don't try now, I'm afraid I'll lose my courage and stay that snivelin' coward forever."

If ever the devil tempted him, thought Brandon, this had to be it. He looked her over. No horns, no reddish glow, no forked tail...in fact, no tail at all. No, she wasn't the devil, just a bruised soul, tarnished through no fault of her own; and here she was before him, nearly thirty, and by her own admission, still waiting.

She had been thirteen. It was a crime that left scars that he might be able to soften, and maybe over time, eradicate. The plea on her face, her lips, and in her eyes, could not be set aside.

"Alright," he answered, with a throat thick with emotion,

feeling like he was damning his soul to hell. "I'll do what I can."

They stared at each other, their eyes meeting for the first time since his first attempt at loving her. And then he reached for her and saw her eyes widen in fear, her shoulders tense. An anger so deep welled up inside him that someone should reduce a woman so lovely, so genuinely sweet, to this.

He took a deep breath. Anger was not going to help the situation and so he calmed himself, willed himself to focus only on her needs.

"C'mere to me," he said softly, holding his arms out to her, letting her do the moving. It would be less frightening.

She slowly dropped the sheet and moved over to where he sat at the end of his pallet. He put his drink down and she did the same. And then he leaned over, stroked her jaw tenderly, and took her mouth with his, all the while trying to control the feeling of wanting to ravish her. This was for her, he reminded himself. He would only please her. He could get himself off in the woods later and no one would be the wiser, but for now, this was all about her.

The kiss was lovely, thought Aine. If only the rest could be like this, and she sent a silent plea heavenward. She felt his hands stroke the undersides of her breasts, come up and rub across her nipples, making them ruche into tight little peaks. They were sensitive, and each touch was felt enticingly between her legs where her bud throbbed with wanting.

She wanted it all, she knew. But could she achieve that? Could she make it through the entire act without screaming in fear?

He was moving her back onto the bed, pressing her into the soft blankets, tucking the pillow, just so, under her head. Being close to the floor, the smell of new wood inside the house wafted up, tickled her nose, and helped to distract her from her fear as Kathleen's words raced through her mind. *He'll protect ye*, she'd said, and Aine believed her.

Brandon's kisses trailed a path from her mouth, down her throat to her breasts, leaving her with the tangy taste of the brew he'd had. His tongue drew circles around her nipples and then drew one into his mouth to suckle on it like a newborn babe. She thought briefly of the little girl that Kathleen had delivered, of the blessed outcome of that near tragedy, and saw the woman, holding her wee daughter and trying to nurse her, knowing that it was too late for that; too much time had gone by. She'd be a bottle baby and there was nothing wrong with that. They had all survived.

Brandon was rolling her nipple around with his teeth and it brought her back to awareness of what he was doing to her body. He had such a way of making her relax that she really felt at ease with what he was doing. As his mouth did things to her breasts, his hands roved along her sides, across her belly, eliciting wild sensations that were new to her yet familiar. Those long showers alone...

His fingers splayed across her skin, massaging, testing. Would this be the move that made her scream in fear? No? Then move on. And so it went, him moving, testing. Her experiencing those sensations, sometimes flinching, at which point Brandon would change tactics.

And sometimes sighing, where he would pause and continue what she was enjoying.

And then he was stroking her thighs, spreading her legs, rubbing her box until she spread her legs wider with wanting and began to breathe more deeply.

Brandon moved deeper, more deliberate, as if every move was calculated to observe her reaction and then move on. And stop. This was it. The point of no return.

She helped him remove his jeans until he was wonderfully nude before her, an Adonis come to life. His lad was chubbed up, standing upright like a steadfast soldier, just for her.

With slightly shaking fingers, she handed him the rubber; helped him put it on. Rolled it down his flute as if she'd been instructing a group at a clinic. Only this was real. He would take that rod that she'd felt with her hands, that she'd rolled that piece of latex over, and slide it inside her where the OTHER MAN had hurt her.

And did it hurt because it was that OTHER MAN, or did it hurt because she had been thirteen and a virgin? And scared. It shouldn't have happened, but it did.

But this was Brandon, and she loved him.

He moved his lips to kiss her abdomen, and despite her fears, she wanted him to kiss her there, where his rubber-wrapped flute should go. She wanted something more. She didn't quite know what.

His lips traced a path, his tongue enticed her to new heights, excited her to the point where she was gasping for breath. What was he doing that had her so enthralled?

And then he touched her little bud of womanhood with his tongue. That part that the showerhead awakened whenever she felt the need come over her, and she felt the waves come. No darkness, no pain, just waves of pleasure, over and over…

And then he was there, inside her, and she hadn't even known. He was over her, in her, pumping, joining her in her climax, a feeling made all the more intense because he was inside her.

Then came the fall to earth. The reality. The guilt. Oh yes, the guilt. She'd made him break his promise.

He collapsed on her, breathing as hard as she was.

She stroked his head, his neck, his back where dampness met her fingers, the sweat of his lovemaking. "Oh, Brandon. Ye've no idea what ye've done to me." But she didn't get a chance to finish.

"I know what I've done," he said, and only then did she realize he was choked with emotion. With guilt. "I've broken my promise. I've not kept my word. And now, I've likely passed on whatever those bastards gave me to you. How fair is that?"

"No, don't ye ever say that, ye hear?" She grasped his head in both her hands and looked into his eyes. She could read the guilt in them as clearly as if it was written across his forehead. "Ye've helped me. Do ye hear? Helped me! For God's sake, Brandon, ye're the first man since I was raped to shove his lad inside me, so get over the guilt and recognize what ye've done for me. Ye've freed me. I'm free. I know there's a real life out there without pain, without fear. And you were the one that's done it. No one else. Just you!" And with that, she took his face, brought it to her own, and kissed him senseless.

He couldn't help himself, he knew. He'd wanted to do it, but had intended only to make her come; use his hands, his mouth, everything but that. But in the end, he'd lost the battle. He'd felt her hands on him, pulling him, inviting him in; and whether she knew it or not, it was her hands on him that pushed him over the edge.

At the time, he wanted to believe her words, words from a clinician that said how rubbers worked when used properly. He hoped to God she was right!

And then he'd slid into her and was…lost. That was the only thing that made sense. His body took over when his mind quit working and he had no thought, no rationale for his actions. Only mindless pleasure that he was where he wanted to be, where he needed to be, in the arms of the one person he truly loved and who had just said that she loved him.

* * *

They woke in the early morning to the smell of wood smoke, and Brandon's head came up suddenly, sniffing the air. Without warning, Aine's t-shirt and bra came flying through the window, with Hank's voice saying, "Thought you might need these."

"Thanks," mumbled Brandon, staring down into eyes as soft as the dawn outside. "Good mornin'," he whispered and then put his mouth to hers.

"Mm," she answered. "I will be mortified to go outside

after that."

"What? Hank throwing our stuff through the window?" She nodded. "Well, he's of age, know's what it's all about. In fact, I'm sure that was his plan all along, dropping ye off here last night as he did."

"Still," she rubbed her hands across her face. "God, I could use a shower right now."

Brandon brightened at that. "I have one. Here."

"A shower? Here?"

"Yeah. Maybe not the kind ye're thinkin' on but it's a shower. Just in the bush, there," he pointed out the window with his thumb to where he knew Hank was stirring up a campfire, putting bacon in a cast-iron pan, making breakfast for them. He could hear the sizzling, smell the bacon.

"Later," she decided, "once Hank is gone."

"Oh, he'll likely be here the day. Maybe Laura will come with the baby." And then he looked at her, wanted nothing more than to snuggle back down under the blankets with her, but he knew Hank was outside cooking for them.

"Tell ye what. I'll let ye rise, get dressed, and join us outside for some breakfast, Canadian style. Hank assures me this is how they do it when they go campin'. It's great craic, too!"

She seemed mollified by that, raising one sculpted brow to accompany the smirk she gave him. "It does smell good," she commented, sniffing the air appreciatively.

"The bacon is different from ours. More fat, less meat, and often smoked with maple. But they also have something they call 'Canadian' bacon, which looks more like Irish rashers, only half the size."

"I'll take yer word on it."

Her eyes still looked half asleep and he laughed and kissed her again. "Right, then, see ye outside."

Aine watched as Brandon dressed, couldn't take her eyes off the male beauty that he was. His strong shoulders and arms were sculpted like a model's and she didn't doubt that he could be a good one if he wanted that sort of attention. He was certainly built that way.

Her eyes traveled down to the six-pack of his stomach muscles, not quite like a weightlifter's but only, she suspected, because what he displayed was natural and not the product of steroids or weight training. His legs, long and muscular, bent slightly as he picked up his clothing from the floor, pulling his knickers up, tucking his flute and nads inside. They formed an impressive package.

He drew his jeans on next and it was all Aine could do to refrain from helping him zip up. He grabbed his socks, then drew them on and stuffed his feet into his boots. Then picking up his t-shirt from where it lay, he winked at her and left.

Aine wanted him again. Now that she had banished the past, got beyond the fear that had always held her back, she wanted to experience more. She knew the past would always haunt her, always be just a bad experience away, and would surface when she least expected it. But she had power now, she had control. It was evident Brandon didn't quite understand the gift he'd given her.

They'd made love again during the night, only that time, Brandon brought her off without going inside her. He had absolutely refused, saying that it wouldn't make right what he'd already done to her and he didn't need to compound it any further. Afterward, he'd let her bring him off, which was also a new experience for her. She'd wanted to take him in her mouth, to taste him, to know what that was all about but he'd held her off, remembering the doctor's cautions. It was then he'd taken her with him to the edge of the bush and where he'd let her give him a hand job.

It had been embarrassing for her and was still when she thought about it. She felt the blush begin to take over and grinned to herself. She was beginning to enjoy her newfound freedom.

Brandon had thought it funny and had said so. She supposed he'd done a lot worse in his time, so for that reason, she'd laughed it off, too. They were together. He wouldn't be doing those things anymore. It was all behind him. Or would be, as soon as they knew for sure. The specter of disease hung over them like a storm cloud, potentially marring what could be a perfect relationship.

But life wasn't perfect, Aine knew. She'd gladly take second best, as long as it had Brandon in it. But as many times as she'd told Brandon she loved him, he hadn't reciprocated, hadn't said anything. Did that mean he wasn't in love with her, even though his every action seemed to say that he was? Was he a man of action only, with few words, if any, of love?

"Aine? Did ye go back to sleep?" came Brandon's query

through the window.

"On my way," she said, brushing the thought from her mind and hurriedly pulling on her clothing to join the two men outside.

Chapter Twenty

Babies were cute but a lot of work, thought Brandon as he and Aine watched Laura clean up yet another spit-up from young Ryan. He was fussing and squalling and making all kinds of unpleasant noises and Laura looked frazzled, somewhere between frustrated that nothing seemed to soothe the baby, and herself in need of a good sleep. She'd been up several times during the night, Hank informed them when they walked through the door earlier. Ryan was teething.

Without hesitation, Aine strode over to where Laura sat with the baby and calmly held out her arms. "Here, give him over to me and you go get yourself cleaned up. There's not much I can do to feed him but I can take care of his squabbles as well as any. Off ye go."

The look of relief on Laura's face was evident as she handed her son into Aine's care.

"Where's Hank?" asked Brandon, hoping he was somewhere outside so he could avoid the baby's harsh cries.

"Out back, assembling the swing-set we got for Ryan. We're kind of hoping the swinging will keep him happy during teething when nothing else does," Laura explained on her way upstairs.

Brandon looked to Aine, who asked him to bring her a shot of whiskey before she shooed him off. His last glimpse before going outside was of his lady, standing and rocking the baby, her finger inside Ryan's mouth, gently massaging his gums. The wee lad was going to be a fine Irishman, Canadian or not. He loved the taste of that drink.

Brandon found Hank in the massive back yard, spanner in hand as he put the final touch on the last bolt, looking up in time to see Brandon approach.

"Those windows workin' good?" asked Hank, referring to the fact that the last two days had been spent installing windows and doors on the new cabin.

"They keep the weather out. Glad to have had it last night with the rain blowin' like it did. Nice day today, though," he answered looking up at the wide expanse of blue sky overhead. And it was nice. Bright sunlight beamed out of the cloudless sky, hot and slightly humid.

"Takin' a break from buildin', are ye?" asked Hank as he grinned at his half brother. Brandon knew Hank was appreciative of all the help he'd given. With the installation of windows and doors, the cabin was now clad to the weather.

"Actually, I have a question for ye." He helped Hank attach the double-seated swing to the upper bar and continued talking as they worked. There was an easy camaraderie between them now, as if Aine's presence had put paid to Brandon's depression. "Is there a nice restaurant in town I could take Aine to? I think I've run out of barbeque options."

Hank laughed as he fitted the bolt. "Hang on, let me think." He fiddled with the bolt, got it set and tightened, and then both men dropped their arms and shook off the tension of holding their arms above their heads for so long. Anyone watching would have seen the similarity in their movements, the likeness of their features, and known them for brothers.

"There's a lovely restaurant overlooking the lake at the far side of town. Ye'll need reservations to get the seat ye want. I suggest sittin' outside."

Brandon waited while Hank pulled out his mobile phone, flipped through a few apps, found what he wanted, and made the reservations for Brandon, right then and there.

Putting his phone away after a few minutes, he told Brandon, "Nothin' available tonight but I don't think ye'll mind waitin' a couple of days. It's a great place." He gave Brandon the date and then they both went back into the house where Aine held up her finger to her lips on seeing them enter. She indicated the sleeping baby in her arms and pointed upstairs meaningfully.

"I sent Laura to bed, too," she smiled. "They both need a nap."

Hank walked over to Aine and retrieved his sleeping son from her arms. "He gets heavy after a while," Hank said in tones just above a whisper. "Let me take him and tuck him in. You guys go have some fun. Spend the time however ye like. Brandon's been workin' on the cabin like the devil's been chasin' him, and deserves some time away."

As they left the house, Brandon couldn't help remembering

the look of Aine while she held the baby, the animation in her face as she rubbed his gums and how gentle she was with him. It told him something he knew in his gut, that she'd be a good mam one day. But it also made him wonder if he could have his own child, even if he was infected. Hadn't Aine said something about that being possible? The thought gnawed at his guts and he knew it would turn him inside out if he let it, so he focused instead on staying positive and ignoring the specter his illness presented.

Hank had been right. They had been busy. For two days, they'd worked steadily, outfitting the cabin with new windows, a sometimes difficult task when Hank left the site and it was just Aine and Brandon. They did it, though, and Aine, by the high-five she sported after each one was finished, was thrilled to have learned so much.

The windows, thought Brandon, were a stroke of genius. Although modern in construction, Hank had ordered leaded panes in the two that would flank the big picture window in front. The finished effect was stunning. Between the stone chimney and façade that Brandon and Hank had finally finished with smooth river rocks, the cabin was truly emerging as a little bit of Ireland in Canada.

Aine was learning carpentry skills, had learned how to shim the windows so they were level, and watched as Brandon and Hank hung the doors. She seemed delighted with her newfound knowledge and had begun handing tools to Brandon before he asked for them, just as if she were assisting in an operating room. She was getting bolder, but he was still reluctant to leave her too often without keen supervision.

They drove back to the cabin, having already spent most of the day in town. By the time they pulled up to the site, the afternoon had turned cloudy, the wind had come up, and Brandon knew they were in for a repeat of the last evening's display.

As they left the truck, he gestured to the equipment outside. "I'm going to cover everything before it starts to rain. I think we'll have another storm like last night."

Aine looked up and agreed. "Seems to be comin' in fast. It's a good thing the hibachi is under the shelter of the porch."

"And it's a good thing the porch now has a roof," Brandon laughed. It was true. The roof was on and though not completed, it was effectively sealed against the weather with giant plastic sheets in place until the rest of the shingles could be laid.

While Aine brought in the few groceries they'd picked up, Brandon got the equipment covered and helped prepare the steaks they'd bought to go along with the potatoes and kebabs of fresh vegetables. While they ate, the sky opened up and the rain came pouring down. It instantly made small puddles that soon turned into large ones and it seemed that if it kept coming down, it would threaten to flood the foundation and send the house floating down the mountain.

Then as suddenly as it began, it stopped, the wind died down again, and clouds parted to reveal brilliant sunshine.

"It's gorgeous," Aine breathed, happily admiring the

213

droplets that clung to the trees and undergrowth, shining like glittering gemstones in the sun.

"I love the rain," Brandon said, sniffing the moist air appreciatively, "it's truly the one thing I miss about Ireland. Here, it doesn't rain as often, so things get dusty and dry. Nothing like a good rain to clean everything up."

"It smells so fresh," she agreed.

His arm came up and around her, hugging her to him. They'd been eating as they watched the storm pass, sitting well under cover of the deck, viewing the lightning that pierced the darkened sky. They were sitting on cushions on the porch floor, she, leaning against his lean frame, using him as a back rest. His legs stretched out on either side of her, his back relaxed against the smooth wall of the house. With his arms about her, his hands absentmindedly stroked her breasts, brought the nipples to life, making stiff little peaks under his ministrations.

He went to tuck one hand into the waistband of her jeans but was halted by the snug fit until she helped him out by popping the snap open and shucking them down just a tad. His hand slid down, fingers dipping into her moist heat. She sighed and gave herself over to his talents, his one hand cuddling her breast, tweaking her nipple, the other doing something between her legs that had her sighing contentedly.

She was completely relaxed against him, arms splayed boneless by her side. He'd never seen her so at ease, he thought, as he worked his magic on her. He had her, he knew, and felt a certain pride in his actions. He felt her juices start to flow, knew when she arched her back, thrust her breasts upwards with nipples hardened to little nubs, that she was ready.

His finger slipped inside her, his other hand gently thumbed a nipple as he held her close while she trembled in his arms, softly gasped her climax, then came back to earth. He kept his fingers there, slippery with her moistness, still inside her, still stroking as she came around.

"That was amazing," she breathed. "The only thing missing was having ye in me," she said, eyes dreamily misted.

His answer was to kiss her. They'd been through this before, the wanting, the desire, the almost painful realization that they would never again have each other the same way as that first time until Brandon knew for sure. It made all their other experiences bittersweet, but tempered them with an excitement of something better on the horizon. Neither would admit the possibility of his being infected. It wasn't going to happen.

* * *

The day of their dinner date was hot, as had been the case for all the days previous, the heat only mitigated by the sudden rainstorms during the night. But at midafternoon when they arrived in town, it was hotter still, so Brandon took Aine along the main shopping areas where she had a good look around and they could duck into stores to cool themselves off in the air-conditioned atmosphere. She tried on clothing; they checked out souvenir shops, of which there were a few, and stopped for ice cream before continuing their shopping foray. Store clerks were always asking where they were from, and the feeling of notoriety left them both in high spirits. Aine giggled when one store clerk couldn't understand what Brandon was saying and Aine had to interpret. It seemed her Dublin accent was easier to understand than Brandon's, even though he'd grown up in Inishannon, not so very far away. Accents there were just as soft but Brandon spoke quickly, sometimes too quickly for foreigners to understand.

Eventually, their walk took them back down the street where they'd parked the truck near the pub, having already made the decision as they parked that a drink there before dinner would be grand.

The pub had, like most, a dark interior. Dark wood paneled the walls and dark tiles of some sort covered the ceiling. Two dartboards hung on a far wall and the area behind the bar was lit by hanging lamps, reflected in the mirrors behind the shelves, on which stood a variety of alcoholic choices. Several beers and ales were offered on tap, and were part of the reason the pub was so popular.

Drinks in hand, they chose a table near the window. A few people were at other tables or at the bar, conversing quietly. Sometimes a bout of laughter could be heard as jokes were exchanged between friends. And then the door opened and the threesome that Brandon had joined scant weeks before walked in. One of the girls recognized him and pointed him out to the others.

"Up for another threesome?" she called out crassly, and if Brandon had ever thought he wanted to disappear immediately, this was it.

He wanted to reply, to tell her to eff off; but he knew that it would only inflame things, and so he said nothing and tried to concentrate on what Aine was saying. It was clear she, too, was trying to ignore the insulting outburst.

"Hey, Irish, I'm talking to you," the girl said, louder this time.

Brandon looked her way then, saw the look in her eyes, and decided she'd either had enough to drink already or had taken drugs of some sort. He looked back at Aine, "Let's finish up and go. This could get ugly."

Aine also looked toward the girl, then back at Brandon. "Sure, we're almost done anyway." She stood, but not before the mouthy girl came over to sidle up to Brandon.

"Hey, don't you want us tonight? It was really fun last time."

"Excuse us," he said, brushing past her, "we're just on our way."

"She could come, too, I guess," said the girl, nodding toward Aine.

"I said we're leavin'." He took Aine's hand, brought her before him and out of the way to let her leave first. His only thought was to get her out of the pub and off to the restaurant where he could maybe do some damage control.

"He's no good, y'know," said the girl to Aine, "wouldn't even use his cock. Guess he hasn't got one!" She laughed at her own joke.

Brandon didn't think it funny. He felt embarrassed. It

was bad enough the girl said all those things loud enough that the whole pub knew what he had done. But the fact was he had Aine with him, and now she, too, would know just how depraved he was. Still.

"I'm truly sorry, Aine. I had no idea they'd be there," he said when they finally got through the outer door and heard it close solidly behind them.

It was clear that Aine was trying to make sense of everything. She had a scowl on her face that spoke volumes.

He stopped and turned to look at her. There was no one on the street just then. "Ye must know I'm not the man ye want, Aine. There'll be more of that back home," he gestured to the pub they'd just left. "I've made a real mess of my life. I'm no good, will never be good. And although I love ye as much as I can, because I do love ye, ye must know I'm not worth the effort. If ye want, I'll take ye back up the mountain and ye can stay with Hank and Laura; be comfortable for once, have a hot shower when ye want. Life with me would never be comfortable. I'll always be runnin' from my past."

She seemed to be quivering with anger as she whirled on him. "And what do ye think I've been runnin' from? Brandon, we can't pretend the past didn't happen. I get it that ye've a past that ye don't like. Ye wouldn't be in the dire straits ye find yerself in now if ye didn't. I get it that those women had relations with ye. Ye were free to do that. I was untouchable because of my job and I'd already told ye back home that I couldn't be with ye. Ye had no idea I'd left my job until I got here. And although I'm not thrilled that ye decided to take them on, it fills me with relief that ye had the sense to refuse intercourse."

"I'd made a promise. I keep my promises. Usually. But I've broken that promise with you, so what does that say about me? I can't be trusted and I won't have ye hurt by my actions."

Her countenance softened and she stepped nearer. "If ye recall, I was the one that made ye break that promise. It's my fault ye broke it. I convinced ye when ye wouldn't have gone ahead. So don't talk to me about trustworthiness. Ye promised me ye wouldn't hurt me, and ye didn't. But this, Brandon," she gestured back toward the pub, "this is a part of yer past that we both must face. Don't shut me out just because ye feel embarrassed by what ye did."

"I'm not embarrassed by what I did and maybe that's the problem with me. I don't give a damn. But I am embarrassed for you, that ye had to witness that. It's one thing to admit doin' those things with other women. It's another to have it thrown in the face of the one person I truly love in this whole world."

Aine's face was calm, though her eyes misted with unshed tears. He was worried for a moment that she would cry but she held it in. And what would he do if she did? Yet when she spoke, it was like a whisper, and she rubbed his arm as she did so, following the line of it down to grasp his hand. "Ye must learn to trust me, Brandon. I love ye, and to hear ye love me, too, warms me to the depths of my soul. Whatever ye've done, we'll weather it. I can't say it doesn't bother me, or that I don't feel for ye. But I can say that I'll stay by ye. Now," gripping his hand in hers, she asked, "are ye goin' to take me to dinner or do I have to threaten to let those women have at ye again?"

Brandon couldn't help the grin that spread across his face. "Ye must be daft to want me after that display in there."

"Ah, she was on somethin', I'm certain she was."

"Doesn't mean she wasn't right in what she said."

"Let's put it behind us. I'm hungry."

At that, he put his arm around her and led her to where the truck was parked. "Hop in, my lady, ye're off for a dining experience ye won't forget. And I truly hope that's in a good way."

Aine tried to calm her thoughts. The girl had definitely been on something, whether drugs or alcohol made no difference. She had been crass and ugly in her statements. And as Brandon admitted, there was truth in her words, as nasty as they were.

Aine had promised Brandon she'd stay by him, but what if he was right and this was just the tip of the iceberg? There'd be more, surely, once they were back in Ireland.

She watched the streets go by, feeling strange to be on the opposite side of the road. The signs, lampposts, and other things close to the road shot by her on her right shoulder as they drove. It felt odd and just a bit unnerving, as if her shoulder was going to be scraped off at any moment, so she moved, ever so slightly, toward Brandon, as far as her seatbelt would allow. If Brandon noticed, he didn't say a word.

She thought back to the scene at the pub they'd just left, and compared it to home. There would be stares and comments from people if they were to go certain places, of that she was certain. But depending on the circles they traveled in, they could likely avoid most unpleasantness all together. When she looked at it from her point of view, it didn't seem all that difficult but she was beginning to realize that Brandon didn't have to look too far to find trouble, and could she deal with that? She tried to put it from her mind and just enjoy the moment.

The drive to the restaurant by the lake took all of fifteen minutes, most of it weaving through the streets in town, and she was soon caught up in the sights. As they came over the hill at the edge of the town, the lake came into view, a calm body of water reflecting the early evening sun. It was August. The air was still warm.

They were led to a table at the front of the restaurant on the outside deck, a semi-secluded seating for two with a view of the lake and the moon that was just rising. Darkness would not happen for another while so they watched as boaters, water-skiers and others enjoyed the cool water on this very warm night. Aine was glad they were outside where the breeze cooled them before the perspiration could bead up and roll uncomfortably between her breasts.

When the food arrived, they tucked into it with avid enjoyment. With the exception of the two dinners they'd shared at Hank and Laura's, they'd lived on camp-style food they'd cooked themselves for the last week. And while camping out was fun and the experience delightful, Aine was thrilled that someone else was cooking, that servers brought the food to them, and that, thanks to tall citronella torches, their dinner was relatively bug free.

Sated at the end of the meal, Aine leaned back and patted her stomach. "I don't know when I've felt so full before. That was delicious," she exclaimed, and if the look on Brandon's face was anything to go by, he thought the same.

"It was," he agreed, confirming her opinion and wiping his mouth with his napkin. "Would ye care for anythin' more? Dessert?"

Dessert was the last thing on her mind, or was it? "Hm," she thought, "no, thanks. I really am quite full." She looked wistfully at the lake and sighed.

Brandon seemed to understand what she was thinking. "Want to go for a dip?"

She laughed, "I'd love to. It would be grand to wash the sweat off, but we've no suits with us."

"I can take care of that," he said, and after paying the bill, took her hand and led her back to the truck.

Once inside and on their way back up the mountain road, Brandon said, "There's a small pothole lake part way up the road here. Hank showed it to me not long before ye arrived. We were in town, the sun was hot and the AC unit in the truck had quit for some reason."

"Seems to be working now," she observed, feeling the blessedly cool air flowing from the vents before her.

"Yeah, his buddy, Greg, had a look at it and fixed it. But

on that day, it was hot as Hades and we were wiltin'. He pulled into this wee lake, not a soul around in the middle of the day. Don't even know if many people know of it. Anyway, we shucked our clothes and jumped in. It was grand, just *feckin'* grand."

"Ye know where it is, then?" she asked.

"I do," he said confidently. "Leastwise, I think I do. We should be comin' up on it fairly soon. I seem to remember a strange looking tree, a pine, very large and split into two, halfway up, so it looks like it's got two tops."

"Left or right side?" she asked, and he seemed to know what she meant.

"Oh, on the left, over here. Maybe around this next corner."

In the end, it was a few corners on but Aine didn't care. The tree was exactly as he'd described it and they drove slowly through the bush on something that looked like a cart path, barely wide enough for the pickup truck to make it through. Branches lashed and scraped along the sides as they drove, making Aine glad the windows were rolled up. She couldn't imagine going through with the windows down, having myriad branches swiping at her as they passed.

Just when she thought they'd never find it, the bush ended and a deep swath of slightly rocky beach opened out before them. All around the far shores of the lake, there were only trees. It was dark now, although there was still light from the moon. If there had been campfires, they would have seen them, but there were none. They were alone.

Brandon got out of the truck and wasted no time getting naked. Aine was less brave, checking out the area beyond the front of the truck. "Should we leave the headlights on?" she asked timidly.

He easily dismissed her worries. "Nah. There's the moon to see by. C'mon," he waved with his arm.

She undressed, carefully putting her clothing on the front seat, and then gingerly made her way across the stones to feel the cold water seeping up to wet the bottoms of her feet. It was so cold!

"Are ye sure? It's quite chilly," she said, standing stiffly, ankle deep in the lake.

Brandon had waded in without pause and was up to his waist when he turned and looked at her. "Ah, no bother. Ye'll get used to it. It's only cold at first," he said.

"Liar," she yelled at him but it was hardly an insult when she was laughing.

"Come on," he encouraged her. "It's really not so bad." He strode back to where she stood, him with a god's body limned with moonlight, emerging from the lake like a child of Lir, a swan come to life, one with the water. He splashed water on his chest and arms and ran wet hands down his face. Droplets shone on his tanned skin, the muscles beneath outlined and defined in stark relief.

She stood transfixed as he approached her, not realizing what he was about until it was too late. She'd been focussing on his body, every inch of his maleness, when he suddenly scooped her up to carry her like a baby, then turned his back to the shore, walking determinedly into the water with her in his arms.

She squealed as the water touched her buttocks, gasped as he lowered her partway into the lake and then raised her up again. He was laughing, and she was trying her damnedest to climb higher on his body.

Slowly, he began to lower himself into the water and she struggled out of his grasp to flip around and sit on his shoulders. It worked until he swam out from under her, dropping her fully into the lake.

She stood up gasping, her wet hair plastered across her face, the tendrils like a veil, covering her eyes, temporarily blinding her. He chose that moment to dive and come up between her legs, scaring her, making her think for a moment that some giant fish was attacking her.

Again a squeal, followed by laughter and an unrepentant Brandon standing before her. They were nearly chest deep as he pulled her to him and kissed her deeply. She went into his arms willingly, more for the kiss, she told herself, than the bit of warmth his body offered. Because in fact, his skin was cold to the touch and she doubted she'd get any warmth from him at all.

And then the feel of his fingers inside her box started amorous sensations to build and she couldn't help but reach down and stroke his flute. Despite the cold water, he was getting chubbed up.

Brandon bent over, took her moist nipple into his mouth, and suckled. She couldn't believe how much more erotic

225

everything seemed out here, where any moment, they could be discovered. He had her building toward a climax; she wanted more, she wanted him inside her, but they had no rubbers and he had told her before, he wouldn't put her at risk again.

And so she felt him work her body until, despite her chilly surroundings, she felt her insides quiver, felt his fingers prod her canal, mimicking what his flute would do, and gave herself over to the inevitable.

He was still somewhat chubbed up as he turned and walked with her from the water. She stopped him and took hold of him, looking at his eyes, so black instead of the blue they were, with the moonlight reflected off the water. "What about you, now?" she asked, rubbing his flute with her hand.

He simply shrugged. "No help for me," he said grinning, but she caught the pain and desperation in his voice.

She looked around and found an area of grass, valiantly trying to grow where the rocks exposed a sandy area. It was distinguishable in the moonlight, only because of the boulders right next to it, outlining the tall, grassy stalks in variations of shadow and weak light. "Come with me," she said, and he followed. She wasn't sure if what she had in mind would work, but it was worth a try.

Lying on the grass on her back and scootching around until she found a tolerable patch, she coaxed him down on top of her, shushing him when he would have protested. "Here," she said, grasping his flute and tucking it beneath her into the crack of her buttocks, sandwiching it there along the length of her. "Try that. See how it feels."

He gave it a try and she wondered if the ground would be too rough. She might have a soft arse, which would help on one side, but he'd have to rub against grass and sand on the other.

He moaned in what she was certain was delight.

"Good?"

"Mmf," he answered before taking her mouth with his.

She took his tongue, twirled it with hers, massaged long fingers into the tight muscles of his arse, and felt his flute grow between her buttocks, the strange sensation somehow just as titillating as any foreplay he'd done before. Brandon suddenly picked up the pace. Aine knew he was coming close, and though she felt herself want to go with him, she held back, didn't want to slow him down. She'd already come, and this was for him.

Brandon couldn't believe what Aine was doing for him. This woman, who'd begun her adult life thinking all sex was hurtful, was showing him a way to enjoy it with her without putting herself at risk. He hadn't time to think about what he was doing, he was just enjoying being with her, feeling her beneath him on this patch of ground that was neither soft nor especially comfortable. At least, he didn't think it was. He didn't really know; he wasn't the one who had to lie on it.

But as he felt his body grow taut and the sensation build, he lost all thought of discomfort, of the sand and grass beneath, and thought only of Aine's lovely arse, cradling his flute so he could come.

He loved her. There was no question. He would do anything for her, and with the clarity that clean living had brought him, knew she loved him, too.

Chapter Twenty-One

Ten days had not been long enough. They'd had ten days in which to solidify a relationship that would be torn apart by distance, even if only for the span of another month.

And then Brandon changed his plans. "I'll go back with ye," he said, the day before she was due to leave.

"Ye don't have to. I can manage."

"It's not that I don't think ye can manage. I know ye can manage just fine. It's just that, well, I think I'm done here. It can rain or snow and the house will be just fine, which was Hank's biggest concern. There's a lot more still to be done but I'm sure Hank can manage. I had a chat with him yesterday."

They'd been up on the roof, checking it over and putting on the finishing touches while Aine had been busy below with Laura and the baby, who had come along with Hank for a site visit. Hank had noticed the glance that Aine sent Brandon's way while Brandon wasn't watching. It had been wistful, Hank told him, then said quietly when Aine became distracted by baby Ryan's giggles that Aine didn't want to leave him and why didn't he go back to Ireland with her?

"But we've the house to finish," he'd answered, but Hank

229

had obviously been thinking about it.

"No. You've got the stonework done, the windows and doors are in, and it's clad to the weather. It can stay this way until next spring and be just fine. Ye need to get back home, to sort things out there. It's not that I want ye to leave but I know that ye need to."

Brandon had thought about that and couldn't disagree. "I've got my head on straight now, thanks to Aine. I don't know where I'd be without her."

"She's an amazing woman. Ye'd best do what ye can to keep her. It's like what happened to me with Laura. Seems we've both been blessed by women who love us, in spite of ourselves."

Brandon had laughed then and Hank had joined in. After the laughter died, Hank confessed to Brandon, "I wasn't keen on havin' ye here, and when ye got yerself into trouble with those girls, all I could think of was that I wanted to strangle ye and I should have taken ye by yer clackers and put ye on the first plane home. But ye've redeemed yerself, set yerself on a new path, and I'm proud of the work ye've done. Both on yerself and on the house. There's a wee bit o' the aul' man in ye. Seems to have missed me." This last was said with a mixture of whimsy and thankfulness.

Brandon had mixed feelings himself. He hadn't expected Hank to welcome him with open arms. Hadn't expected to be welcomed at all. And yet, he had been. A bond had been formed, and Hank, being only a few months older, was someone he could look up to, learn from, and even emulate.

Hank had qualities that Brandon didn't. Brandon had talents that Hank was lacking. Brandon was beginning to see that despite the fact they were raised in separate households, they were indeed brothers.

He nodded in acknowledgement of Hank's words, felt the warmth of emotion inside, let it settle, held on to it, a part of him now. "I guess we're done up here." He couldn't disguise the roughness of his voice, thick with emotion.

"Yeah," answered Hank, who seemed to know no further speech was needed. His voice was just as rough.

Aine knew that Brandon had been serious when he told her he wanted to go back to Ireland with her. "Where will ye go back to? Will ye stay in Cork with yer family, or will ye move to Kerry, like Henry did, and make a new life there?" She'd wanted to add the words "with me" to her statement, but something held her back. Was she ready to go back to Ireland with Brandon, and take up a life with him there? Things would be different back home, she knew. There would be no more fairy-tale existence. It would be for real.

"Ah, well, I'll need to sort things out with Sean, in Kinsale, and see where I go from there. I've had a couple of sessions with him while I was here; had one just before you arrived, and I'll be due for one in another couple of weeks. After that, I don't know," he shrugged.

"Well, I'm happy ye want to come back with me. And honestly, the longer ye stay away the more difficult it will be to return, like. And it's pleased I am that ye're still seeing Sean. He's a good man, smart. He'll get ye through this."

"So, it's settled then? Ye'll let me travel back to Ireland with ye?"

She laughed, noted the way he worded his question. He hadn't said "go home" with her, so she nodded in return. Neither one of them, she was certain, was quite ready for a live-in relationship yet. Not until they knew for certain, and that brought up another point. "Ye're nearly due for the first test," she said, and Brandon knew exactly what she meant.

"I am. It's a bit scary, thinkin' I could have that shite."

"For what it's worth," she said, gaining his full attention, "I don't believe ye have it. I won't believe it until there is irrefutable proof."

"And that's the blood test, eh?"

No words were needed. Instead, they both began packing their gear, and Brandon checked the work site and put away tools that Hank had requested be locked up. Everything would be left for Hank to work on when time allowed.

Brandon had mixed feelings about leaving. Hank and Laura had given his life a purpose, made him feel useful and needed again, given him shelter and something to do when he had felt himself at his wits' end. For the first time in months he felt normal, as if Kinsale, as he had begun to refer to the incident that had landed him in hospital, had never happened.

It was his and Aine's last night together, and Brandon wanted to make it special for her. It felt to him like his last night on earth.

Laura and the baby had said their goodbyes at the cabin while Hank played chauffeur. He dropped them off near the airport where Brandon had made reservations at a well-appointed hotel. Their plane left at noon the next day, enabling them to have a decent breakfast without having to wake up so very early.

They enjoyed a lovely meal in a dining room so fancy they almost felt out of place. It was on the tip of Brandon's tongue to suggest they eat in their room but Aine had gazed at her surroundings with a certain amount of pleasure, and seemed much more at ease than Brandon when the maître d' led them to their table. Maybe she was used to this sort of thing? He really didn't know where she came from, other than the Dublin area. It had him wondering suddenly if their cultural status was perhaps miles apart.

His questions about her background soon came to light with the types of dishes she ordered. He hadn't noticed a difference when they had gone to the restaurant by the lake because, as nice as it was, it was a very grassroots sort of place, where people in shorts were as welcome as those in fancier dress and the food, while well prepared, was not *cordon bleu*. He hadn't felt out of place there, but was beginning to here, especially when a couple was seated near them, she sporting a glittering necklace over an outfit that screamed wealth, and her date with a silk suit and tie, if Brandon didn't miss his mark. The owner of the hotel in Kinsale owned such a suit, and boasted that fact to anyone who remarked on the particular sheen to the fabric.

Brandon looked down at his own clothing, the jeans, the dark blue shirt with the collar open at the neck. Despite being

233

clean, he couldn't help wonder what the other diners might think of him, as if he had just come in from working in a garage or some other less illustrious job.

He smiled to himself when he realized the comparison he'd just made. He had, after all, been working on Hank's cabin. And despite the fact that Brandon was unable to work while visiting Canada, Hank had insisted on paying him anyway, and so Brandon had significantly more money in his pocket than when he'd arrived.

As Aine tucked into a delicate shrimp, Brandon thought again on her background. They really didn't know each other, hadn't ever broached the subject, and this was as good a time as any. He began with the usual, "Tell me about yourself," to which she replied with a giggle.

"That sounds so much like a first date."

"Well, I think ye know a helluva lot about me compared with what I know of you. Oh, I know ye're an amazing woman, that ye've way more courage in yer little finger than most folk have in their entire bodies. And I know yer capacity for love is boundless. I've felt it, been the recipient of it. But I don't know about you, yer background, other than ye're from Dublin."

Spearing another shrimp, she smiled and met his eyes. She had gorgeous eyes, he reflected, and describing them as gray would be to describe the sky as blue. There were countless variations and comparisons, but tonight, the softness therein was unmistakeable. She was looking at him with love in her eyes, if he didn't miss his mark, and knew he looked back at her with the same.

She dropped her lashes, swirled the shrimp in the sauce on her plate, "Where to begin," she laughed. "My parents are both doctors, and I'm an only child, no siblings. That was maybe the thing I wanted most in life. I would have died for a sister, but a big brother would have been grand, too!"

"I know what ye mean. I've come to regard Hank as my big brother, which he is, but not having anyone else to rely on for so many years... Oh, there was Henry, o' course. But, well, he didn't count. But now, suddenly, having a whole new family is truly something else. Not just Hank, but Laura and the baby, too." He took a mouthful of his own food, the crab leg tasty, smothered in butter, and he quickly wiped a drop from his chin before it could fall onto his shirt.

Aine giggled and wiped her own chin delicately with her napkin. Their eyes met and held.

Brandon took a deep breath and then let it slowly out. The images in his mind, of licking dripping butter or sauce off her chin, her throat...he felt the reaction to his thoughts between his legs and shifted uncomfortably in his seat. *Back to the subject at hand*, he thought, willing his mind to redirect its thoughts.

"If yer folks were both doctors, didn't ye want to be one, too?"

She shook her head. "No, but in retrospect, I've probably done the same amount of coursework as they did, all told."

"Not a career for ye?"

"No. But I knew I wanted to be in medicine. Just didn't

want to be a doctor. My da was determined I would be, but Mam said I should be what I wanted, and like always, she won."

Brandon took in her words. She'd had parents who truly wanted the best for her, and she had a champion in her mam. Had Brandon ever felt that? He realized with sadness that he'd never felt as if someone had his back. That, despite the closeness he now shared with his own mam, he'd always felt alone, separate from the rest.

Yet all that was beginning to change. He'd found a friend, if not a real connection, with Hank and Hank's family. Hank was the brother that Brandon sometimes wished Henry would be but he was beginning to see Henry's side in all of it, too. Henry, the little boy who'd had to become man of the house at fourteen. The ten-year-old that Brandon had been, already an out-of-control lad, becoming his mother's worst nightmare. They always said that Brandon didn't have to go looking for trouble, that it found him. And they'd been right.

But he was tired of trouble, felt it in the marrow of his bones. It wasn't so much as himself giving up as it was seeing something else out there that deserved his energies so much more. He'd never felt that before.

Not until Aine.

And here she was before him, gazing at him with love in her eyes and telling him about herself as he'd requested. She not only loved him, he thought, as he heard how hard her parents drove her in school and at home, she trusted him. And that realization brought emotions so profound to the surface that he had difficulty swallowing his next bite, and eyes watering, took a deep draught of the beer he'd ordered.

"Are ye okay?" asked Aine, laughter in her eyes.

"Oh yeah, just gone down the wrong pipe," he joked. It was an easy out for what could have become an awkward moment.

"Sounds like yer folks were slave drivers," he remarked, once his throat had cleared.

"Oh, they were hard on me, to be sure, but not without reason. I was lazy. I could do the work, just would rather have spent all my time with friends, or doin' other things, none of which included homework," she laughed.

"I never did any."

"What, homework?"

He nodded. "Nothing. Unless, of course, I was threatened with the switch or kept inside with the headmaster standin' over me. Even then, I only did what I thought I needed to do. The barest minimum. It's a wonder I ever got through school."

"Did ye?"

"Oh yeah. Mam made sure of that, and so did Henry. There was every expectation that I would make it through and I think they did it through sheer energy alone. Maybe somethin' inside me knew I had to do it, or face doin' it later. But once I was through, I vowed never to go back."

"And is that how ye feel now?"

He thought a moment. "Not sure. Guess it depends on what it is. I learned a lot from Hank these past two months, and so maybe if it was that kind of thing, learnin' a new trade like, I'd be okay with it. But actual book learnin? No. I'm not that kind."

"I understand. I didn't have a choice either but I saw it as a means to an end. Ye know what I mean, like? I wanted to go into nursing. I knew I had to do the studying. It was as plain as that."

Brandon hesitated to ask the question uppermost on his mind just then. He wanted to ask about her parents' reaction to her rape. Did they even know? His curiosity would not be quiet and so he steeled himself for her answer as he asked, "Aine, remember when ye told me about what happened to ye?" She nodded, suddenly somber looking. "Well, ye can tell me it's none of my business and I could just eff off, but, did ye ever tell yer folks?"

She was very quiet, as if he'd asked her the worst thing in the world; and who knew, maybe he had. "I didn't have to. They came home not long after and I was still cleanin' up the blood and vomit from the floor."

Immediately, he saw his error. This was not something he should have been asking. At least, not in this way, not here. But it seemed the floodgates had been opened and she began to spill it all.

She spoke quietly, never loud enough for even the nearest table to overhear. "Of course they were angry, upset. Da was like to kill him right then and there but Mam stayed his hand. They talked about going to the garda, laying charges, all kinds of things. In the end, they decided not to do any of that."

Brandon was outraged. "Nothin'? Why not? Why…"

"Because," she broke in, "my folks felt it would be too hard on me to put me in front of judge and jury and say what happened. Da said he had a better way, and it was left at that. I've never asked, and he's never said, but a few weeks later, they found the guy floatin' in the river, sayin' he'd been up to no good in the drug trade and it was likely that's what got him killed. All I cared about was that he couldn't harm me anymore, nor anyone else."

"I'm gobsmacked, I am. Do ye think, I mean, could yer da have had anythin' to do with it?"

She only shrugged. "Don't know. Don't care. I've thought little about it since then. All I know is he got his comeuppance."

Brandon placed his hand on hers, felt the tremble of her fingers as she pretended to be calm. He didn't doubt she'd told him something that she'd never told another living soul, and for that, he felt honored. "I love ye," he said, when her eyes finally met his.

"I know," she answered softly, a Mona Lisa smile on her face, "I love ye, too."

Chapter Twenty-Two

Brandon was waiting for the doctor to come in, wondering what the test had said. Wouldn't he just get a phone call if everything was fine? Wouldn't someone just call and say all was well, come back in another three months for the final one? He realized he was tense when he looked at the magazine he'd been trying to read. The pages were creased where his hands had gripped it and he hadn't read a word.

A knock on the door, and the doctor entered, closed it behind him, and sat down. He was an older man, with a ring of hair, sandy with glints of gray glinting in the harshness of the overhead light. The glasses on his nose were the kind that had no frame around the bottom of the lenses and the top was a stylish thin black line, giving him a distinguished air. He looked at the computer screen, leaned back in his chair, arms folded across his chest, and cleared his throat.

"How are you feeling?" he asked, and Brandon felt the sweat trickle down his spine. The day hadn't been especially warm but it was hot inside the little room.

Unable to hide the nerves that were plaguing him, he answered, "Fine, nothin' out of the ordinary."

"Not tired? Any flu-like symptoms?"

"No, nothin'." He'd caught a cold when he first arrived in Canada but it had been over and done within a week.

"Hm." The doctor pushed his glasses up his nose, got up and grabbed the blood pressure cuff, and went about checking Brandon over. First his blood pressure, then his lungs and heart. "No discomfort rectally? No discharge?"

"No, everythin's fine." He was beginning to wonder where it was all leading. This was not the doctor who'd done the surgery, and although it was normal for him to want to make certain all was well, Brandon couldn't help the worry that began to gnaw at him.

"Hm," the doctor said again and then, "I wish I could give you better news. The test has come back positive, although right now, you're healthy."

Brandon felt himself pale, a feeling of the floor beneath him falling away, wanted to throw up. His head began to spin and he began to shake. "No," he heard himself say. "It can't be."

"I'm afraid it's true. The test was positive for antibodies. Brandon, you have HIV."

Brandon stood. The urge to fight, to hit something was almost uncontrollable. "I said no, ye've got the wrong man!"

"Sit down, sir!" the doctor ordered, and Brandon sat, felt the fear that he'd been harboring all these months creep up his spine, felt the fingers of illness spread through his veins, infect his awareness of who he was. "Can ye re-do the test? It's got to be a mistake," he said.

241

The doctor cocked his head. "We can. But the results won't be any different. It's your name, your test results. Brandon, I'm very sorry to be the one to tell you, but now we have to get on to talk about treatment. Right now, you aren't sick. By your own admission, you have not had a fever or other flu symptoms, you aren't tired, your energy is good. These are all positive signs. But we need to start you on medication right away. Now, let me get you a prescription for those medicines and we'll go from there."

Brandon finally left the clinic after receiving his prescriptions and having a lengthy chat with the doctor. There were all the reinforcements of instructions he'd received the last time; no sexual relations without a rubber, with the added, "You must inform your partner you have HIV." How could he? How could he tell Aine that they could never be together? She wouldn't want him now that he had tested positive, he was sure of it. Better she get over him, meet someone else, learn to love someone else. He sat in his car for what seemed like forever, refusing to answer his phone when his mam called. She'd want to know the results and he hadn't the heart to tell her.

In time, he started the car and turned it toward Garrettstown. He'd gone back to his grandparents' home when he and Aine returned to Ireland. She had gone on to her new life in Killarney, and now Brandon knew he'd never see her again.

Well, it was better this way, he thought.

His grandparents weren't home. That was just as well, too.

Inside the room he'd lived for the last while, he stuffed his clothing into a duffle bag and, glancing around to see if he needed anything else, went to his gran's kitchen, took some paper and a pen, and scrawled a note to let them know he'd be gone for a while. He couldn't tell them he had no plans to come back.

He then walked out the front door, leaving behind the home he'd grown to love. He'd never return.

* * *

"Henry, have ye heard from Brandon?" asked Kathleen, her fingers gripping the phone tightly as she spoke. She was anxious to know, wanted to hear from Brandon himself before she broke protocol and talked to the doctor.

Henry had answered with a simple, "No," and then, "why? Should I have heard?"

"No, I just thought he might have rung. He was to hear his results today and I can't get hold of him on his mobile. He's not answering."

"Well, maybe he's off to the pub, celebratin' or some such thing. Ye know Brandon, he'll not tell anyone anythin' unless he has to."

"What about Aine, have ye seen her?"

"Not since she got back. Is there somethin' ye're not tellin' me, Mam?"

Kathleen felt the panic build and tried vainly to keep her attitude professional. But this was her son, dammit! "It's just, I'm concerned. It's not like him to not answer when I ring him."

"Ah, I'm sure all's well. Maybe he left it at home or maybe he's turned it off. Ye never know with him. He could be off surfin', too," added Henry. They all knew Brandon never turned down a good wave if it could be helped.

"I hadn't thought of that," said Kathleen, but the feeling of something wrong just wouldn't go away. "Okay, well, ye'll tell me if ye hear from him?"

"I will, but I've got to get back to work now. Ye're alright?"

"Of course I'm alright. I'm just, well, I'm just concerned for Brandon is all."

"Ah, he'll be fine. No bother."

"Right, then," she said, and hung up the phone.

She received the same response when she finally connected with Aine and the two decided to meet the following day, when both had time off.

The drive from Inishannon to Killarney scarcely gave Kathleen time to think. Her parents hadn't seen Brandon either, but had found the note, which had said only that he was going away for a while. They had thought perhaps he was going to Killarney, to be of help to Henry.

Kathleen was now truly worried, and she said as much to Aine when they met. Aine poured coffee and then put a good dollop of Irish whiskey into it. They'd need it, she'd said.

It was only then that Kathleen realized her hands were shaking. "I can't believe he'd just up and leave," she said to Aine after the first good sip of coffee hit her stomach and she felt the whiskey warm its way through her gut.

Aine placed her hand over Kathleen's and squeezed lightly. "He'll come back when he's ready," she said, but Kathleen saw the worry in her eyes, reflecting her own.

"Have ye spoken to the doctor yet?" asked Aine, concerned, caring.

Kathleen nodded. "He said the test was positive. Oh, God, Aine, how can that be? Not my beautiful boy…not my boyo." Despite her resolve not to cry, she felt the tears roll down her cheeks and the tissue being thrust into her hand. "Thanks, love," she said, taking the tissue from Aine and dabbing her eyes.

"Do ye have any idea of where he'd go?" Aine wondered.

Kathleen shook her head. "Henry's going to check a few places but if I know my son, he's goin' to go where no one will find him. He'll go where no one knows him."

"That could be anywhere."

"Aye, that could be."

They both sat in silence, neither giving in to the dark thoughts that were invading.

"Have ye heard from yer friend? Ye know, the one who was counselin' him?" asked Kathleen when the silence had stretched on for what seemed like forever.

Aine shook her head. "I placed a call, asked him to ring immediately, but still haven't heard."

"Did ye tell him, when ye left the message, what it's about, like?"

She nodded and said, "It's maybe why he hasn't called. Sean's good about gettin' back to me, he is. If he's got any

245

information, he'll soon be in touch. But I'm thinkin' he's chasin' down ideas. Maybe goin' through the notes he made from the sessions he's had. Brandon was doin' so well until this." She hesitated, and then asked, very quietly, "Ye don't think he'll do somethin' bad, do ye?"

Kathleen's facial expression must have shown all because Aine turned her eyes away to look out the window.

"I don't believe he'd do anything," Aine said, when Kathleen didn't speak. "I don't believe he'd be stupid enough to harm himself. That's not the Brandon I know. Ye know what I think?" She didn't wait for Kathleen to answer but continued on. "I think he's taken himself off north, maybe Galway, Mayo, even Donegal. Somewhere where he isn't known. He'll find a job he can do, keep his nose clean, and bury himself in work. He's done fishin' before, he told me. Maybe he'll do that?"

Kathleen looked at Aine and wished she had the kind of hope that was written on Aine's features. "I honestly don't know," she said. And then Aine's phone rang, and as the young nurse picked it up, she hurriedly checked it, and the hope in her eyes grew.

"Sean, have ye heard anything?" she asked.

He hadn't. Kathleen could tell by the way Aine's face fell, and she knew a depth of despair she hadn't felt since losing her husband. What would he have done, had he been alive to hear the news?

"No, nothin' then," said Aine. "Anything that might tell us what he'd do, where he'd go?" Again, the silence and the fallen features. "No. Okay. Yes, we'll keep in touch, and if ye hear anything…of course. Thanks, and bye." She hit the disconnect button and placed her phone back on the table.

"No one has seen or heard from him. Sean says there's nothing really that indicates where he would go, although he remembers Brandon telling him once that he liked his alone time. So, Sean and I, we're both thinkin' he may have taken himself off somewhere, like a dog would, to lick his wounds until he feels better."

"But he's not goin' to feel better," exclaimed Kathleen, and new tears began to fall. "He's only goin' to feel worse. And I don't know that he's even filled his prescriptions and without those drugs, he'll only get worse for certain. Oh, I'll kill him if I ever lay eyes on him again!"

Aine started to laugh at the irony of her statement, and the tension in the room eased when Kathleen joined in.

* * *

Later that night, Aine gazed out the back door of her little cottage. It was tucked away on an acre of land, just out of the town, an area she had grown fond of. It was her little piece of heaven, even though the cottage itself was almost rustic. It had everything she needed but was in need of updating. The cooker was old, as were the cabinets. There was no dishwasher, as in her flat in Cork, but she didn't mind so much. It was just her. She wondered if she should get a cat for company. She'd rather enjoyed Hank's cat, although he'd been aloof when she first met the big orange beast.

The night sky told her nothing, although she sat on a chair

and gazed up at the stars for what seemed like hours. A star shot through the sky and she watched in awe as it streaked through the heavens before disappearing out of sight. It was a beautiful night, for September.

In the distance, she could see darker shapes on the horizon, and knew that they'd have rain before morning. It rained more in Killarney than it did in Cork, but it was often a short rain followed by periods of sun. But it was moving into autumn, and she knew the weather would soon turn.

And where was Brandon? He'd left the yellow Mini that he loved to drive around at his grandparents' home. He'd left on foot, taking only the barest of items with him, according to them. They were all worried about Brandon, and Aine added the grandparents to her list. They were elderly. How would they take it if the worst thing happened?

No, she scolded herself, she wouldn't go down that road. That way led to madness and she wouldn't go there. Brandon would be okay, of that she felt certain. And even if he had HIV, which she still hadn't reconciled within herself, he'd be alright. Once he got used to the idea he was sick, he'd be alright. He just needed time. Time in which to adjust to his new reality. And he couldn't do that with people all around him, people that he knew and loved and had given them every reason to reject him. They wouldn't reject him, though. She knew that in the very marrow of her bones, but did Brandon know that?

A glance at her watch in the reflected light of the kitchen window told her it was late. She had an early morning shift and if she wanted to be awake for it, she'd better head off to bed.

She took another glance at the sky but the star or comet, or whatever it was, had disappeared for good, and she wondered briefly if Brandon had done the same.

Sadness filled her and she stemmed the tears that threatened. She wouldn't believe he'd leave her and not give her some indication of his plans. And she wouldn't believe he'd be upset enough to take his own life. She knew that was what everyone was thinking, that he'd harm himself. But that wasn't the Brandon she knew. He didn't think that way. He was more likely to fight, to challenge anyone who looked at him the wrong way than he was to run from it.

No, Brandon hadn't gone off to do himself in. But if he'd gone off, and he so very obviously had, then where? And why hadn't he told her? He said he loved her. She believed him. So why leave her in the dark?

Why, indeed, she thought, standing in the very dark of the porch, out of the light of the kitchen window.

"Brandon," she spoke quietly to the night, "if ye can hear me, come home to me. I love ye. I don't care ye might be sick or not. I love ye anyway."

There was no sound but the rustle of the wind in the trees. The clouds were moving in. Rain would start soon.

She turned her back on the garden and went inside to go to bed.

From his secluded spot beneath the trees, Brandon heard her words. He'd wanted to see her, just one more time, and to hear the words she'd just spoken. That she loved him, that she wanted him regardless of his HIV status, had nearly broken his heart.

He'd show them, he thought. He'd show them all he wasn't sick. He'd go away until the next test was due and then he'd prove he was well. He'd show them.

He slid into the darkness, a new determination in his heart.

Chapter Twenty-Three

B randon had been gone almost two months, thought Kathleen, making her way down to the Emergency Department. Two months in which no one had heard anything. *But no body had been found, either*, said a small voice in her head. There was still hope. Hope he'd turn up.

Amid the busy department, a pregnant woman had been brought in, the victim of a motor vehicle mishap and while being checked out by the ED physician, her water broke and there was no time to move her to Maternity. Kathleen had been there, just in time, and soon after, a healthy baby was born. Kathleen was just cleaning up the area when a scuffle sounded behind her and she noted the garda and an intern, wrestling with a patient on a gurney. "Name's O'Farrell," said the garda once they'd had the man subdued. "He's a regular, he is."

Kathleen went immediately to look at the man on the gurney, her heart pounding. Dark hair matted with blood reminded her of that other time and she held her breath, hoping it was Brandon so the search would be over, hoping it wasn't. She didn't want to see her boy beat up again. She peeked over the sheet, noted the bruising and swelling of the cheek, the obviously broken nose.

Not Brandon. The relief that swept through her made her feel faint. Relief, tempered with disappointment.

She caught the name on the paperwork as she stood beside the intern. "Brendan O'Farrell" it read.

Kathleen took a deep breath. "May I see that, for a moment?" she asked, and the intern, new to the unit, handed her the paperwork while he did an assessment of the man, who appeared uninjured with the exception of the facial wounds.

The paperwork had notes scrawled on it, something about getting facial wounds from a brawl and the words "HIV+" next to the comments.

She looked at the name again and wondered, her mind working. Handing the papers back to the intern, she quickly headed back to maternity to complete her shift.

* * *

Henry couldn't believe what his mam was saying. "I'm tellin' ye, Henry, there was a mix-up in the bloodwork. Brandon didn't test positive. His test was negative, but the other fella had the same name almost. Except his name was Brendan with an "*e*" and then an "*a*," not Brandon. But the same last name and no relation! I saw the paperwork myself and then contacted the lab."

"Jaysus, Mary and Bride, all this time the poor fella's been thinkin' he's infected, and he's not. And what were the odds ye'd be on shift in that exact spot when they brought the other one in?"

252

"Must be the good Lord lookin' out for us, I'd say," she answered.

"Amen to that," said Henry, crossing himself. "We have to find him," he said over the phone. "We've got to let him know he's okay. God knows where he is or what he's doin' but we need to locate him before he gives up."

"I pray to God he hasn't given up already," said Kathleen.

"No. Don't even think it. I was down Dingle way two days ago and someone said they thought they saw him. Said they thought I was him, so that's a good bet he's around there somewhere. I'm goin' to go back today, take a couple of photos with me. Maybe I'll get a hit."

"Right, then. I've only got a few minutes left on my break but I'll call ye if I find out anythin' else. Oh, and just to let ye know, I spoke with both Niall and Liam. Liam is up Donegal way, shooting for some commercial or something, but said he'd keep an eye open up there. If anyone has seen him, he'll know. And as for Niall, well, ye know he's always got his nose in some computer manual or somethin'. He wouldn't know if a bomb went off unless it destroyed whatever program he was workin' on."

"That's our Niall, to be sure. And good to know where Liam is. Did he say where in Donegal?"

"No. But they'll be movin' to Galway in the next couple of days, so he'll have a chance to watch around there as well. Henry, he could be anywhere."

Henry nodded. If Brandon wanted to hide, and it seemed he did, no one would find him.

He hung up the phone then and thought of ringing Liam.
Liam, his younger brother, was outgoing, all dark good looks
and deep navy eyes, a lady's man to be sure. The other twin,
Niall, was introverted, a geek if ever there was one. Not only
that, Niall was a computer whiz. There wasn't a system he
didn't know, not a server he couldn't hack. It had nearly got
him into trouble as a lad when he'd hacked into a local finance
company's server. He'd done it as a lark, had never meant any
harm, and had got out of it without corrupting the system. But
then his conscience had got the better of him. If he could do
it, so could others, he'd reasoned, and so he'd owned up to
being the hacker and had then gone on to help the company
build a better system.

Yes, thought Henry, if anyone could find Brandon within
a system, Niall could.

Several days later, Henry was back on the road, this time
heading northwest. He stopped in at Dingle, asked around
the town and then down along the shore, hoping that maybe
Brandon had taken to giving tours as he'd done in Kinsale.

"Oh, aye," said an old fisherman. "He was here. Got
hisself a craic job, leading tourists a merry game. Was here
a month or more. Haven't seen him these few days past,
though."

Henry thanked the man, and after getting the name of the
tour company, paid the office a visit.

"He picked up his pay and left," said the office
coordinator. "Said he needed to move on. Came up sudden
like, his needin' to leave, and too bad. He was a good 'un,"

she said, "tourists really liked him. Always took his guitar along with him, sang to them at times and had them all singin' along. Seems they like the old rebel songs the best, accordin' to Brandon." She had a wistful look in her eye and if Henry interpreted the situation properly, the woman had it big for his little brother. And did Brandon…?

No, he wouldn't go there. If he left Aine because of the threat of HIV, he certainly wouldn't have relations with a stranger, *unless he was at his wits end*, said a little voice inside his head.

Bollocks! Henry wouldn't believe it, and since there was no more to be learned from the tour company, he left. But where to look next?

Calling Niall, he learned that Brandon had purchased a motorcycle shortly after he'd decided to disappear. There was a registration in Dingle for one such vehicle. So, with that in mind, he knew for certain that Brandon was somewhere, and he was alive. All good news. But where in hell Brandon went after Dingle, Henry didn't know. The only other thought keeping him going was the fact that Brandon had bought another guitar. But did this fit the pattern he'd lived before? He was working for a tour company again, singing to his clients and entertaining them. Did it follow that he was sleeping with them, too? Was he going down the road that had led him to so much misery? Henry didn't know, and the not knowing was almost as bad as not finding his brother.

He got himself a room for the night and settled in to call his mam. She'd be worried, wondering if he'd found anything.

After that call, he placed one to Aine but was unable to tell her much. He felt somehow inadequate, not having something more positive to say, but the fact that he knew Brandon was alive was more than what they'd known before.

"I'm coming to meet ye," she said, just before Henry signed off.

"What do ye mean?"

"I'm going to help ye look. I can't stay here and do nothin'. It's drivin' me insane."

"I understand that, but there's no sense both of us chasin' rumors. Niall's still searching databases and whatever else he can think of. I'll call ye if he hears of anything else."

He'd finally coaxed her off the phone with his promise of calling her again but didn't know if he'd be calling any time soon. Niall may know computers backward and foreword, but even he couldn't invent data where there was none. He was just about to get himself a shower when his mobile went off. It was Niall.

"I've a hit," he exclaimed to Henry. "He's in Kilrush. My guess is he's signed on to take visitors by boat to Scattery Island. Seems like somethin' he'd do."

A chill went up Henry's spine that had nothing to do with ruins on islands and medieval churches. It felt right, he knew. It was remote. It was a place to hide where no one knew him.

Thanking Niall, he called Aine back.

"I'll be there tomorrow," she said, and hung up the phone.

Was it a pipe dream? Would they really find him? Alive? And would he, like Niall supposed, be taking tourists around?

Sleep. He needed sleep. He laid down on the hotel bed, feeling the mattress stiff beneath him, and didn't care that he hadn't undressed. As soon as he could, he'd be up and moving. He had to get to Kilrush, and daylight couldn't come fast enough.

* * *

Brandon was listening to the small band in the pub. He'd been enjoying the music and whiskey and the attentions of the barmaid. She kept winking at him, wanting to chat him up but Brandon wasn't interested. She'd be great company on a cold night, of that he was certain. She was all rounded curves, soft and warm, he had no doubt. But he wasn't there for that.

He'd found himself a comfortable existence in the last week. The boat he'd rented for the winter had a small galley and sleeping bunk, and a few extra amenities. It was not large, but it was enough for him. He'd take tourists out in the bigger tour boat when the weather was good, and once the winter was over, decide where to go next. By October, the weather would be too cold and stormy to allow for sailing back and forth to the island but there would still be the odd tourist, wanting to visit the Cliffs of Mohr or some other such thing and he could do those easily enough. The tour company he'd signed on with was happy to have someone equally at home with either driving a boat or a bus. And one that entertained visitors with rebel songs and other Irish ditties was a good catch indeed.

So far, he'd made a good wage from tips because the actual wage wasn't much. It fed him, sheltered him, but left little else to live on. The tips, however, were what kept him going.

Tomorrow, if the weather changed for the better, he'd take another group out to Scattery Island. They liked to see the ruins of the churches, no less than five, and the round tower, the tallest in the country he would tell them proudly, as if he, himself, had been the one to build it.

He downed the rest of his whiskey, said goodnight to the barmaid, and left the pub. Walking back to his home through the driving rain was not pleasant but it wasn't a far walk. The boat he'd rented was moored close by, although, without a working radio it wasn't going anywhere, and he was fine with that. He only needed a place to lay his head and it had come cheap enough.

He thought of Aine, of making her a part of his past and moving on. He told himself that he could have another woman, that Aine would be free to live her own life, find someone new, and if so, wouldn't he, too? But it had been a hollow thought with no substance.

His mind was preoccupied as he made his way down the dock, not really concentrating on his surroundings so he hadn't noticed the figure on his boat until he was quite close. His first thought was that someone had come to call, although who that might be on such a night as this was beyond his reckoning. And then he realized that the person was trying to get into the cabin. He hurried along, the noise of the storm masking his presence, and surprised the intruder by grabbing him from behind, arms around the man's chest, groping for a handhold on his skinny frame.

And that was when he discovered that "he" was a "she."

His hands had come across nubile bumps, not contained in any bra beneath a sodden t-shirt; she hadn't any coat on. Christ, she must have been half frozen dressed like that. He didn't waste any time once he figured out she was a woman, and managed to subdue her enough to get her inside and turn on the light for his first good look at her.

Woman? She was barely that. Maybe sixteen and skinny as an eel. She could easily pass for a boy but Brandon knew for certain she was female. And she was completely safe with him. He could no more have shagged the girl, even if she was thirty and a looker, than he could have pulled gold from his arse. She was clearly a waif. A runaway, if he didn't miss his guess.

She stood dripping, making large puddles on the floor as if he'd just pulled her from the ocean, and she was shivering. So rather than hand her the towel, he pushed her toward the shower, turned it on, and told her to stay there until she was warm.

The door closed with a bang and eventually a few pieces of clothing landed with a splat outside the shower room door.

He then took her wet clothing as she tossed it from the shower, wrung out as much water as he could in the small galley sink, and hung them from the curtain rods. There was no other place and the one wardrobe was packed full of his own gear.

When he heard the shower turn off, he stayed outside

the tiny enclosure, handing her a towel, a dry shirt, which would no doubt be more like a dress on her, and some socks to warm her feet. He had nothing he could provide in the way of knickers or even pants.

In the meantime, he saw her emerge from the shower and got his first good look at her. Her cropped hair was orange in places, red in others, as if she'd tried to dye it but hadn't quite got it all. Dark brown roots were showing through, giving her a modern punk look, which was probably what she liked, he thought.

"Hungry?" he asked, and saw her lick her lips and look at the frying pan where the bangers were cooking.

"Yeah," she nodded.

"Have a seat. Spuds are done. I'll get ye a plate." Moments later, he saw her tuck into the food like it was her first meal in days, and likely was, he reflected.

The t-shirt he'd given her had long sleeves, which she'd rolled up several times, and the socks on her feet came up to her knees but were warm, he knew. They were wool, made for seamen, and would retain warmth, even if wet.

He was starkly aware of her nudity beneath the shirt. And she'd had no knickers of her own to speak of, just a t-shirt and jeans and socks with holes in soggy running shoes.

"Who are ye and where're ye from?" he asked, eyeing her as he took a sip of the hot tea he'd brewed. Pushing a cup before her, he received a look of dangerous loathing. If he didn't miss his guess, she'd rather slit his throat than tell him.

She kept eating.

He waited until she'd finished and then asked again. "I want to know, and if ye don't tell me, I'll take ye out right now to yon garda and let them deal with ye. It's no never mind to me. Ye're a complication I don't need, so spill it or suffer. Your choice."

Silence was her answer but it looked as if she was thinking about telling…or not.

"Look, I promise I won't take ye to the garda if ye tell me what ye were doin', tryin' to break into my boat. Ye look like a runaway to me, so what, or who, are ye runnin' from?"

An eternity of silence ensued, and finally, "My da," she said, quietly, angrily, as if to say, "so there!."

Brandon felt an anger well up inside him at the thought of what that could mean, but he needed to know more. "So what's the story?"

Again, silence, as if she was trying to determine how much or how little to tell. And then that quiet voice again, "He's mean."

"Mmf," said Brandon, wondering if "mean" meant beatings. And with her attitude, maybe she deserved one. But he didn't say that. Instead, he took in the waif-like features and knew she'd been running for some time. "Well, I can't promise ye won't end up back where ye came from but I've got to get ye to the authorities. Ye can't stay here," he said, standing and putting dishes in the sink.

"Please, please let me stay," she exclaimed, and jumped up from the table to plaster herself against him. "I can make it worth yer while," she stated, rubbing up against him in unmistakable gestures.

He tried unwinding her arms from his neck. "Leave off," he yelled, but she'd have none of it and thrust one lanky leg between his thighs, rubbing his nads so hard he felt as if she would crush them. Far from turning him on, he was disgusted by her actions.

"Cop on!" he yelled and pushed her from him, so hard that she fell against the table, leaving him feeling horrible about what he'd done. She'd have a bruise from that, he was certain, and there was no place for either of them to go. No sanctuary from each other, the cabin was too small.

She began to hike up the t-shirt.

"Leave it," hissed Brandon. "I'm not the kind that takes a child to bed," he exclaimed, nearly at his wits' end. What was he to do with such a wildcat?

"I'm not a child, I'm eighteen," she lied.

"Bollocks, that's what that is. Ye're sixteen if a day. Likely younger, and I'll not have rape on my head. If it wasn't such a foul night, I'd throw ye out. Now get into yon bed over there and stay there. And don't even think of leavin'. I'll deal wit' ye's in the mornin'." Why did anger make him slur his words together so badly? His mam would wash his mouth if she'd heard him just now, but then he remembered it was Mam who sometimes resorted to a less than cultured sound, especially when dealing with himself.

The girl, he noted with a silent prayer of thanks, crawled into the bed and drew the covers up to her chin. Her hair, once plastered against her skull, now stood out in all directions, red and orange with two-inch-long dark roots. It was like looking at Peter Pan in his bed and he amended her age. Maybe fourteen. Her eyes closed, reluctantly it seemed, and he soon heard the breathing of deep sleep.

Checking his mobile phone, he noted there was still no service; the storm had knocked it out earlier that evening so he couldn't even call the garda now if he'd wanted to, which he did. He had a bad feeling about the creature in the bed but it would have to wait until morning. Hopefully, service would be restored by then.

He poured a finger of whiskey into a glass and tossed it back, felt the liquor slide down his throat and soothe him. He'd been so angry when she assaulted him, angry enough that had she been older, he might have backhanded her. But he'd learned a few things these past months. He'd learned a lot.

Leaning back against the cushions of the seat behind the small table, he stretched his long legs out to rest on the opposite side and put his head back. As soon as daylight came, he'd take her to the garda. They'd know what to do with her. Maybe they could figure out her name because in all the kafuffle, she'd never said it.

He closed his eyes, determined to get some sleep even though he was far from comfortable. He wasn't concerned with her at the moment. She was out. And the cabin was so small, he'd hear her if she tried to leave.

Just in case, he locked the door, which he knew gave a loud enough click to wake the dead. She stirred in sleep as he turned the lock, rolled over, and was soon snoring softly once again. He settled down, propped against the squabs of the built-in table seating, and felt sleep overtake him.

Chapter Twenty-Four

Brandon woke to the sound of something moving in the cabin. He'd been dreaming of rats scurrying around his small boat. He was at sea and it was just a dory. The rats were everywhere.

He came fully awake when the little wildcat he'd captured dropped his guitar, the very guitar he'd bought in Dingle to replace his other one. He'd finally found one he liked. She'd been holding it clumsily but quickly grabbed it again, swinging it high overhead. It hit the ceiling and Brandon looked up just in time to see the thing come down toward his head. He shot forward out of his seat and the arc of the guitar missed him, breaking apart at the neck as it hit the small table.

Stunned as he was for a moment at the shattering of his second guitar, it gave the girl the split second she needed. She grasped at the lock and turned it with an audible click. Brandon recovered his balance and grabbed her, held her close though she was determined to run from him. *No way*, he thought angrily, *no way was this little hellcat going to dash and run*. He'd get her to the authorities without delay. He just wasn't sure how he would do it on a motorbike.

They struggled and he realized she was still wearing the t-shirt he'd given her the night before. The wet clothing was still on the curtain rods, still damp, he noted when he'd brushed against them as he tried to grab her.

She hit the latch, the door swung open letting in cold, damp air from the sea. She bolted, wearing only his shirt and socks!

He swore and grabbed at her but she eluded his grasp and hightailed it up the stairs to the deck. He was after her in two strides and nearly caught up to her in three. She'd hit the dock running and as her feet gained solid earth, he grabbed her from behind, swinging her round with the impetus of their flight.

* * *

Aine and Hank had finally closed in on Brandon. It had taken some sleuthing, but with Niall's help, they'd located him in a small marina in Kilrush. Now their only obstacle was to reason out which boat he might have rented for his own, and was it docked. The harbormaster soon cleared up any confusion. "It's the *Stormy Lady*, berth three. Ye can just see her from here," he said pointing.

They looked and could see a small sailboat, maybe a thirty-footer if an inch, and made their way toward the dock.

Aine felt a rush of excitement, so close to seeing Brandon again, to be able to tell him he was okay, they'd got the samples mixed up. To see him smile, to be held in his arms again, to feel the solid lines of his body next to hers in sleep. Images filled her head and so she hadn't noticed that Henry had stopped walking.

"What in hell…" said Henry, squinting as two figures wrestled on the ground. The one on the bottom had her shirt hitched up and seemed to have no care that her white arse was exposed for all the world to see. Over her, Brandon had her arms in a grip, looked as if he was trying to sit on her, or get between her legs…

Aine froze. All she saw was Brandon with a woman on the ground. She couldn't take it in, couldn't see it for what it was; only saw Brandon with another woman. Tears pricked her eyes and she cursed herself for being all kinds of a fool. She'd trusted him and this was where it had led.

"Let's go back," she said to Henry, who seemed to be enjoying the show. "I've no desire to see any more. I've seen enough as it is."

She turned to go but Henry stopped her, his hand gripping her arm. "No, wait."

But she didn't want to wait. And suddenly there were sirens and the garda rushing to the scene, hauling a loudly cursing Brandon off the woman.

And then the voice yelling, "Rape! He was tryin' to rape me!"

"Oh, Christ," muttered Henry.

The next thing Aine saw was Brandon being taken away in cuffs and the girl being wrapped in a blanket to be led away to a different car.

Girl, thought Aine. *She was just a girl.*

Aine looked at Henry. Neither knew what to say but

Henry sprang into action. "C'mon," he said, "we'll follow them to the station."

The girl, they noted when they arrived at the station, was seated in an office, the blanket still wrapped around her. Aine was glad for that. But what on earth had she been wearing? Why didn't she have any other clothing on and especially, why was Brandon over her like that? Even if rape was his intent, which, in retrospect, she highly doubted, he wouldn't attempt it on the ground in broad daylight, in view of everyone. It didn't make sense. Not even Brandon was that brazen.

"Wait here," she said in an aside to Henry. She had an idea that had to be tried. If not, they could lose Brandon to the justice system, and with his history…well, anything could happen.

Walking up to the desk, she drew her wallet from her purse and handed a card to the officer on duty. "I'm a rape counselor. I'm here to speak with the girl in that room."

"Wait here," was the command, and so she did, trying her best to look official and not give in to the panic she felt.

The officer had a word with one of his co-workers, who spoke to another officer, a woman who, Aine surmised, had been assigned to look after the girl. The woman approached her, and Aine stood as tall as her five and half feet would allow. The female officer was an Amazon.

A brief discussion ensued in which Aine explained her interest in the case. She'd heard the girl scream, and as she had been a highly qualified nurse and counselor with Cork University Hospital, and of late, Killarney Hospital, and was on holiday in the area, she would like to offer her services, especially since it was unlikely there would be someone of her calibre in Kilrush.

The officer agreed. They were just a small outpost with extreme cases being moved to a much larger center, she'd explained. They were in the process of moving the girl to the nearest hospital, so they would be grateful for any help Miss Donohue might provide.

Aine stepped into the room and began her work.

Henry watched from his seat near the main door. He didn't want anyone thinking he and Aine were together. At least not yet. When the officer on duty went back to the desk, he approached and asked about Brandon.

"I hear my brother was just brought in. Can I see him?"

The officer looked him over. "Wait here, please."

What seemed like an hour later, another officer came and said, "Follow me."

They went through a hallway to a room in the back where Brandon was seated at a table, hands clasped together, the cuffs clanking against the metal tabletop.

Henry sat on the opposite side and looked at his brother. He hadn't seen him in almost three months and the man he saw now had changed little from the Brandon of three months ago. That was the good part. He was tanned from being on the water much of that time, he thought, and his hair could use a good trimming, but there was no denying it was his little brother. And Brandon needed his help.

"What the hell happened?" he asked softly. He wanted to

reach out, pull his brother into a hug, but he knew it wouldn't be allowed. He hoped the tone of his voice would keep things calm and convey what he couldn't put into words, at least, not here.

There was little surprise in his countenance as Brandon looked at Henry, acknowledging his brother with a slight nod. Brandon appeared grim-faced and completely sober, although he bore the signs around his eyes of little sleep. "I got home last night to find that little hellcat trying to break into the boat. Was only when I got her inside that I realized she was a girl, and a young one at that. I gave her shelter, fed her, and that's it. I tried to call the garda myself last night but mobile service was still down. I wish to God I'd been able to reach someone. Maybe if I had, then this," he jangled the cuffs on his wrists, "would never have happened."

Henry cocked his head in thought. "How did yon hellcat end up in your shirt and outside on the ground the way ye were?" He hesitated to say more. He didn't want to provide anyone with information that could possibly be used against his brother.

"She was sodden when I got her inside. She'd no coat, was shiverin' like, so I offered her the shower to warm up and then tossed her some things to dress in whilst her clothes were drying. Only, I don't have a dryer on board, so I hung her jeans and t-shirt up on the curtain rods. If the garda want to check that out they can. It'll be as I said."

"But, Brandon, I overheard them. They're charging ye with rape."

"I never touched her," he answered, head down, defeated. "Henry, I never touched her. I've been celibate since I got back from Canada and that's the god's truth. If they want to pin rape on me, they'll have to prove it."

"And that bit when ye were arrested? How did that come about?"

"She was trying to flee. She broke my guitar and I just saw red. I was so angry that she'd take the one thing I treasured and try to break it over my head just because she wanted away."

"Why didn't ye just let her go?"

"Well, for one thing, she's underage and needs help. I'd intended to turn her in to this station today and she knew that. She didn't want to go but somethin' inside said I must try. So after she broke my guitar, I determined that she wouldn't get away with it. I'd make her pay by takin' her here, let the authorities deal with the little witch. She'd tried to break into my place, after all."

Henry nodded. It fit Brandon's character to want to look after her. For all his faults, Brandon was a caretaker of souls. All kinds of souls, even to his detriment.

"Look, I'll find ye some legal counsel and we'll get ye out of here. Can't promise anything, but for what it's worth, I believe ye."

By the time Henry had finished with Brandon it was to see Aine waiting just outside the station doors. She was hugging her purse to herself as if she were shivering with cold. She was shivering, noted Henry, but soon found out she

271

wasn't cold. She was furious.

"She was raped over and over," she said before Henry could get a word in. "From the time she was little, that child has been abused. It sickens me. I don't think I've ever come across such a heinous crime in all my years of counseling. I knew there were perverts out there who did this sort of thing, but this is the first time I've come across it myself, and it sickens me to death. I just want to throw up."

If he'd been Brandon, he knew he'd put his arms around her and offer comfort, but he wasn't his brother, this wasn't his lady, and so all he could do was acknowledge her words and offer a few of his own. "Ye must know it wasn't Brandon. He never touched her, he said, and I believe him."

"I don't doubt Brandon's words but only a DNA test will confirm that. They've taken her off to the hospital. I'll go and provide a report. I went in there to help Brandon, to figure out what went wrong, and I found something else instead."

They began walking toward Henry's car. "What else did ye find?"

She got in the car, put on her seatbelt, and waited for Henry to get in, too. "I found myself, Henry," she said. "These past couple of months at my new job have taught me that I miss the counseling, that it's a part of me that I've shut out. I can help people like this poor girl. She's nasty, no doubt, but she has a reason to be. She's as much a victim as is our Brandon. And she needs help, too."

Henry started the car. "Right. I'll drop ye off at the hospital and then I'm goin' in search of a good lawyer. I've some buddies I can call and ye can ring me when ye're done. I'll come and get ye and we'll figure out the next move."

Chapter Twenty-Five

Brandon stood on the bow of the little sailboat he'd come to call home, although it had been that for only a few weeks. The winter was settling in, frost had dotted the landscape, and the day was calm. The scent of the sea was in his nostrils, and he breathed deeply of the salty air.

It was all over. Finally. He'd been cleared of any wrongdoing although the charges of unlawful confinement were a close thing. But his intent, as his lawyer put it, was to keep the girl safe from further harm with respect of getting her help as soon as he was able. The fact that there had been no mobile service went in his favor, as did the fact that the boat he was on was considered a houseboat, confined to the dock for the season, and therefore not equipped with a working radio. Brandon had been told that when he rented it. So many puzzle pieces had all come together to make one great catastrophe. Or nearly.

The girl, it had turned out, had indeed been the owner of a juvenile record a mile long as well as a runaway. Brandon was very certain the two things were connected. Fortunately, and as he had suspected, the tests taken at the hospital had confirmed the story she'd told Aine. The best part was that Brandon was cleared of all charges.

He looked around the boat and checked to make certain nothing was left behind. He didn't have much to begin with and now, without a guitar once again, the motorbike ride back to Kerry would be easier.

Brandon didn't know what life had in store for him anymore. He seemed to be damned to stay on the bad side of life, finding trouble wherever he went, despite his efforts at staying on the straight and narrow. The part he missed most was Aine. He'd told her in no uncertain terms that they were finished. He was done making her life miserable and refused to be responsible for any more pain on her part. It was clear that he was bad news for any woman. A part of him thought he'd be better off in a monastery but doubted he'd be allowed entry, even if he could find one. He hadn't been the best Catholic the world had ever produced. A saint he wasn't, and he'd left her standing there after his acquittal, looking as beautiful as ever but with a sadness about her that tore at his heart.

Perhaps this was what his ancestor had felt, he wondered, the two- or three-times-great uncle that had taken himself out to sea, never to be seen again after losing his beloved wife to illness. Henry had found relatives in the graveyard at Killegy and discovered that before the family settled in Cork, they'd lived for generations in Kerry. And that was where Henry lived now, with his wife, Siobhan, and their adopted daughter, Emily. Emily, who was Hank's niece, so in reality, his niece, too. Such a good kid. She didn't deserve to have an uncle like him. He'd stay away from everyone, not wanting to taint them with his bad luck.

The frosty air stung his nostrils, and he noted the sun trying bravely to poke its nose through ivory clouds above. Thin patches of blue were daring to show the promise of a brighter afternoon than the morning had been. But he couldn't stay any longer. Even though he'd been cleared of charges, he could feel the eyes of the folk about him, glancing sideways, always wondering if he'd lied to get off. A child rapist, after all.

Time to go. He left the little boat with a pang of wistfulness. Until the girl arrived, he'd been content. And that had been enough.

The only bright spot through the entire ordeal was that he'd had his test for HIV and it had come back negative. Henry had told him what their mam had found out; how the names had been so close and the lab had got the results mixed up. Any elation he felt at being vindicated were washed away by the tragedy of recent events.

His grandparents had wanted him to go back to their home, to live there until he got himself sorted out, but Brandon couldn't do that. He thought perhaps he'd go back to Cahersiveen. Nothing bad had happened there and there seemed to be an opportunity he could take advantage of come spring. He could get a flat and go back to working for the tour company he'd been with. He'd have to get another guitar, though. He loved to entertain, loved to see the smiles and hear the laughter of his clients as he drove them around the countryside. He loved Ireland, felt himself a part of the land like no other. He belonged here. And while he'd enjoyed staying with Hank in Canada, he knew that he could never leave his own patch of soil and start over as Hank had done.

Having secured his meagre belongings to the back of his motorbike, he hopped on, and without a backward glance, headed south to Cahersiveen.

* * *

Aine stood on her back porch under cover of the small overhang and looked at the rain pouring down into her back garden. The grass was long and needed cutting but it wouldn't be getting cut any time soon. The flower garden was done, even the asters had given up; but she'd been able to tidy the flowerbed up before the rain came. At least it didn't look as disheveled as her feelings were.

Her new job was working out well, and since the events in Kilrush, her desire to work with rape victims had been renewed and she'd been able to transition her original job into one similar to what she'd left behind in Cork. But that was as far as the good part went. There was so much more that was absent from her life.

She missed Brandon with a pain that went bone deep. She loved him so much but he'd been adamant that he didn't want her. That was a lie, she knew. He was trying to make the ultimate sacrifice, to give her up so she could have a better life.

That was a lot of malarkey. She'd never have another man

in her life. Never. Brandon had been the one to take her fear of a sexual relationship away but how could she tell him that it only worked with him? The thought of being with anyone else was abhorrent to her. She couldn't imagine another man touching her the way Brandon did. Of making her feel the way he did. He could melt her with just a look.

Thunder rolled across the sky and she stepped back inside. An idea was brewing and she'd made the decision to follow it through. Christmas was coming up, the perfect time for what she'd planned.

That decided, she turned out the lights and went to bed.

* * *

The following week found Aine wending her way down the road to Cahersiveen. She'd been up to Firies to purchase a brand new guitar from a fellow there who'd come highly recommended. She'd liked his shop, liked his way with the guitars as he checked the one she'd chosen for Brandon. He'd held it like the quality instrument it was and reminded her of Brandon when he stroked the strings.

She watched as he sat and checked the tuning, played a few chords and then a riff up the strings. His fingers were like magic as the music poured forth from the sound box. He looked up and winked. "Now that's a fine piece," he'd said, nodding as he stood and, grabbing a soft cloth, gave it a final polish before putting it into the hard case she'd purchased with it. Looking as if he was giving up one of his children, he handed it over to her with another wink and a smile.

After her stop in Firies, she left for Cahersiveen where

278

she knew Brandon was now residing. He was living near the water in a small, whitewashed cottage, much like the one she had in Killarney. It was located on a spit of land rolling down to the sea, with a view of Ballycarbery Castle out one window. It wasn't especially isolated as there were other cottages close by, but it was a thinly populated area, which would suit the brooding man she'd come to love.

As she drove toward the sea and saw the white cottages come into view, she noted the yellow Mini, a gift from Brandon's grandparents that they'd insisted he take, according to Henry. She knew, without a doubt, that he was home. Pulling up beside his vehicle, she went around to the back of the house to knock on the door. Only strangers went to the front. In her hand, she carried the new guitar, encased in a hard violin top case that would protect it from anyone who chose to break it over something, even something as hard as his head.

Brandon heard the knock on the door and waited. Maybe they had the wrong cottage, he thought, or maybe they were out to check to see if his television was legal. He discounted those thoughts, though. Those kind of folk, the ones who didn't know you, usually went to the front door and tried to peer in the windows. Nosey parkers, most of them.

The knocking repeated itself, however, and he gave a quick glance out the front window to see a familiar car parked behind the Mini. At least, he thought it looked familiar. He wouldn't know until he opened the door and he braced himself for who he might see.

As the door opened and Aine's eyes met his, his first thought was to gather her into his arms. But that was quickly overridden by common sense. He'd told her he couldn't be the man she wanted, no matter how much she wanted it, and yet one look in her eyes and he knew she hadn't given up.

Brandon did the only thing he could. He opened the door wider to let her in. Only then did he notice what she was carrying.

"I brought this for ye," she said, nodding at the guitar case she'd put down by her feet. She then removed her gloves and unbuttoned the coat she'd donned against the windy December day. A bright red scarf was wrapped around her throat, guarding against any cold draughts that penetrated the slightly open collar of the coat and added color to her cheeks, already kissed pink by the raw wind outside. Brandon helped her with her coat and automatically went to put the kettle on the hob.

"Tea?" he asked.

"Ah, lovely, thanks," she said brightly. And were those tears in her eyes or had the wind made them water?

He looked at the guitar case on the floor and said, "If that's for me, I've nothin' to put in it." He hadn't found the right guitar yet, although he'd been looking.

"Ye neddy," she jibed, "open it. Ye don't think I'd be so daft as to get ye a case and nothin' else?"

Brandon went to the black guitar case, ran his hands along the raised violin top, and began to undo the latches, all five of them, and then the clasp that locked. Opening it slowly, he looked inside at the blonde wood, the scroll of ivory that followed the curve of the guitar body, and the coloration of the wood itself, much brighter than if it had been a darker finish.

He couldn't help it. He picked the instrument up and held it, put his fingers to the strings and strummed.

The guitar sang.

Brandon felt the tears prick the back of his eyes as he began to work the strings. The resonance was more than he could have hoped for, more than he would ever have dreamed possible. He didn't deserve such an instrument. And it was brand-new. He'd only ever owned used instruments, had never owned a new one. But this was new. And now it was his.

Or so he wondered. His eyes met Aine's, saw the tears reflected there, and had to ask. "For me?" At her nod, he asked the obvious. "Why?"

She, lady that she was, stood there solidly and without wavering, said simply, "Because I love ye. Because I've always loved ye, and will never stop."

He put the guitar down reluctantly. It was too much. He couldn't take such a gift from her. From anyone. He wasn't worthy of it. Shaking his head, he replied, "I can't keep it, Aine. I don't de…"

"Bollocks," she interrupted what he was about to say. "Ye deserve it, Brandon. Ye deserve all the good things that come yer way. Ye're not a bad person, never were, and it's time ye stopped seein' yerself that way. Ye've a good heart, ye mean well, and ye've got yerself straightened around and respectable, like. People like ye. They love to hear ye sing, and if ye're ever goin' to get that business of yers off the ground, ye'll need a guitar to play on, to entertain the masses as ye've always liked to do. That's what ye're good at, ye feckin' eejit!" She was crying with her last words.

He stood and looked at her, unable to process all the things he was thinking. She loved him. Still. After all he'd done. She hadn't abandoned him, hadn't left him like his da had.

And then he knew. He'd been running since he was ten and the feeling of abandonment that he'd felt at that tender age had dogged him ever since.

"Ye want me? Still? After everything?"

She took a step toward him. "Brandon, I never wanted to leave ye but ye'd have none of it. None of me. Ye had some crazy notion that ye weren't worthy, that ye didn't deserve anything. I was even worried for a bit that ye thought ye didn't deserve to live. We feared for ye. All of us. Me. Yer family. The only thing that kept us sane was yer sister Ciara, saying ye'd make it through okay. She couldn't tell us when or where. We just had to believe her. She's quite special, Ciara is."

Brandon nodded. "Yeah. Always has been. Freaks us out at times with what she sees but she saw Laura and Hank marrying, of the baby that was to follow, and that was before Laura had even agreed to marry him."

"Well, she saw a few things for us, too."

It was his turn to step toward her. "Like what?"

She went to the stove to turn off the hob and quiet the kettle that had begun to boil. Turning back to Brandon, she held out her arms.

He didn't need to be told twice, and stepped toward her.

"I want ye, Brandon. I want ye in every way possible. Can't ye see that? I don't care what ye've done, where ye've been, or what's happened. The past is done. You and I have a future. We can make it good," she said.

"C'mere to me," he whispered, and she took the final step into his arms, just as his lips came down over hers. One kiss, and then a deeper one, a kiss that had both give and take, and Brandon knew exactly where he wanted to take her. "This way," he said, and led her from the kitchen and down the hallway to his bedroom at the front of the house. "It isn't fancy," he said, "but the bed's comfortable, and I guarantee we won't have to worry about rubbers."

He could tell he got her with that remark. The question, "why?" was etched in the way she held her mouth, the way her brows arched. "I think we need to see if we fit. If it's as good as we remember."

"And if it is?" she had the cheekiness to ask.

"Well, then, I suppose we should do somethin' about that, eh?"

He stood before her and took his time removing her clothing. He wanted to make love to her properly, worship her body as was his right, and hers. They had only truly made love once, although he'd loved her many different ways since that night. She deserved to be pampered, and he was going to make certain she felt pampered and loved every day of their lives together.

Lifting her jumper off over her head, he then went to work on the buttons of her blouse. It soon opened up to reveal the creamy mounds of her breasts half hidden by the bra she wore, the one whose clasp came magically undone.

She sighed and let it drop to the floor with her other garments and rubbed her hands on his bare skin beneath the shirt he was wearing. As her fingers found his small male nipples, he slid his hands into her jeans, released the snap, and pushed them down. Her knickers went with them, and before long, he had her naked before him.

She caressed his torso with long fingers, feather soft on his skin, paused only long enough for him to release his own jeans before cupping him in her hand, rolling his nads through her fingers, and stroking his flute. He was chubbed up from her touch, but if he was honest, he'd been that way since seeing her in the doorway.

They moved to the bed and he pulled the covers aside, following her down to the clean sheets. He thanked Ciara for ringing yesterday and specifically telling him he needed to change the sheets on his bed. He'd long since learned to do as she said and not ask questions. He'd soon enough learn why, or learn to regret that he hadn't followed through.

The bed gave lightly under their weight as he pressed her into the mattress. Their lips met, held. His hands stroked her sides, teased the nipples as he caressed her breasts and then took a rosy peak into his mouth and suckled, releasing a sigh of contentment from her half-opened mouth.

He kissed down the length of her while she speared her fingers through his hair, and when he stroked a particularly sensitive spot with his tongue, she held him there momentarily. Eventually, she released him and let him continue his ministrations.

He moved between her legs and down her thighs to the sensitive spot behind her knees. She widened her legs at his touch, was open for him to do what he would. She'd given him carte blanche, and he knew it.

As he kissed the inside of her thighs, his fingers found the moist pearl between the folds of her sex and began rubbing her juices lightly across its surface. Once again, a sigh escaped her lips, deeper, more vocal. He pressed a kiss to her mound and then dropped down to feast on the flow. She was so wet for him. It was all he could do to hold back and wait, just a little longer.

"This time," he said softly to her eyes, half-lidded with love, "we'll be skin to skin. No rubber. Just you and me." A few more strokes and he could hear her breath hitch, feel her stomach muscles tighten. Moving into position, he placed his flute at her entrance with a breathy, "Ready?" At her nod, he slid home, felt the skin of his flute slide into her, felt the ripples of her canal, her muscles gripping and tensing.

She'd begun to gasp and he knew she was more than ready so he began to slide back out, then in and out again, building the rhythm that would take them both home. He felt the pressure build at the base of his spine, felt it take over and heard her cry out her release. She was gripping his arse, fingers digging into his muscles as she pulled him into her. And then his body went rigid as he spent himself within her, as if the effort it took to come had encompassed his entire body, his mind, his soul.

He lay atop her, stroked the hair back from her forehead, brushed her cheek with the back of his fingers, and felt the tear that had seeped from her eye.

"Are ye alright?" he asked, worried that he'd somehow hurt her.

"About as right as you are," she smiled, running a finger across his cheekbone. Only then did he realize that he had let go a tear or two himself.

"It was *that* good," he remarked, chuckling.

"It was," she agreed.

"Whiskey? To celebrate?" he asked, and at her nod, left her to get the bottle from the other room. He brought it back to the bedroom with two small glasses, poured a little in each, and handed her one. "Sláinte," he said, and touched his glass to hers.

"Sláinte," she answered, and took a sip.

"Sleepy?"

"A little."

"Me, too," he said, and pulled her close. "Get some kip. We need to plan a weddin' in the mornin', but 'tween now and then, we have a whole lot of lovin' left to do."

Her response was a throaty chuckle.

Epilogue

They were all gathered at the castle ruins near the sea. In fact, it appeared as if the combined populations of Inishannon, Garrettstown, Kinsale, and Killarney had infiltrated the meadow, the very same meadow where Hank and Laura had exchanged their vows less than two years before, and within months of that, the celebration of the twins' marriages. *How could that be?* thought Brandon. So much had happened, so much had changed. He wasn't the same man he'd been. To say he had changed was an understatement. He'd done a one-eighty. And to see that there were people from his past there to see him wed—people he thought would have turned their backs on him and run in the opposite direction—was almost more than he could take.

The meadow was filled with well-wishers. It was like the medieval fair the family had held when the twins tied the knot, the only thing missing were the stalls and hawkers selling their wares.

Brandon had to laugh. Liam had thought to create the same kind of atmosphere of Hank and Laura's wedding. And while they'd re-created a chapel inside the structure itself for Hank and Laura, Brandon's wedding could not be contained within four small walls. For his wedding, they used the backdrop of the castle itself, the outer wall of the bawn with its hidden tunnel and plant-covered stone enforcements. He remembered crawling along the inside that wall as a lad, and up through to the top to view the landscape below from about fifteen feet. Not a great deal of height but the wall was narrow, the wind was up, and a fall from fifteen feet, no matter the ground was well grassed, was still a hard landing. He was lucky he hadn't broken his neck, or anything else, so Mam had said.

But today was different. Today, any boyo climbing the walls, inside or out, would be taken to task. The ruins might be good craic on any other day but today this particular castle was like a church, as rustic as it got. The good Father had mentioned that if the parents were to provide a fine donation, he would consider it an honor to perform the service within the keep's shadow.

Brandon's twin brothers, Liam and Niall, were in attendance with their spouses, Sine and Michael. The somewhat unusual foursome always drew eyes, both for the twins' identical looks and because Niall and Michael were so very obviously together.

Gran and Grandda were here, and oh, how happy Brandon was about that. He worried about them. They were getting on in years. They'd been his staunch supporters always, even when no one else was.

Henry stood near Siobhan, lecturing young Emily about something. The young lady had her eye on someone, though

Brandon wasn't sure who. They'd have to watch that girl if they wanted to keep her on the straight and narrow.

Hank and Laura had flown over from Canada, not wanting to miss out on yet another celebration at the castle where Hank had proposed on that misty morning not so long ago. They'd brought wee Ryan with them, and were so patently a happy family.

And then there was Ciara. She was with the same young man that had caught her eye at Hank and Laura's wedding. Although Brandon hadn't kept in touch with Ciara over the past year of his messy life, he hadn't worried because she'd been living with Mam and… It was only then that Brandon realized how free Ciara had been. It scared him half to death. But still, she'd been able to ring him and tell him to change his sheets, and just in time, too. Aine had turned up the following day. It was as if by changing his bedding he'd changed his life, changed the direction of his path, and set himself on a proper course. When Aine showed up on his doorstep, the gift of a guitar in her hand, he could no more have refused whatever she'd wanted than he could have turned the sea to land. Something had changed and he hadn't fought it.

And here they all were, assembled on the grassy lawn beside the most amazing castle in all of County Kerry in his mind. A child squealed in delight, someone laughed, and the portable organ began to play.

He watched as Aine's da escorted her up the grassy verge to where he stood. Covered in beautiful Irish lace from head to toe, she was a vision of delight, and he'd never get enough of her. As the service commenced and they got to the point of, "Do you, Brandon, take…," all Brandon could think of was, "Yes. Oh, yes."

* * *

Sunlight glinted off the water and laughter could be heard from the beach as the first weekend in July brought with it a true summer heat wave. Children splashed and played, and Hank and Laura's little boy, now a giggling toddler, ran after other children on the beach. Emily, employed as his babysitter, happily ran after him. It wouldn't be too long, thought Brandon, and they'd have to mind where Emily herself was going. She was lovely to look at, with a sweet and generous spirit, a good catch for the right fella.

Laura got up to run after them. Another six months, and she'd have baby number two to rock in her arms. The family had bets as to when the second child would be born.

Brandon looked at Siobhan and Henry. He doubted they'd ever have kids. Emily seemed enough for them and neither had ever mentioned wanting a child of their own.

Mam was having the time of her life, acting as Gran to the weyan, Ryan. She was going to love it when more grandchildren began to come along because neither he nor Aine were taking any precautions. They both wanted children, and the sooner, the better.

Everyone was to meet at Gran and Grandda's house later, where a huge family dinner was being prepared. Liam and Sine were there already. The twins had had a rocky year but their marriages seemed to have settled them both. Liam's leg, accidentally broken during his latest film, was finally healed, and Niall, who'd reluctantly taken his brother's place in that film, had sworn off acting. He'd been quite clear and very forthright to Liam when he'd said that he didn't think he'd ever get the taste of lipstick out of his mouth. Michael had been none too happy about it, either, saying that watching Niall on set with a woman in his arms was just wrong. It had nearly torn them apart, and while Brandon couldn't imagine loving another man the way Niall loved Michael, he, maybe more than anyone, understood it. Love was love.

Brandon was happy to be back at the beach in Garrettstown, staying up at the big house for the weekend along with Aine and everyone else. The following week, they were all to assemble in Dingle, where Brandon's new boat would take them on a tour of the peninsula if the weather was fair. Aine had opened a clinic in Cahersiveen and made the jaunt to Killarney once a week to work in the clinic there. No more late nights and crazy shifts for his lady love, and that suited him just fine.

A group of surfers were taking their boards out to the water and Brandon watched them for a time. He recognized Sheila, but she never acknowledged him and he was okay with that. The group paddled their boards out to where the breakers were just swells and then sat, as they always did, chatting before deciding which wave to catch.

"Do ye miss goin' out?" asked Aine by his side. He hadn't heard her come up to him.

"I do and I don't. I miss sitting out on the board, the view of this headland from the water. But I don't miss them," he pointed to the group on the water. "There's more to life than surfin' dawn to dusk, drinkin' and partyin'. I've learned that."

Aine didn't say anything and he wondered what she was thinking, so he asked her, "Are ye sorry ye've taken me away from all this?"

Her answer was a grin as she squinted into the sunlight off the water. "This?" She indicated the beach, the foaming waves upon the sand. "Or just them? Because I don't think I could ever take the beach out of ye. Wouldn't want to. I love to surf as much as the next person but I don't regret that ye're not a part of them anymore. And if ye want to go back and be with that crowd, ye'll be doin' it on yer own."

He put his arm around her and drew her close, allowing the surf to tickle and tease their toes, half burying their feet as the waves pulsed in and out. The tide was out and there was a goodly portion of wet sand showing.

"I will never choose between them and you. There is no contest. I have no desire to ever trade what I've found with you and what we have together. I nearly lost it all and I'd never forgive myself if we parted over the likes of them. They aren't bad people, just in a whole other world."

Aine rested her head on his shoulder, and he took her mouth with his. For two pins he'd take her whole body, right here on the beach.

"Care for a hot tub?" he asked when the kiss finally ended, unable to help the grin that he knew was spread across his face.

"Jaysus, Brandon, ye're a plonker, if ye think I'm doin' that with ye now!"

"What? I just asked if ye wanted to go into the hot tub?"

"Don't look all innocent on me, I know what ye meant. And the answer is no. Ye'll have to wait until later. We can sneak out to the hot tub yer grandda set up later, when everyone's asleep."

He liked the way her mind worked.

"I don't think so," said a deep voice standing over his head.

Brandon looked up to see Niall and Michael, standing behind them. They'd overheard everything.

"I wouldn't go into that tub and do what ye're plannin'. Too many others are plannin' the same thing," Niall said. "In fact, Michael and I are goin' up there now. Mostly to see if any help is needed but also for a bit of time alone. It's fair crowded here today," he indicated the beach and waves beyond.

Brandon looked at the beach. It wasn't as packed as it could be but he understood what Niall was getting at. The family was taking up a large part of it, and in any case, there was nowhere for a couple to be alone. "Well, off with ye then, and we'll be along shortly. I imagine folk are beginnin' to get hungry."

"That's what I'm thinkin' as well," answered Niall, taking Michael's hand and walking to where they'd parked the car behind the stone wall.

"Did ye want to go, too?" Brandon asked Aine.

"No, not yet. I'd much sooner wait here in the sun with you. We could be the last to leave. We could be the last on the beach and rent that hot tub that's here."

"Ah, ye're a woman after my own heart, y'are," he said, kissing the top of her head and pulling her closer.

He heard a car drive away and wondered if Niall would sneak Michael off to his room for a quick one before supper. He hadn't missed the longing in Michael's eyes when he gazed at Niall's swimsuit clad body.

The sun was lowering in the afternoon sky and family members were gathering their things together, making for the line of cars. Brandon watched them go, remaining where he was to draw Aine into his embrace. "Ye know, if anyone had told me a year ago that we'd be standin' here, watchin' the family like this, I'd have said they were sadly mistaken. But look at them. Everyone is here, and furthermore, they're all happy."

"Especially us," smiled Aine.

Brandon couldn't argue with that, and kissed her softly, seeing his love reflected in her soft gray eyes. "I guess we just have to wait to see if Ciara marries that great Dane of hers," joked Brandon.

"Oh, ye mean Cian? Funny how their names are so similar. Ye think they're serious?" They watched as those two negotiated the larger rocks near the wall, hand in hand, laughing at some private joke they shared.

"I do. Look at them, not a care in the world and eyes only for each other," Brandon murmured next to her ear.

"Ye mean like us?"

"Us? Maybe. I think we've got one over on them, though."

"Oh? How?"

"Well," he said, pulling her closer, "I'll have to prove it to ye in yon hot tub."

Laughing, Brandon planted a kiss behind Aine's ear. "I think we're very lucky."

Aine's answer was to meet his lips with hers and kiss him back.

The family was turning out alright after all, thought Brandon, as he took her hand and led her to the hot tub tent.

Ciara and Cian had reached the stairs and were on their way to their car when Ciara stopped in mid-stride as if she'd just run into a wall.

"What's the matter?" asked Cian, a perplexed look on his Viking features.

She shook her head as if to clear it, as if she'd been somewhere else for a time. "Not sure," she said, suddenly serious when she had been laughing only moments before. "I thought I saw something. Just a glimpse." She hesitated, as if catching a dream just before it flickered out. "I think it was you. Dressed in some sort of armor."

Cian laughed at that. "Could be. I've a role in that series they're making. Seventeenth century stuff and all that. Supposed to start in another couple of weeks."

"Maybe," she said, but didn't sound convinced. Then, shaking her head again, she laughed about it. "That must have been it. Let's go."

As they passed the hot tub tent near their parked car, the unmistakeable sounds of laughter from inside could be heard. Brandon's marriage was going well.

A knowing smile passed between Ciara and Cian.

THE END

Read on for an excerpt from the next exciting installment of the O'Farrell Legacy series, *A Winter Sky*.

A WINTER SKY

Book Four of
the O'Farrell Legacy

Chapter One

The November wind added a realistic chill to the film set, an accompaniment that no one particularly enjoyed. The Galway coast was not a warm section of land at this time of year, what with the wind whipping the waves to a froth as they crashed against the rugged coastline, bringing precipitation in the form of sleet and ice pellets when the skies decided to let loose their cache.

They were in the final stages of an ancient battle scene of Irish warriors and enemy intruders, they being the collection of actors and actresses who brought the scene to life. They wore the costumes of the day, and despite the cold temperatures, some of the actors bore the appearances of irritating sweat rolling into their eyes as they blinked it away, the exertion of their own efforts lifting and swinging the heavy props of shields, long swords, and cudgels only adding to the stress. Just off the set were two large smoke machines, manufacturing enough fake smoke to fully replicate the warlike atmosphere, that billowed and mingled with the acrid smoke of real fire from the burning of seventeenth-century-type battering rams and rigged, wooden towers, to irritate already sensitive eyes.

An actor gave under the crack of a sword across his body. From where Ciara stood watching, well back of any line of action, it appeared as though the sword had run the man through. Yet that one action seemed to be the catalyst for a group cheer, and the swarm of actors that had held back suddenly surged forward in a victorious yell, rising to a deafening level and blotting out all other sound.

There was some sort of discussion and nonverbal communication going on behind the scenes and then, through the amplification of a bull horn, the word "Cut!" was heard.

To a man, they all stopped what they were doing, dropped their arms laden with swords, shields, clubs, and body armor as if they were suddenly too heavy to handle, and stood still or walked in circles, breathing hard. Those who had been delegated to the surf ran up the shore to grab blankets before heading toward tents and trailers set up for the transformation of battle-weary soldiers to modern day citizens.

"That's a wrap. Good work, thank you everybody." The director turned from where he'd been standing and walked away toward the production trailer, and everyone let out a celebratory whoop. There was a lot of laughing and congratulations and as Ciara watched the final moments of a television series in the making, she noted key components of the crew were already unplugging things, rolling up cables, and generally clearing the area. Tomorrow, from what she understood, the real striking of sets and cleanup would occur.

By then, she and Cian would be long gone, on their way to Denmark to visit his parents. As if thoughts of Cian called to him, she saw him striding toward her where she'd waited, staying out of the way of cameras, boom operators, and lighting assistants. Cian's bared legs were covered in dirt, emphasizing the well-sculpted muscles rather than detracting from them. The armor that cloaked his body, showing off arms every bit as filthy and honed as his legs, only seemed to make him handsomer than ever. Even the dirt on his face and fake blood down the side of his head could not take away from his Viking good looks. Cian was as Danish as could be.

As he neared, she lifted her arms to enfold his wet, armor-clad body to her own but instead of reaching for him, her hands moved toward her own face, covering her mouth in a giant intake of breath while tears suddenly burst forth and a keening cry erupted from her throat.

"Ciara!" Cian was at her side in moments, lifting her crumbling form into his arms, holding her close as her gulps for air through her sobs gradually subsided. "Ciara, what's up? What happened?"

Cian had been told of her psychic sense, her images of things that were likely to happen. Her family had said she hadn't been wrong yet, but so far, all her visions had been easy for her to explain. Was this a vision, or something else? Because if it was a vision, it shook Cian to his very soul.

"Ciara?"

Her breathing was returning to normal as she curled into his chest. As light as a child in his strong arms, she slowly straightened her legs, and he let her slip to stand on the ground. Her legs took her weight, wobbling slightly, so he held her close until she was steady.

"It's okay. I'm okay now," she said, although from the sound of her voice, she was anything but.

Cian observed her features: the emerald green eyes, the blonde hair with its tinge of red that hung in waves down her back, a contrast to her brothers, who were raven-haired and blue-eyed to a man.

Liam, one of her brothers and older than Ciara by four years, ran quickly to her side. "Christ, Ciara! Are ye alright? Was it a, ye know, a…" He let his voice trail off, knowing how she hated to be looked at as an oddity. His twin brother, Niall, completely the opposite of Liam as mirror twins were, also hated being viewed as such. Niall was gay, as shy and introverted as ever, while Liam was an outgoing actor, as was his best friend, Cian Nicolaisen, Ciara's boyfriend for over a year now. What Liam wasn't sure of was how much Ciara might have told Cian about her visions of the future.

He looked at his sister, at her haunted eyes and pale features. He'd never seen her appear so unlike herself before. "Ciara?"

His sister looked around. Her cries had brought everyone to a silent halt and Liam leapt to her defense. "It's okay, everyone. Cian just challenged her to scream as if a Viking were ravaging her, so she did. It's just an act. Sorry if she made it seem too real," he joked. He sported a huge grin and nodded at them as the rest of the cast and crew withdrew and went about their business. One bold voice was heard to exclaim, "Sign her for the next episode, she was brilliant!"

A tentative smile curved Ciara's full lips and her green eyes pinned her brother's as she clung to Cian's arms, his strong limbs hugging her safely to his side. "It's, em, yeah. It was a vision." She spoke quietly, as if unwilling to let anyone overhear what really happened.

"This wasn't like anything I've ever seen you go through before. This was different," objected Liam.

Ciara agreed. "It was…different."

Liam didn't miss the hesitation in her voice. "How?" He held her gaze, daring her to dismiss this vision as just another one.

"Can we go somewhere else? Somewhere private?" she asked, and Cian, with his arm around her shoulder and holding her to him, agreed.

"Yeah. Let me and Liam change out of costume and we'll go to the flat."

She nodded, and taking the car keys from her pocket, said she'd wait in the vheicle, where it was private.

And quiet.

"Liam! Cian! Join us at the pub?" came the call from another cast member.

"Maybe later," Liam called back.

With a nod and a wave and within a short space of time, they met Ciara at the car and were on their way to Cian's flat.

* * *

Ciara held the mug of steaming tea between her hands and waited for Cian to join her on the settee. Her brother had already settled himself in the big armchair, his long legs stretched out before him, his feet crossed at the ankles.

Eventually, Cian joined them, handed Liam a beer, and settled himself beside Ciara. He took a long draught of his own beer, set it on the table near the settee, and laid his arm possessively across her shoulders. Ciara wanted the contact. She needed it, just now. Still unnerved by her vision, she knew she would have to tell them something, but how much should she reveal of something she didn't wholly understand herself?

"Maybe it wasn't a vision," she began, and immediately Liam harrumphed his opinion. "No, really, I mean it," she said. Again, her brother's raised brow said others might be so gullible but not him.

"Ciara, I was there when you predicted Brandon's misadventures. It wasn't anything like this," observed Cian. "Then, you were calm, laughing even. This was a very different reaction."

Liam agreed and once more gave her a look that said she'd better come clean.

"The vision of Brandon was different," she agreed. Brandon was the second son born into the family, six years older than Ciara and as wild as they came. He gave the term "bad boy" a whole new meaning. Ciara had seen a dark sky envelope him, the clouds roiling around his boneless form, twisting him about before flinging him off to an unknown future, only to be rescued by a beam of light that dropped him gently to the ground. She knew he'd go through hell, but also knew he'd survive; that someone, or something, would come to his rescue. And it had happened just that way.

This vision was nothing like Brandon's, nor like anything else she'd ever seen. It was like she was there, in a different place, and seeing all kinds of carnage, like a real battle scene. But it had been brief, so brief. Just a flash, and it was gone. Yet what she'd seen had chilled her to her core.

"Ciara, ye're daydreamin'," chided Liam.

"I'm not. I'm thinkin."

"Well, think out loud so we all can hear."

She cast a mutinous glance at Liam and felt Cian's fingers stroke her neck, a calming motion. "It wasn't like my visions before, where I saw others in them," she began. "Ye know I've never been able to see anythin' about my own future. Not even when I was nearly hit by that car the day I decided to take my bicycle out on the road after Mam expressly forbid it."

"Ye're lucky Brandon came to yer rescue, and just in time, too," said Liam.

She nodded and looked to Cian for support.

"It's okay; you're here, in this room, and no one's going anywhere. I'll always keep you safe."

As if Cian's words gave her strength, Ciara continued. "Remember that day on the beach at Garrettstown, and I had that funny vision of you in armor?"

Cian nodded.

"Well it was like that, only worse, more intense. It was awful and scary, like a real battlefield."

"Maybe it was," Liam interrupted. "After all, we'd just finished that last sequence and that was definitely a battlefield. Maybe that sparked it off?"

Ciara shook her head. "No. This was too real. It was like I was there. Really there. In a real battle. And nothin' was familiar, like. It reminded me of…". Her voice trailed away.

"Like…?" Liam prompted.

Shaking her head again, she said, "No. It's gone. I don't know." It was true. The vision was fading almost as fast as it had come on, and now that she was trying to recall it, it seemed to be slipping away, like vapors from the smoke machines on the film set, drifting into the wind, mingling with the clouds. Gone.

"Well, whatever it was, try letting it go. I can tell it's upset you but we have a good week to look forward to. You'll love Denmark," Cian said, trying to cheer her up.

Ciara took another sip of tea and leaned into his embrace, feeling him kiss the top of her head in a familiar fashion. "Ye're right. I'm makin' too much of it. And I am lookin' forward to seeing Denmark. Everyone says it's so beautiful."

"And meeting my parents?" asked Cian, a crooked grin spreading across his angular face.

It was a sore spot between them. She loved Cian, at least, she thought she did, and she was pretty sure he had feelings for her, too. But meeting his parents was like a formal declaration, to see if she passed inspection. Could she trust Cian in a full-time, forever relationship? She wasn't so certain he wouldn't drop her at the first sign of a cute costar to come his way, and yet he hadn't even glanced at another woman, as far as she knew, since they'd begun dating. Had, in fact, made it quite clear that he wanted only her.

So why was she hesitating? At the ripe old age of twenty-nine, she'd started to get the feeling it was time to settle down. Time to start thinking about a family. And Cian had been the only man she'd ever met that made her heart sing.

Yes, she thought, she loved him. But did he love her? He hadn't ever said so. Furthermore, did he want marriage, children, a dog or a cat? She wanted all that and more but she was no more certain of his love than she was of the vision that had scared her so badly.

A vision that was slowly losing its grip on her.

"Yes, and meetin' yer parents, too," she chuckled, because she knew it was inevitable.

Liam downed the rest of his beer, stood and stretched, his long arms reaching almost to the ceiling. "If ye're feelin' better, Ciara, I'll take myself off, then. Sine's waitin' for me to pick her up. She was done on the set two days ago and has been chomping at the bit, waitin' for us to finish up here so we can celebrate. Will ye join us?"

Ciara felt Cian's eyes on her, and knew the choice to go or to stay would be up to her. "You go ahead, Cian. Ye deserve to celebrate with the rest. I'd just feel like a groupie if I went."

Liam shook off his stretch and eyed his sister skeptically. "A groupie? You? Hah, ye'd no more be taken for a groupie than Cian or myself. Ye're a much-accepted part of the package, just like any spouse of any actor there, and well ye know it."

"I do. But…"

"Oh, c'mon. Just for a bit. It'll put ye in a good mood

for yer flight tomorrow," coaxed Liam.

Ciara crooked an eyebrow at her brother but he had her, and she knew it.

"Fine," she said, causing both men to break out in laughter.

"Always pay attention when a woman says, fine," laughed Cian, and Liam gave him a sideways glance that spoke volumes.

"We may as well go," said Ciara, downing the rest of her tea. "The tea is gone, yer beer is done, and I'm famished, with nothin' in here to eat. Christ, Cian, but ye're a poor host!"

"Hey, not my fault. You live here, too. And you were the one who said not to buy anything else until we got back because you didn't want it to spoil," he said in defense of himself. "I'm just following orders."

No one could argue that, so Ciara took her mug over to the sink and ran water into it, just as Liam's phone rang. As she pulled her jacket on, her mind still trying to recapture the lost moments of her vision, she heard him say, "Sick? What kind of sick? I thought ye wanted to go out tonight?"

Immediately an image intruded on Ciara's senses and she grinned to herself as it was quickly followed up with an idea. As Liam hung up, a look of disappointment on his face, she said, "How about we all go to your place instead? We can pick up something at the chipper for ourselves and Sine. Filmin' starts up again in another couple of weeks anyway. Ye don't have to go tonight, do ye?"

Liam cast his sister a telling glance and added his grin to hers. "Right ye are. What say ye, oh Viking king? Are ye for something from the chipper? Burger? Fish? They've great fare there and Sine was sayin' as how she was feelin' like havin' some fish and chips."

Ciara hid a broad smile as Cian piped up, "The chipper sounds great. Haven't been there for months and to tell the truth, I was not really looking forward to another evening in the same pub. It's nice, great food, great craic, but I think I could use a change."

An hour later they pulled up to the house that Liam shared with Sine, his wife of one year. She'd been on the production with them in her first lead role, opposite Liam's role as the hero. Her last scene had been shot two days ago and today she greeted them at the door, a delighted squeal of pleasure when she saw they'd brought fish and chips.

"Fabulous!" she exclaimed in her slight American accent, "I've been craving those for days but didn't want my waistline to increase during production, so I stayed away from anything that was fried."

Ciara noted that Sine's accent had begun to take on an Irish lilt the longer she stayed in the country. Fried came out sounding more clipped, less drawn out than before. She also noted the trim figure her brother's wife usually sported was hidden beneath the bulk of a large woolly jumper that hung down past her bum.

"Let's all get inside," said Liam, prodding them through the door like cattle jammed at a gate, "it's gettin' cooler outside and the food will be, too, if we don't all get in and start eatin'."

At that, they flooded in through the great front door that looked like a medieval entry, with meter-long black hinges bolted across the gothic-arched wooden door. Ciara loved her brother's home, especially now that he was married to Sine, who had quickly become one of Ciara's best friends.

The two women embraced and Ciara shared a look, eye to eye, and knew her earlier intuition hadn't been a mistake. They stepped quickly into the spacious kitchen, pulled barstools up to the counter, and began doling out fish and chips for all.

Later, a satiated Sine stood and stretched, placing a hand on her back as she did so, leaving Ciara to hide a grin with her last mouthful.

"You go sit in the other room and I'll make us some tea. I think the boys could use some bondin' time before Cian and I head off tomorrow," said Ciara, clearing up the disposable food boxes and getting a thankful nod from everyone.

"Grab yer beer, Cian, there's somethin' in my office I think ye should see. It's another script I'm considerin'…". Liam's voice trailed off and Ciara watched them leave, thankful for the privacy. After filling the kettle, she sat in the sitting room with Sine, the room that overlooked the cliffs and the stormy weather that often hit the Galway coast in the winter months.

"I wouldn't be surprised to see some sleet or snow in the next few days. God, but it was cold out there today. Ye'll be glad ye didn't have to work in that," she said to Sine.

"I know. I love location work but sometimes it's so freaking cold, and running in and out of tents to warm up doesn't always do it."

Ciara watched her for a moment, wondering if she should ask. Not the question of "are you," but "did you know," because sometimes, as was the case with Hank's wife, Laura, they didn't always know yet. They chatted on for a few minutes and then the kettle boiled, prompting Sine to rise and make the tea. Coming back with two steaming mugs, she handed one to Ciara and sat back down.

Ciara sniffed the tea, noted it was herbal, and stifled another grin. She hadn't been blind to the fact that Sine had refused alcohol at supper, something unusual for her. Ever since her first taste of Irish whiskey, she'd often enjoy a glass in the evening over any other drink. Unless they were at the pub, and then it was the black stuff, all the way.

"So," she began, not content to wait any longer, "when are ye goin' to tell Liam?"

Sine held the cup away from her lips, cast a glance

to where the boys were ensconced over the new script, and met Ciara's eyes. "Soon," was all she said. If she was surprised by Ciara's knowledge, she hid it well.

"Why not now? What are ye waitin' for?"

Sine shrugged. "The right time. Not sure when that is but it'll be soon. Maybe I'll wait until we're in the middle of a big argument and then I'll just throw it out there, especially if I feel like I'm about to lose the fight."

They both chuckled over that and Sine asked, "How did you find out? I haven't told a soul."

"It was this afternoon. I had a couple of visions today. One was about you, the other..." Her voice seemed to fail her. The feeling was still strong, enveloping her as if she only had to recall she'd had the vision, not necessarily what it was. It was as if that moment in time was tagged with a cloud of darkness.

Clearly, Sine wanted to know more. "Go on," she prodded. "I won't tell."

Ciara shook her head. "I can't explain it any more. It could even have been because they'd just finished the battle scene and there was the fake blood and the smoke machine was goin', as was the fog machine, so the air was filled with vapors just as if they'd really come off a battle scene a few centuries ago. And the mud! Ye should have seen the mud. It was everywhere, they were covered in it. I waited in the car while they showered and changed. If it was just Cian in there, I would have waited inside but I thought Liam could use the privacy," she joked.

"What was the vision? You haven't really said."

Ciara sipped the tea appreciatively, tasted the camomile, the rose-hip accents, the touch of lemongrass, and braced herself against the onslaught of a memory she didn't want. "It was awful. I think...no, I'm not sure. I remember it was a battle, I don't know who I was looking at. I just remember the blood, the mess of battle, much like the scene done today. And death. All about me, death. And the stench. I can't explain the stench." She finished with a shudder, and Sine's face reflected what Ciara felt. Fear.

"Oh, my God, Ciara. Why? Do you know what it was? Or maybe the more important question...when?"

"I don't know. I've never had a vision like this before. Anythin' I've had has always been to do with friends or family, or once in a while something about to happen right in front of me. I've never had any kind of vision that didn't pertain to the here and now. And I seriously don't think whatever it was I saw was either here or now. It just wasn't."

They both sat uncomfortably for a time, sipping tea, deep in thought. Ciara's vision had clearly unsettled them both.

As a distraction and to shake off the distressing mood, she turned the talk back to the baby. "Speakin' of when," she began, and gave Sine a pointed look.

"Oh, that," Sine laughed. "Well, I think I'm really only at the six-week mark but I'll know more after tomorrow."

"What's tomorrow?"

"The doctor appointment, of course."

"What doctor appointment?" asked Liam, coming to join them in the sitting room with Cian bringing up the rear.

"Oh, nothing special," said Sine, "just a doctor's appointment I made a while back. Yearly checkup and all that," she lied.

Liam gave her a funny look. "I thought ye had one of those just recently."

Sine opened her mouth to say something and then suddenly got up and left the room as if the devil himself were chasing her.

"What the…?" said Liam, and Ciara began to giggle.

"What's so funny?" asked Liam, clearly flummoxed by Sine's hasty departure.

"Ye'll maybe want to see if she's okay," said Ciara. "In the meantime, Cian and I should get going. We've a bit of packing left to do."

"But Sine? Is she sick?"

"No. Yes. But not how ye think. Don't be a plonker, Liam, just go see her," she chided and ushered Cian toward the door.

"Ciara, what aren't ye tellin' me?"

"It's not for me to tell ye, big brother. That's for Sine. Now go. Cian and I will see ourselves out, and we'll call once we're back in Ireland. If ye need me for anythin', we'll both have our mobiles." With a last look at her brother and a blown kiss at the door, she closed it fast against the brightness from within and glanced up at Cian, who sported a wry look.

"I may be a male, but even I believe I know the cause of her sudden sickness," he said as they walked to the car, and at Ciara's silence, said, "She's expecting, isn't she."

Ciara knew it wasn't a question. Cian was sometimes as tuned in to his own intuition as she was to hers. "Yeah. Isn't it grand?"

His arm came about her and he hugged her close. "Maybe that'll be you and me one day."

Ciara wanted to agree, to jump up and down with joy and acknowledge the love she felt in her heart at his words. But all she could think of was the spectre of a battlefield and death all around.

END OF EXCERPT

A Winter Sky is the fourth installment of the O'Farrell Legacy series and is now available.

www.smcross.net

ABOUT THE AUTHOR

The daughter of an Air Force family, and therefore an extensive world traveler, Ms. Cross has been writing since the age of fifteen, creating stories around the places she has lived and visited. After writing an editorial column for a newspaper for fifteen years, she is now retired and living in Canada's north with her children, grandchildren and an assortment of cats and dogs.

BOOKS BY THE AUTHOR

The O'Farrell Legacy Series:
Mulligan's Dream
Double Take
Brandon: Bad Boy of Kinsale
A Winter Sky
C'Mere to Me

IRISH AND IRISH SLANG
Usage and Pronunciation

a chroi — (uh kree) my heart

a mhac — (uh wak) my son

a stor — (uh shtor - like 'store' with an 'h added) my treasure

An bpósfaidh tú mé? — (on bohs-ee thoo may) Will you marry me?

banjaxed — broken, usually irreparable

bean sidhe — banshee – In Irish folklore, the Bean Sidhe (woman of the hills) is a spirit or fairy who presages a death by wailing.

black stuff — Guinness

bowsie — thug, scumbag, wife-beater

box — vagina

boyo — boy, lad

cáilin — (colleen) girl

chipper — a place for burgers or fish 'n chips

chubbed — erection

Claddagh — a design on a ring, of two hands clasping a crowned heart

	between them
clot-heid	(clot-hade) cloth head - another word for idiot, more Scottish than Irish but used all the same
cop on	smarten up, leave off, settle down, etc.
craic	(crack) fun
eejit	idiot
fáilte	(FAHL-cheh) welcome - also the National Tourism Development Authority
fella	your guy, partner/husband/boyfriend
flange/fanny	women's genitals
flute	penis
gabh transna ort fhéin	(gave tras orth hayn) go fuck yourself - literal - 'go sideways on yourself"
Garda/Gardai	police, also called shades
Gligeen	stupid person
gobsmacked	surprised
gonch	underwear
Gráim thú	(ghraw hoo) I love you
grá mo chroi	(yraw muh kree) Love of my heart
hoer	(Dutch) whore
horned up	horny
Is tú mo ghrá	(Is too moh Greah - the eah like in "yeah") I love you
jammered	stolen
jarveys	men who drive the jaunting cars
kip	sleep
lack	girlfriend
lad	penis
langer	multiple meanings – in the books

	it is sometimes used as a term for penis, as are 'lad' and 'flute'
loo	toilet
manky	dirty, flithy, disgusting
mo cáilin	(muh colleen) – my girl
mo chroi	(muh kree) my heart
mo chuisle	(muh kishla) my pulse
mo dheartháir	(Muh ghrih-hawr) my brother
moggie	cat
nads/clackers	gonads; balls
neddy	idiot, fool
Oiche mhaith agus codladh sámh (EE-hyeh WY(h) ogg-uss KOLL-oo SAA-oo) good night and sleep well
pennyboy	menial worker
plonker	country bumpkin, slow on the uptake
póg mo thóin'	(pogue muh hone) kiss my ass
poot	(Dutch) homosexual man
ráicleach/raaklochk (rack lock) slut
shandy	beer mixed with another drink - lemonade, ginger ale, etc.
skank	untrustworthy, low-life criminal type
sláinte	(slawnt-ye) health
sláinte mhaith	(slawnt-ye wa) good health
Striapach	whore
Tá tú go h-álainn.(TAW too guh HAW-linn) you are beautiful
Táim I ngrá leat (TAW-im ing graw let) I'm in love with you
thick	extremely stupid ('brick' is also used)
wankers/gormless	idiots